Grateful for Gabe

HART'S CREEK STORIES - BOOK FOUR

by

Suzie Peters

GWL
PUBLISHING

First Published in 2023
by GWL Publishing
an imprint of Great War Literature Publishing LLP

Produced in United Kingdom

Cover designs and artwork by GWL Creative.

ISBN 978-1-915109-41-5 Paperback Edition

GWL Publishing
Chichester, United Kingdom

www.gwlpublishing.co.uk

Dedication

For S.

Chapter One

Remi

How To Wed a Prince?

Honestly… where do they think up these titles?

I study the cover for a moment. It's illustrated with what appears to be a stately home in the background, and a young couple in the foreground. Their clothes suggest a Regency setting, and the way they're gazing into each other's eyes implies his thoughts aren't very regal, and that they probably won't be wearing those clothes beyond about chapter three.

I smile, sliding the book back onto the shelf, between *Heart's Ecstasy*, and *How To Win a Rascal*, which sounds a lot more fun than wedding a prince, if you ask me. I think those two must be part of a series, but I'm not interested enough to find out. There's no time, either. I've still got several more books to put away, and it's nearly time to close up the library.

At least I get to leave the Romantic Fiction section now. My next book belongs in Arts and Crafts. It's about quilting, a hobby of which I've never been a fan, although judging by the number of books there are on the shelves, I guess many people around here find it fascinating.

A quick foray into the History section disposes of four more titles, and then I return to the fiction aisles to complete my task, taking a moment to admire one of the covers. Science fiction may not be my 'thing', but I often think the cover designs are the most inventive and eye-catching, and this one is no exception. There are lots of scrolls, birds, butterflies and flowers, all beautifully illustrated and embossed, curling around each other to form a frame that surrounds the title. I'm about to open the book when my attention is diverted by voices. Very familiar ones...

"Colin doesn't get it."

That's Audrey. She works here, too, alongside Camilla, who I know will be standing with her by the counter, the two of them no doubt ready to go home and filling the last few minutes of the day with idle gossip. And why shouldn't they? It's what they do the rest of the time.

"Men don't," Camilla replies, and I imagine her rolling her eyes. They both do that a lot, especially when they're talking about men in general and their husbands in particular.

"I told him we need to speak to Marcus about the way he lets that woman talk to little Cody, but he says it's none of our business."

"I guess it was always gonna be difficult when Marcus and Lily split up."

"That's the problem these days, though, isn't it? I remember saying to Colin just before Marcus and Lily got married... I said to him, I knew it was a mistake."

That was optimistic.

"I know. You said the same thing to me."

"And I was right, wasn't I? It was clear for anyone to see. They'd only known each other for five minutes. And look where they've ended up? Divorced. Both of them with new partners, and a two-year-old who doesn't know which way to turn half the time."

"I suppose I should count myself lucky that Emma and Jack haven't had any kids. Yet."

"Are they still fighting about it?"

"They are. She may be my daughter, but I think she's being completely unreasonable. Jack earns more than enough for them to start a family. But, no… that's not enough for Emma. She has to have a career." I can hear the sarcasm dripping off of her tongue as she says that last word, even though I can't see her.

"That's modern women for you. They don't know when they're well off."

I hear Camilla sigh… or I assume it's Camilla. "Sometimes I wonder where I went wrong with my girls. Emma doesn't seem to understand what being married is all about, and as for Karen…" She lets her voice fade and I wonder – not for the first time – what it is with Karen. She's Camilla's younger daughter, and although I don't know why, she's always spoken of between the two women in whispered tones of deep disappointment. The possibilities are endless.

"You're not responsible," Audrey says. "You gave them everything they ever asked for."

Maybe that was where she went wrong…

"I know. You did the same for Marcus."

I hear a door opening, and as they continue to commiserate, their voices diminish. They'll have gone into the staff room to collect their things, and I take a last glance down at the book, which is still in my hand. The cover really is beautiful. I've got no idea what it's about, or how it qualifies to have a 'Sci-Fi' label on its spine, but I slide it onto the shelf, in its rightful place, before returning to the counter.

It's at the back of the vast space that forms the library, which is in one of the oldest buildings in town, situated at one end of Main Street. There are book shelves around all the walls, even either side of the enormous wooden double doors that form the entrance, and the space between is filled with racks, a couple of couches, and some desks. When I first started work here, back in the spring, I asked why there were no computers.

"Surely there should be public access to the Internet," I said, and Audrey looked at me with a sympathetic smile.

"We tried it once," she said. "It didn't catch on."

"It didn't?"

She shook her head. "There wasn't much call for it."

In a way, I wasn't that surprised. The library here is caught in a time warp, and although it can be frustrating, in a way, I quite like it. Books are a passion of mine, and even if I'm not averse to electronic devices, I also like the idea of turning a page.

It's one of my many old-fashioned idiosyncrasies. I have a few of them. The way I dress is probably the most obvious. I'm not all tweeds and buttoned-up blouses, but I've never worn a miniskirt, and I don't own a pair of jeans, either. Or leggings. They're not my style.

I grab my keys from the drawer behind the counter, where I left them this morning, and wander to the front door, locking it, but leaving the keys behind. We don't want any visitors at this time of night, but Audrey and Camilla will need to let themselves out, and in the meantime, I need to clear up.

It's something they could have been doing while they were talking, but I guess they were otherwise occupied.

They usually are…

I noticed that on my very first day here. While I was busy learning the ropes, getting the hang of the systems, and establishing what needed to be done, they were both sitting back and doing as little as possible.

It's been that way ever since.

I'm not saying I do all the work. Just most of it.

They fill their time with gossip, discussing their husbands, their children, and in Audrey's case, her grandson, too. Their interests don't end with their families, though. They also delight in discussing what they watched on television the previous evening, dissecting the plots of every soap and drama, until I know them backwards, even though I've never seen them.

Another favorite topic is food. They'll tell each other what they've cooked, how they've cooked it – in infinite detail – and whether it was good, or bad, how they might adjust the recipe next time, what Colin or David thought – if they gave a verdict – and then they'll bemoan the fact that their latest diet isn't working. With the holidays approaching, this has become a more regular feature in their conversations, as they both prepare for the forthcoming feast they obviously intend indulging in. It all seems a little paradoxical to me… as does the fact that Camilla spent nearly an hour this afternoon telling Audrey that she'd got nothing to wear because none of her clothes fitted properly, and then went over to the coffee shop to buy them both a brownie. She offered to get me one, to be fair, but I declined, even though she told me how good they are. Twice.

I know how good the brownies are. I've eaten a few of them myself, but I wasn't in the mood for one today, and I watched Camilla leave, shaking my head, because I knew she'd come back, eat the brownie, and then beat herself up over it for the next hour.

In reality, that's exactly what she did.

I wanted to yell. Because that happens every time.

It isn't just infuriating. It's so much worse than that. The fact is, neither of them needs to lose weight in the first place. But the really annoying part is, all of their moaning is just an excuse to gossip, instead of doing the thing they're paid for… namely, working.

I guess it's too late to change them now, though.

They're both part of the furniture of this place, having come back to work once their kids left home for college, never to return, it seems.

In their mid-sixties now, they're far too set in their ways to listen to the likes of me. And why would they? I'm Nora's replacement.

That's how they see me.

Nora had been working here since printing was invented. That's how it feels when they speak of her, as though she were still here, hiding behind one of the racks, their tones hushed in reverence of everything she ever did, every word she ever uttered.

Do they resent me?

Maybe. A little.

It's not my fault, though.

Nora retired. She wasn't forced out. It was her choice, and she stayed on until I'd been here for a couple of weeks, just to help me get used to the place. It was kind of her, and we got along okay. Once she'd gone, though, I realized how much she did… and how much of an outsider I was.

I still am, really.

Not just because I'm Nora's replacement, but because I'm not from Hart's Creek.

I moved here straight from college, when I got this job, hoping to start afresh.

I had such high hopes, but it hasn't been as easy as I'd thought it might be.

Perhaps that's because I haven't met anyone of my own age yet. Not really. The lady who serves me in the coffee shop is probably in her late twenties, and she always greets me with a smile, but I never know how to take it any further. It's the same in the delicatessen and the florist's. At least some of the people who work there are young enough, but we never seem to get the chance to talk.

As for the people who come to the library… they're much older.

They talk enough – or rather, they whisper – but I'm unlikely to make friends with any of them. They're here to borrow a book, or to bring one back. If they want to talk, or even ask a question, they'll go to Camilla or Audrey. They trust them. I'm too new to be trusted. Too new for conversation.

I guess that's why my days have become a little formulaic. It stops me thinking about being 'too new', 'too young', 'too shy'. If I look busy and feel busy, then I don't have time to think, do I?

That's why I get up at the same time every day. Seven o'clock, on the dot. I shower, dry my hair, get dressed and have breakfast… all before seven-forty-five. I leave the house at eight, even though I don't need to be at work that early, and use the time before Audrey and Camilla arrive to check everything here is set-up and ready for the day ahead.

The days themselves are different, and can be unpredictable, depending on who comes in to the library, but at lunchtime, I go to the delicatessen and buy a sandwich. I vary the filling. I'm not that boring. And I take it back to work and eat in the staff room.

At the end of each day, although we all have a set of keys, I'm the one who locks up before going home and cooking myself something for dinner. Again, I vary that, just so life doesn't become too mundane. Then I watch a movie or read for a while, and go to bed by ten.

It's not the most exciting life, but it's my life. And it's better than it could have been.

"Maybe you and David should come over at the weekend."

Audrey comes through the staff room door ahead of Camilla. It's at the back of the building, marked with a sign that says 'Private – Employees Only', and it takes a moment or two before they appear between the racks.

Audrey is the shorter of the two, with mid-length dark hair that's peppered with gray. She's wearing a thick winter coat and is pulling black woolen gloves over her hands as she speaks.

"Sounds great. Saturday would be best for us. Emma mentioned something about coming over on Sunday."

Camilla is right behind her, and as Audrey steps aside, she comes into view. Her hair is blonde, without a trace of gray, and she's wrapping a scarf around her neck, both of them prepared for the cold evening, it seems.

I know from listening in on their conversations that they both live down Beech Road, so they don't have far to walk.

"Call me later. The Patriots are playing tonight, so Colin won't have a word to say on any subject worth talking about."

"David will be the same."

Both women shake their heads, although they're smiling. "We'll talk then, shall we?"

What on earth about? You've done nothing but talk all day.

They turn to me.

"Have a good evening," Audrey says, giving me a nod.

"See you tomorrow." Camilla smiles in my direction, and the two of them head toward the door, unlocking it and letting themselves out.

For a moment, the silence feels deafening, but then I remember the door's unlocked. Anyone could walk in, and the sooner I get out of here, the better.

It's not that I'm scared of being in the library alone. Hart's Creek isn't the kind of place where you can feel scared. It's lovely here, not too dissimilar from the Connecticut town where I grew up. Although I heard a rumor about a man being arrested here a few months ago for running a fake dating agency. Audrey was the one who seemed to know all about it. She was outraged because he lived just a few doors away from her, and although she'd been away visiting Emma and Jack when all the excitement of the actual arrest had taken place, she gleaned a little information by asking around. It seems the man concerned had been getting women to sign up with this agency of his, and then he'd claimed to have matched them with someone, but would go to the dates himself, drugging the women and taking them back to his place. Audrey didn't know what he did with them when he got them there, but it didn't sound good.

As far as I'm concerned, it's another reason for meeting people the old-fashioned way…

If only I could.

Still, standing here feeling sorry for myself won't achieve anything. It won't even get me home.

I quickly tidy the counter, then go to the staff room for my purse and coat, although as I flick on the light, it's hard not to tut out loud. The space is quite cramped, with three armchairs squeezed into the room, along with the closet where we hang our coats and leave our belongings. There's also a sink in the corner, with a coffee machine on the small countertop beside it. I'm not irritable because of the lack of space, but because it's absurdly messy in here. The wastepaper basket could do with emptying, and there are a few coffee cups that need washing, as well as a couple of old newspapers, lying around. I wouldn't have thought it would hurt Audrey or Camilla to tidy up, but I guess I can deal with it all in the morning. It'll give me something to do.

I shut out the lights and close the door behind me, shrugging on my coat before I make my way to the door. Admittedly, it feels a little spooky in here when there's no-one else around, and the place is in darkness, the moonlight casting strange shadows through the tall windows and between the racks… but that's just my imagination running away with me.

Outside, once I've locked the door and put the keys firmly away in my purse, I turn and make my way down the steps, my breath misting in front of my face. I think I preferred it in the summer and fall, when I could walk home. As it is, I've taken to driving, even though I only live in Maple Street, which isn't that far away. Nowhere in Hart's Creek is that far away, but it's too cold to walk home now, and I'm relieved to get into my Toyota Corolla. It was ten years old when I bought it last year, but it does everything I ask of it… like starting in freezing cold weather.

My drive home takes no time at all.

Like I said, nowhere is that far away, and I take the turn into Maple Street, off of Main Street, parking outside my neat little house on the left-hand side. It may be small, but it's home, and it was the best I could afford when I moved here.

I wanted to buy instead of renting… to feel I was putting down roots, rather than looking to move on at a moment's notice, and fortunately, having worked my way through college, but failed to have a life for most of it, I had some savings… enough for a deposit, anyway.

Besides which, I got lucky. This place needed fixing up and was within my budget. It had been rented out for a few years, and had seen better days, and although I'm nowhere near finished, I'm pleased with what I've achieved so far. It keeps me busy on the weekends, too.

I close the car door and glance around at the other houses, all of them decorated with Christmas lights, some more gaudy than others. The one right next door is particularly bright and colorful, and while that's not necessarily to my taste, it puts my place to shame.

Mine is the only house I can see from here that isn't decorated, and there's no denying, it looks really lost and depressing, and I feel embarrassed by that.

What's wrong with me?

I like Christmas. I really do.

It's my favorite time of the year.

Although this is the first time I'll be getting ready for the holidays all by myself, which is nearly as sad as the state of my house.

It's hard for me to think back to childhood Christmases. They're so at odds with how things are now, but even once I'd left home and gone to college, I still enjoyed the build-up to the holidays. I shared a small house with two friends, Sofia and Alex, and we had great fun decorating our rooms, holding dinner parties that made us feel so sophisticated, and shopping...

Man, did we shop.

I won't be seeing them this year. We all went our separate ways after graduation. Alex returned to her folks in Austin, where she found a job as a secretary at an electronics company. As for Sofia, she moved to Arizona. That came as quite a surprise, considering she's from Boston, where the three of us had spent the previous four years of our lives. But she'd met Tate by then... and I think you can guess where he's from. She couldn't be convinced that remaining in Boston would make her happy, so now she works for an advertising agency in Tucson, and lives with Tate... and according to the messages the three of us exchange on a fairly regular basis, she's deliriously happy.

Am I jealous of Sofia?

Sometimes.

But I never let it show.

Perhaps that's why it's harder to raise the enthusiasm for the holidays this year.

Having no-one at all to share it with makes it seem less important.

Even in my first year at college, before I met Alex and Sofia, I had someone. Or I thought I did.

Except it didn't work out.

He didn't ruin Christmas for me... not single-handedly, anyway.

And I have to admit, I've enjoyed all the Christmases since, so I can't blame him for my lack of interest this year.

I look around again, unable to stop the smile from forming on my lips as the inflatable snowman in the front yard opposite sways in the breeze, like he's nodding his head at me.

Okay, okay.

I'll do something.

There are still over two weeks until Christmas, so maybe at the weekend I can get hold of some lights and a tree. They're selling them at the flower shop and although most of the trees are way too big for my tiny living room, I'm sure I'll find something to fit.

This is sounding like a plan, and as I let myself in, the warmth of my home surrounding me, I nod my head.

With today being Thursday, at least I've only got one more day of living in the saddest house in Hart's Creek.

Chapter Two

>>><<<

Gabe

"This is the best meatloaf I've ever tasted."

I put down my knife and fork, taking a sip of red wine, which is almost as good as the meatloaf, to be fair.

"It's meatloaf," Peony says with a shrug.

"You say that, but you've never tasted my mother's version of it."

She shakes her head. "I can't believe you said that. Your mother would be so hurt."

Ryan chuckles, reaching across the table to take her hand. "No, she wouldn't. It's become a family joke over the years. I've tasted Gwen's meatloaf. Trust me, it's terrible."

Peony frowns, looking at me, even though she keeps hold of Ryan's hand. "But meatloaf is so easy."

"I know that, you know that... but my mom's from England. She doesn't get it."

Peony's face clears slightly, although her brow is still furrowed. "Don't they have meatloaf over there?"

"It's not a huge tradition, no."

"But they have mashed potatoes, right?" she says, handing me the dish to take some more.

13

"Sure. And my mom's are incredible, although she doesn't put cheese in them like this. She's a purist when it comes to potatoes."

Peony laughs, taking the dish back from me and offering it to Ryan, who takes a spoonful of mashed potatoes, putting them onto his plate.

Peony's meatloaf really is good, although I'd love being here, even if it wasn't.

Ryan is my oldest friend, and I've worked with him since we both left college. I say 'with' not 'for' even though it's his company, and it was his father's before that. Ryan never treats me like an employee, though. He treats me like a friend who just happens to share office space with him.

And we both like it that way.

Of course, things used to be very different.

We haven't always spent our Thursday evenings sitting in a farmhouse on an apple orchard, eating meatloaf together.

Not that long ago, we used to go out a lot more, and not just on Thursdays. We'd go out every night of the week. We'd drink, have dinner, pick up women, and generally behave like most single men of our age in a big city.

The big city was Boston, and to be honest, I thought we'd spend the rest of our lives doing what we'd always done… and doing it very well, I might add.

We probably would have done, if Ryan hadn't come up here to Hart's Creek to buy a plot of land. He was desperate to prove he hadn't lost his negotiating skills. I don't really know why that was so important to him, but it was, and while I'm his friend and not his employee, I wasn't about to argue with him… even if I thought he was crazy.

What neither of us had expected was that he'd find love, or that he'd find it with the woman whose land he was supposed to be buying. She didn't want to sell, and in the end, he didn't want to buy, if it meant losing her.

So, here we are, on a Thursday night, eating meatloaf.

And not only does Ryan now live here, but so do I.

Not at the farmhouse, you understand, but in Hart's Creek.

Because even though I'm a friend and not an employee, when my boss decided to move his entire operation here just so he could be with the woman he loves, I couldn't really say 'no'.

I could have said, "Are you sure about this?" But I already knew the question was irrelevant. He'd made up his mind and wasn't about to change it. He was in love with Peony and he wanted to make a life with her.

I could have resigned, I guess. With my experience, it would have been easy to find work somewhere else.

But where would I find a boss as amenable as my oldest friend?

And besides, at the time, it all felt so far away. Not Hart's Creek itself, but the entire business of moving. When Ryan first told me of his plans, he'd already found two new offices just outside the town, in a small industrial area, but they both needed work to make them habitable. That was going to take time. My job was to organize that, and to arrange the closure of our Boston office, alongside the re-opening of a new, smaller one. We couldn't afford not to have some kind of presence in the city, but it didn't need to be on the same scale, and with all of that to do, plus re-structuring the company, re-locating the employees, finding somewhere to live up here, and selling my apartment down there, it felt like it would take forever before I'd be able to move.

Of course, 'forever' wasn't really that long, and by the summer, everything was ready. Ryan was already living here by then, unable to stay away from Peony any longer than was strictly necessary. He painted a picture of the idyllic life they had planned at the farm and, although I wasn't jealous, I was intrigued.

The first time I came here, I have to say, I was also surprised.

Sure, it's pretty and quaint, and as apple orchards go, it's everything I'd expected it to be. But it's also run-down and in need of a lot of work. It's nothing like the modern penthouse apartment Ryan used to call home, or even like my own place in the city, which was similar to his, but less palatial.

I couldn't believe he'd ever be happy here, and yet, he was.

He explained that he'd already had the roof fixed, but that they'd put everything else on hold while they focused on their new venture.

"What new venture?" I asked.

We were standing outside on the porch at the time, while Peony was in here, in the kitchen, fixing us something to eat. The view across the orchard was breathtaking, especially given the beautiful sunset streaking across the evening skyline. There wasn't another building in sight, and I'll admit, for someone who works in property development, that made me a little nervous.

"Weddings," he replied, trying not to smile.

"Weddings?"

He nodded his head. "We're gonna convert one of the barns into a wedding venue."

"Are you serious?"

"Absolutely. Peony needs a sideline, and this is perfect."

It wasn't my idea of perfect, but what could I say? It was nothing to do with me, even if I barely recognized my oldest friend anymore. Gone was the aloof man who treated his business dealings with ruthless precision… the man who, on a personal level, had never committed to anything more serious than a one-night stand. In front of me was a stranger, who was looking forward to domestic bliss, and welcoming the bonds of matrimony with open arms.

It beggared belief.

Or so I thought…

Because not only has Ryan moved heaven and earth, and his entire life to be with Peony, but they've converted the barn, they've set up the wedding venue as a completely separate business, and they've started taking bookings.

The first one isn't until the spring, but the trial run will be their own wedding, which is due to take place next weekend.

That's one of the reasons I'm here tonight… aside from the meatloaf. As best man, it's part of my job to make sure everything is ready for the ceremony, and so far, it seems to be.

"Is there anything you need me to do before next weekend?" I ask, finishing my dinner and pushing the plate aside. "Have the heaters arrived?"

Ryan nods his head. "They got here on Tuesday, thank God."

We can all agree on that sentiment. When they first told me they were getting married in a barn a week before Christmas, I questioned their sanity, as well as their willingness to turn their guests into popsicles. They assured me the barn would be well heated, and that Christmas was the best time for them… well, for Peony, anyway. I'm pretty sure Ryan would have married her sooner, but the apple orchard doesn't need so much attention during the winter months, so for her to take a few weeks off to be on her honeymoon is much less of a problem then than it would be at any other time of year.

"What about everything else?"

Peony sucks in a breath and frowns, like she's thinking. I have to admit, it's a cute look, and judging by the expression on Ryan's face, he seems to agree. "We're all set, I think," she says. "Oh, except the chairs haven't been delivered yet."

"The chairs?" I flip around, looking at her.

To be fair to Ryan, it's easy to see why he was prepared to turn his life upside down for her. She's stunning, her long blonde hair hanging wildly around her shoulders, and her startling blue eyes fixed on mine as she bites her bottom lip.

"I know," she says. "It's not ideal."

"Not ideal? That's one way of putting it. Where are your guests gonna sit if there aren't any chairs?"

"We've got over a week until the day itself. I'm sure they'll get here."

I admire her optimism. The chairs in question aren't just going to be used for Ryan and Peony's wedding. They're for all the future ones, too, and I just hope she's right, because I know at least one of the couples who've booked to hold their ceremony here will be attending next weekend. It won't look good if everyone has to stand.

"Have you taken any more bookings?" I ask, for a slight change of subject.

Peony shakes her head. "No. But I imagine people are busy getting ready for the holidays now."

"You don't think they get engaged at Christmas, then?" Ryan asks, giving her a twenty-four carat smile.

"Of course." She smiles back, and I wonder if I should offer to leave. "But would they really start planning the wedding straight away? Surely they'd wait until after New Year."

"That depends how desperate they are to get married."

I can't imagine why anyone would be 'desperate' to get hitched, but looking at Ryan, I think he might be. Either that, or he's just desperate to get Peony into bed tonight. I can't be sure which.

Peony gets up to clear the dishes, but before she's even started stacking them, Ryan takes over, which makes me smile. He doesn't seem to notice and I sit back in my chair, watching him. I never would have thought he'd be like this. I'm not just talking about him being so domesticated, but about him being happy.

He was always really distant in the past. That's a trait I think he inherited from his dad, and he carried it well – with just about everyone except me. Now, he couldn't be more different. He's so happy… and I guess that's because of Peony. And his love for her.

I'm not jealous. Of course I'm not.

This isn't the life for me.

But I'm pleased for him.

I'm pleased for both of them.

"I meant to ask," he says, turning away from the dishwasher to face me. "Did you hear anything back from Nate Newton? I had to leave early, and sent him a message canceling our appointment this afternoon, but I haven't had a reply and wondered if he'd called the office."

"Were you seeing Nate?" Peony says before I can answer.

"Yes. He's asked me to take a last look at the plans for his new house."

"I see." She tilts her head. "But you left the office early, did you?"

"Yes. I'm getting married next weekend. There are things I need to organize."

"Like what?" She's trying not to smile and failing dismally.

"That would be telling, babe." He raises his eyebrows, then blows her a kiss, and after she's blown one right back, she turns to me.

"Do you know about this?"

"The secret? Sure I do."

"And?"

"And that's the whole point of it being a secret. I'm not allowed to tell." Even though I'm more than aware of the brand new pick-up Ryan's ordered for Peony. It's not the most romantic of gifts, as I pointed out to him when he told me, but her old one is only just holding itself together, and he's been wanting to replace it since he moved up here. The problem with that is, Peony isn't great at letting Ryan spend his money on her. He's got more than enough of it, but the way he explained it to me, she'd never take anything as expensive as a car, if he didn't have a reason for giving it. Getting married feels like a good enough reason... at least, it does to Ryan.

"You're no fun, Gabe Sullivan." She narrows her eyes at me, although I can tell she's only kidding.

"I know."

Ryan chuckles and we both turn to face him. "He's not meant to be fun. He's meant to be telling me whether Nate called the office."

"He did. Just before I left. He said it was fine, and asked if he could see you tomorrow morning at ten. I checked your calendar and you don't have anything scheduled, so I said it would be fine."

He nods his head. "Thanks."

"Is there something wrong with Nate's plans?" Peony asks, taking a sip of wine and wrinkling her nose. "Is it me, or does this taste strange?"

"It tastes fantastic to me," I say. It's so good, I wish I didn't have to drive home, because I'd quite like to have some more of it myself.

"I guess it must be me then." She smiles and turns to her future husband. "So... what's going on with Nate's house?"

"Nothing." Ryan comes back to the table.

"So you're not getting involved?"

"No, baby. Residential construction isn't really our thing."

"But I thought that was why you bought the second office when you moved up here."

"It was."

"And now you don't need it?" she says, looking confused.

"We can always use office space," he replies, and I nod my head in agreement. It's true. We seem to need more and more of it all the time. "Whether or not we stay in the residential business remains to be seen."

"But aren't you already building houses on that site up in… wherever it is, in Vermont?"

"We are, but it's proving to be very problematic. It feels like one hold-up after another."

"Haven't you started work yet, then?" she asks, clearly surprised.

"We're trying to," I say, finishing the last of my wine. "The problem is we're not actually building anything. We're still going through the nightmare of getting the planning consents."

She frowns. "Is that why Nate wants to see you? Because he's having the same problems?"

Ryan shakes his head, sitting back at the table and topping up his wineglass. He offers me some, but I shake my head.

"I'm driving."

He nods, putting down the bottle, and turns back to Peony.

"No. Nate just wants me to take a last look at everything, to make sure it's all okay. His permissions have already been granted."

"That was quick," she says, as though she knows all about such things. She doesn't, but I love that she shows so much interest in Ryan's business… just like he does in hers.

"It's a simple construction. There's nothing complicated about it."

"So he'll be able to start work on it soon?"

"Straight after Christmas. I recommended a company to do the work for him. The guy who owns it is an old acquaintance of my dad's, so I know he'll do a good job."

I nod my head. I'm familiar with the company in question and their work is excellent. "Do you need me there tomorrow?" I ask.

"No. I'll be fine. I don't think it'll take too long, and Nate and I are gonna talk about weddings, too."

"His, or yours?"

"Neither, I suppose."

"That doesn't make the slightest sense."

He smiles. "I know. I didn't explain myself very well. A while back, Nate agreed to run a promotional piece for us on the wedding venue, and we're gonna talk about that. It's won't be about our specific wedding, although I think he's planning to take some photographs of the barn once it's all set up. The article itself won't feature us, though. It'll be about weddings in general, and this place in particular."

It's so strange hearing him talk like this, about something as romantic as weddings, but I guess he's looking at this from a business perspective, as a marketing opportunity… and that's much more like the Ryan I know. He's good at seeing the potential in things. Although I have to say, that's usually land, and what he can turn it into, not other people's wedded bliss.

Or even his own.

Still, he's making himself at home here, which is more than can be said for me.

I may have lived here since the summer, but I still feel like a fish out of water. I guess that's because he's found love, while I haven't even found anyone of my own age to spend any time with.

Sure, he and Peony are here, and they've introduced me to Nate and Taylor, and Walker and Imogen. But they're all part of a couple, and I'm far more interested in single people… well, single women, anyway.

Ryan offers to make coffee, but I sense Peony's tired, and to be honest, I could do with getting to bed myself. The last few days of chasing bureaucrats in Vermont have taken their toll, and the frustration of not being able to get the permissions through on this plot of land is getting to me.

It's not my fault. In fact, I'm not sure it's anyone's fault, other than Adrian Marsh, the negotiator who bought this albatross of a plot of land in the first place. He knew we'd never gone in for residential development. He knew he shouldn't have been bidding on the plot… and yet he did it, anyway. His folly has cost the company half a million dollars of hard cash, and thousands more in man hours, and now it's my job to fix it, and limit any further damage, although I'm not doing a great job so far.

I clench my fists.

I need to stop thinking about it. If I don't, I'll need more wine, and that's not practical when I've still got to drive home.

"I'll see you out," Ryan says as we all get to our feet. I nod my head and give Peony a quick kiss on the cheek. She smiles up at me, looking every inch the beautiful bride to be, and then I grab my coat from the back of the couch, where I threw it earlier, and follow Ryan out through the front door.

It's freezing out here, and I shrug on my coat, although Ryan seems oblivious to the chilly night air. I guess that's what love does for you.

"I'm sorry," he says, surprising me, and I turn, frowning at him.

"You're sorry? What the hell for?"

"For being such an absentee boss over the last few weeks. I know I've left a lot of the work to you… especially on this goddamn Vermont project, but I promise things will be different after the wedding."

"You mean after the honeymoon."

He smiles. "Yeah. That too. And you know, even when I'm not in the office, you can still call me."

"I'm not calling you on your honeymoon."

He chuckles. "You'd better not. But you shouldn't need to. We're closing the offices, so you'll be able to take a break, too."

"I could use it."

He smiles. "What I meant was, during next week, if I'm not around for whatever reason, you can still call."

"I know. But I also know you trust me to run the place in your absence."

He smiles, nodding his head. "I do."

I like that. I like the authority he gives me and the trust he has in me. It means a lot.

"How does it feel to be getting married?" I ask. I'll admit to feeling intrigued by the change in him, and we go so far back, I don't think he'll mind me asking.

"I can't wait," he says, grinning. "I never thought I'd say this, but settling down is the best thing in the world."

I'm pretty sure it isn't, but I don't say anything, except goodnight. I'm not about to burst his bubble, no matter how unrealistic Ryan's being. Let's face it, what man in his right mind wants to wake up beside the same woman every single day for the rest of his life? I know I don't. I like variety, the excitement of never knowing what will happen next. It must be so boring doing the same things all the time, having sex in the same way, with the same person, day in, day out.

Although, to be fair, it's been a while since I've had sex at all.

I start my car and set off down the track that leads from the farmhouse to the main road, thinking about the last time...

It was when I went to our Boston offices, about a month ago, which could explain why I'm feeling a little edgy at the moment. A month is a long time for me, and I would have gone back sooner to relive the experience, except Ryan insisted on going himself. One of us has to visit our offices in Boston roughly every two weeks, and usually it's me, but on this occasion, Ryan said he needed to take Peony to the city. The dresses for her, the matron of honor and the flower girl had to be collected, and Peony didn't trust Ryan not to peek. He had plenty of business to attend to, and they made a weekend of it.

That's what I'd done when I'd gone the previous time, my visit starting on a Thursday. I was due to come back on the Saturday morning after a late Friday meeting, but in the end I stayed over until the Sunday evening, for the simple reason that I'd met a woman at the hotel. We both had rooms there, but spent all our time in my suite.

Man… she was hot. She could give head like a pro, and the way she rode my dick still sends shivers down my spine.

Driving back here on the Sunday night, I had to wonder why I'd never thought of doing that before. My previous visits to Boston had all been mid-week, lasting only a day or two at most. I'd kept them strictly business, too, the schedule ensuring I didn't have time for much else. But what was wrong with going at the end of the week instead? Why shouldn't I stay a little longer on my own time? And where was the harm in having some fun while I was there?

It might not have been a long-term solution to the lack of female company in my life, but it would certainly take the edge off, and by the time I got back here, I'd formulated the plan in my mind. From then on, my visits would be longer, and considerably more satisfying.

I looked forward to going back, and would have done, if Ryan hadn't announced he needed to go instead.

The frustration has been immense, especially as we're winding things down for the holidays, and there's no reason for me to go back to Boston until the new year.

No official reason, that is. Sure, I could go back on any weekend of my choosing, just to get laid. But do I really want to become that man? Am I really that desperate?

Not yet.

Although I still need something to take the edge off, because just thinking about that weekend still has the power to drive me crazy.

My meeting on the Friday afternoon had gone on far too long. It was unnecessarily stressful and by the time I got back to the hotel, I was ready for a drink, a shower and a sleep. The drink came first, in the hotel bar, and I was sitting by myself, sipping a glass of chilled white wine when she came in. She caught my eye, but that wasn't difficult. Her long blonde hair and pouting lips made staring inevitable, but it was her tight-fitting business suit that really did it for me. It was one that hugged every inch of her sexy body, and just about every man in the room joined me in admiring her. The difference was, she seemed to enjoy my attentions more than anyone else's, to the extent that, once she'd ordered a glass of red wine, she came over and introduced herself as Macie. It was a ballsy move, but I liked it, inviting her to sit with me, and when we'd finished our drinks, I offered her another.

"No thanks," she said, tilting her head in a way that was open to interpretation.

"Okay." I wasn't about to jump to conclusions, regardless of how tempting she looked.

"That doesn't mean the night has to end," she whispered.

"It doesn't?"

She shook her head, licking her lips in a way that wasn't open to any kind of interpretation, and I smiled, standing up to take her hand.

The elevator couldn't come quickly enough for either of us, and once inside, we gave in to the sexual tension, our bodies craving release. We'd already removed jackets and undone shirts and blouses by the time the doors opened, and I grabbed our clothing from the floor before I tugged her into the hall, both of us running to my room.

Once inside, the desperation of so many dry months got the better of me. I pushed her back against the wall, yanked up her short skirt, paying scant attention to her stockings and garter belt, and just nudged her panties aside before freeing my straining dick. I needed to fuck her, but even then, common sense prevailed and I pulled a condom from my wallet, rolling it over my cock before I entered her. Hard.

"Oh, fuck," she screamed, shuddering. "You're fucking huge." She was clutching at me, her need just as urgent as mine, and we both came loudly within minutes.

I wondered if she might want to leave then, her thirst slaked… but it seemed not. She wanted to stay. And I wasn't about to say 'no'.

I might have intended heading for home on the Saturday morning, but a quick call to the management secured me the suite until the Sunday evening. Macie gave up her room, moving her things into mine, and we enjoyed each other all weekend. I even fucked her over the end of the bed while we were trying to pack.

"I can't. I need to go," she said, although she parted her legs as she bent over and wiggled her naked ass at me.

I'd already put on a condom in anticipation, and I nudged my cock against her entrance. "Sure about that?"

She pushed back against me, making it clear that her need to go wasn't as great as her need to feel my cock inside her. I obliged, and afterwards, she stood upright and turned to face me, letting her arms rest on my shoulders, her hands clasped behind my head.

"That was good," she said, with a satisfied smile on her face.

"Yeah, it was."

"Can we finish packing now?"

"Sure."

We did, and then we got dressed and left, shaking hands in the hotel lobby before we finally parted. That was probably the most surreal moment of the entire weekend.

I never knew her last name, and I have no idea where she was from, or what she did for a living. We didn't ask questions, or exchange life stories, or even phone numbers. It wasn't like that for either of us. We both just wanted to have sex. So we did.

She may have gone home to an empty apartment, or to a husband and two kids. I've got no idea. That's what made it so perfect. It was anonymous.

It was just how sex should be... all about pleasure, and nothing to do with emotions and baggage and angst.

I mean... where's the fun in that?

I park outside my house, going inside and hooking up my coat in the closet behind the door, closing it and letting out a sigh as I turn and look around the lobby.

I have to admit, even though I'm still unsure about Hart's Creek, I like my house. It has four bedrooms upstairs, but it was the downstairs that won me over when I first viewed the place online. It's probably no different from any other property on this street, but I like the simple layout, the large separate rooms, and the fact that the living room has an enormous fireplace. The kitchen's pretty special too, but I don't need to go in there. Instead, I head for the living room, debating between turning on the table lamps, or the Christmas tree lights. I opt for the latter, and stand back.

Although I say so myself, I did a pretty good job with decorating this. I never usually bother with decorations. Living in an apartment on the tenth floor, Christmas in Boston was something I chose to ignore. Somehow, living here, it seemed appropriate to make the effort.

The tree is real and around eight feet tall, so roughly the same height as the one at Ryan and Peony's place. That's the only similarity, though, because while they've used more traditional decorations, which I imagine have been in Peony's family for generations, I've gone a little more modern. I've used white lights and gold baubles. Nothing else. It's simple, but I like it and I sit down on the couch, admiring my handiwork. I put the tree up and decorated the outside of the house on the weekend that Ryan and Peony went to Boston. It took my mind off what I was missing.

And I really am missing it.

My cock is hard, just from thinking about having sex. It's the memories of Macie that are responsible for that. Not that I miss her. Other than her hair, her breasts and her pussy, I can barely remember what she looked like. No, I don't miss her at all. I just miss sex.

A lot.

I unfasten my jeans and lower my zipper, releasing my cock and letting out a sigh of relief. Instinctively, I clasp my hand around my shaft, stroking my length, letting my head fill with images, not just of Macie, but of other women... lots of women, all of them wanting to please me. I close my eyes and imagine a scene where I can pass from woman to woman, taking each one in a different way. This isn't a mental orgy. I'm not sharing a bed with multiple women, or even watching them enjoy each other. In my mind, they're lined up, waiting for me, anticipating, taking turns. It's like every woman from my past has come back to please me... individually, but all at once. Each one of them feels unique, and in my imagination, I fuck them from every angle I can think of...

"Yes... yes..." I grind out the words, come spurting up my chest.

I'd like to say I feel better for that, but I don't, and I guess that's what my overactive imagination is trying to tell me.

I miss the company of women.

*

I woke up late this morning, still feeling a little depressed. I guess that's because, even though I know what's wrong, there isn't very much I can do about it. Not immediately, anyway.

Sure, I can take weekends in Boston to recharge my batteries, but I won't be going back there until January, and in any event, that's not a long-term solution, is it?

As I get into my car to make the short drive to the office, though, I'm not sure there is a long-term solution. I mean… what am I supposed to do? Hart's Creek doesn't appear to be overflowing with single women who want no strings sex. The women here seem to think in terms of relationships, settling down, marriage, and – God forbid – kids. The thought makes my blood freeze, and I shudder against it, reversing off of my driveway.

It's cold today – even aside from my now frozen blood – and I turn up the heater, making my way down Cedar Street.

I have to stop at the end, waiting for a few cars to pass, and I glance across at Hart's Green, which is opposite. There's a sign advertising the Christmas Fair. It's due to be held tomorrow, and there's evidence already of stalls being set out on the far side of the enormous patch of grass.

They had a Fall Festival here a couple of months ago, and although I didn't go to that, I wonder if maybe I should attend this latest event.

I ought to try to integrate better. Sitting at home won't get me very far, and while I know there's no chance of meeting anyone who's female, single, and into the same things as me, I still have to live here. I need to make friends. Sure, I've got Ryan and Peony, and the people they've introduced me to, but it would be good to socialize with friends of my own, too… preferably ones who aren't part of a couple.

A truck stops, blocking my exit, and although that's annoying, I take the time to glance to my right at the Hart's Creek Hotel, a smile touching my lips.

I'd only been living here for a week or so, when I noticed that almost everywhere in town is called 'Hart's' something or other, including Peony's apple orchard. It's her name, too, and when I mentioned it to Ryan, he laughed.

"There's been a Hart in Hart's Creek since the dawn of time," he said. "Or for a few generations, anyway."

"There won't be once you're married," I reminded him, and he smiled.

"Yes, there will." I frowned, confused by his answer. "Peony and I have talked it through. I know what her heritage means to her, and we've agreed she'll keep her own name."

I was surprised by that, but it's just another way Ryan's changed since he met Peony.

I can't imagine being like that myself, or letting a woman change me in any way. I like my freedom far too much to sacrifice it for anyone. But Ryan's happy, and I guess we can't all be the same.

The truck moves and as the sign for the Christmas Fair comes back into view, I nod my head, deciding I'll probably pay it a visit, as I pull out of the turning onto Main Street.

It's busy today, but that seems to be how it is on Fridays, and I'm running a little late. I wonder about getting a takeout from the French restaurant tonight. I don't feel like cooking, and…

The movement of the car pulling out of Maple Street catches my eye just in time. It has to cross my path, and whoever's driving has cut it really fine. Still, it's okay. We'll make it. Except it's stopped. *What the fuck?* Who in their right mind would stop there, right in the middle of the street? I see the driver's face. It's a woman. A young woman. She looks terrified, and for a moment

I'm paralyzed, mesmerized... then I remember to swerve, to brake. It's too late though, and I brace myself for the impact.

Chapter Three

⟫⟫⟪⟪

Remi

This is not the best way to start my day.

I was already running late because – for once – my car wouldn't start, and I suppose that's why I risked pulling out of Maple Street when I did, even though I'd seen that big black Range Rover heading straight for me. I thought I could make it out in time… and I would have done if my engine hadn't cut out. Why it did that is anyone's guess, but it did, and now I'm paying for my impatience.

I might have seen the car approaching, but it was like everything went into slow motion. I couldn't move… couldn't do anything except stare, and grip the steering wheel, hoping for the best. The man who was driving tried to swerve, and he braked, but he still hit me. Or he hit my car, and thanks to his quick reactions, it wasn't as bad as I thought it might be.

I'm okay, other than feeling like a fool, and I climb out of the car, taking a deep breath.

He'll be mad at me. I know he will. I should have just waited for him to pass and then pulled out. It was an idiotic thing for me to have done, and whatever he says, I'll deserve it.

I wait, letting him reverse back a little, and I study the front of his gleaming beast of a car. There doesn't seem to be too much damage, other than a scratch of silver paintwork from mine, which I suppose is something. It's too much to hope that my Toyota will have fared as well, and I glance down, grimacing when I see the crumpled fender.

It looks bad, but I know it could have been worse. Much worse.

"Are you okay?"

I turn to face the man as he climbs from his vehicle, coming straight toward me. He's tall, wearing a very smart gray suit, with a light blue tie, and has reddish-brown hair, which he pushes his fingers through, while staring down at me.

"I'm fine," I say, surprised that he seems concerned and not angry.

He blinks, frowning. "You're not hurt?"

"No." He looks me up and down, like he doesn't believe me, and needing something to do with my hands, I tuck my hair behind my ears. It's a habit of mine. "I'm okay. Honestly."

He nods his head, finally convinced, it seems, and turns his attention to my damaged car.

"I'm so sorry."

Is he serious? He's apologizing? I shake my head, gazing up into emerald green eyes. "This wasn't your fault. It was mine."

"No, it wasn't. I should have done more to avoid you. My only defense is that I was… distracted." He hesitates over his last word, frowning again, like he's confused.

I'm not sure what had distracted him. It could have been something on the radio, his phone ringing… anything, really. He doesn't seem to want to say, and to be honest, it's none of my business. It's also irrelevant.

"I should never have pulled out in the first place, but I was late for work, and I… I took a chance." I sigh, scratching my head as

I look back at the fender. "This is awful. I really don't need it right now."

It's true. I don't. I have no idea how much it'll cost to repair, which is a worry in itself, but there's also the problem of being without a car… especially just before the holidays, and when it's so cold. There's nothing for it. I'll have to wrap up warm and walk to work, I guess. I sigh again, and the man moves a little closer.

"I'll pay for the damage, if that's what you're worried about."

"You can't. It wasn't your fault."

"I think we've already established that it was."

I frown up at him. "No, we haven't, and I can't let you pay."

"Yeah, you can. Look… why don't we get your car to the auto repair shop? It's right here." He nods over his shoulder. "They'll take care of it, and I'll cover the cost."

"But…"

"But nothing. This is my responsibility."

"It really isn't. My engine cut out. I don't know why, but you can't be held responsible for that."

"Neither can you." He looks around. "Come on… we're blocking the street. Let's at least take it to the shop and see what they say."

I nod my head, seeing his point, and he opens my car door, waiting for me to climb back behind the wheel.

"It wouldn't start earlier," I say, giving it a try. It turns over, but fails to ignite, and I look up at him.

"Try it again." I do as he says and this time it sparks to life. I smile up at him and he smiles back. "Drive it across the street, and I'll follow you."

He closes the door before I can reply, going back to his car. He hasn't even checked what damage has been done to his vehicle yet, which seems odd, but I can't sit here all day. Like he said, I'm blocking the street. I edge forward, the car moving easily now it doesn't matter so much, and make my way to the auto repair shop.

To be honest, I half expect the man to drive off, but he doesn't. He follows me, and as I park up just inside the gates, he pulls in behind, both of us getting out at the same time.

A man dressed in dark blue coveralls comes out through a door in a wooden building over to the right, the word 'office' printed on a sign to one side. He's wiping his hands on a towel, and tilts his head to one side as he walks over, studying my car.

"Oh, dear," he says with a smile. "I thought I heard a crunch just now." He nods to the damaged fender. "This explains it." He studies me for a second, a slight frown forming on his face. "I'm Levi, by the way. This is my garage."

I nod my head, wondering if I'm supposed to introduce myself. It feels unnecessary in the circumstances, and for some reason, I'm a little nervous. I feel shy, too, but that's normal for me. As for the nerves? That's ridiculous, really. Levi's nice enough.

The man in the Range Rover steps forward, my nerves abating slightly as I look up at him. He has a friendly and very handsome face, and there's something about that and his self-assurance that makes me feel at ease.

"Can you fix this lady's car for her?" he asks.

Levi nods his head and steps up a little closer to my car, bending and then crouching for a more detailed inspection. "It looks worse than it is," he says, standing up and turning back around to face us. He glances at me again, frowning just like he did before. "I've seen you around, haven't I?"

The man in the Range Rover steps a little closer as I nod my head. "You might have done. I work in the library."

Levi smiles. "That's it. I remember now. You're Nora's replacement."

I want to yell that I'm a lot more than that, but I smile instead. "Yes, I am. I moved here in May."

"And how are you finding it?"

"Fine, thanks."

I can hardly tell him I'm bored and lonely, and in dire need of friendship, can I? He'd think I was crazy.

"Getting back to the car," the man in the Range Rover says, and Levi looks up at him. "Can you fix it?"

"Sure, I can. I just need to replace the fender."

The man nods his head. "The engine cut out, and it doesn't start very reliably, so could you check that out, too?"

"No, really…" I say, but the man holds up a hand, silencing me.

"We might as well get everything done at once."

"But I…"

He shakes his head. "It's on me."

"No. You can't do that."

He smiles, showing off perfect white teeth. "Yeah, I can." He turns back to Levi. "If you can check over the engine, fix whatever needs fixing, repair the damage, and let me know how much it costs?"

As he's speaking, he pulls out his wallet and hands a business card to Levi, who takes it, checking it over before he puts it away in one of his many pockets.

"It might take a while," he says, pulling a face, like he knows I'll be disappointed. "I'm real busy right now, and with the holidays coming up…"

"How long is a while?" I ask.

"A week?" My face falls and he obviously notices "I'll do my best to get it done sooner, but it depends on what's wrong with the engine, and if I need to order any parts, other than the replacement fender."

"That's fine."

The man with the Range Rover steps forward. "Are you sure?"

"Of course. It can't be helped if Levi's busy, can it?"

"What I mean is, I can arrange a rental for you, if it helps."

I'm tempted, but I can't accept. "No, really. You're already doing too much."

He shakes his head, but before he can contradict me again, or repeat for the umpteenth time that he feels the accident was his fault, I turn to Levi.

"Do you want my number, too, so you can let me know when the car's ready?" It's fine for the man to pay for it, but I'll need to pick it up, won't I?

Levi nods and pulls out his phone from yet another of his pockets, making a note of my number as I reel it off, along with the car's make and registration. I guess that's more memorable for him than my name might be.

"We'll let you get on." The man with the Range Rover turns toward his car, and I give Levi a smile. There's no point in hanging around here anymore. I need to get to work.

I also need to thank the man, and once Levi has gone back into his office, I look up at him again. He sucks in a breath, but before he can say a word, I get there first.

"You really don't have to do this, you know, but as you don't seem to be very good at taking no for an answer, thank you."

He smiles. "You're welcome. Can I give you a ride to work?"

I shake my head. "It's fine. I've only got to walk to the library."

"Oh, yeah… you said."

I step back, but he moves forward, making me stop in my tracks. "Is something wrong?" I ask.

"No. It's just, I forgot to introduce myself. My name's Gabe Sullivan. I live in Cedar Street, and I work for Andrews and Son Properties."

"I see. Is there a reason you're telling me this?"

He shrugs his shoulders. "I guess I just wanted you to know that I live here, too... and I'm not about to run out on you without paying for the repairs to your car."

"I wouldn't have blamed you if you had. It wasn't..."

He raises his hand, resting his forefinger against my lips and I fall silent, a tingle running down my spine. I've never been touched quite like that before, not even by someone I know well... let alone by a complete stranger, and I don't know what to make of it. He gazes at my mouth, just for a second, his eyes widening, and then he suddenly pulls his hand away.

"Sorry," he says, and I tip my head, unsure what he's apologizing for. "You were going to say it wasn't my fault again, weren't you?"

"Yes, because..."

This time, although he raises his hand, his finger only dusts over my lip, rather than resting there. I'm not sure which sensation is the more confusing. Either way, I feel like my brain just froze.

"Let me do this," he says, slowly lowering his hand.

"It doesn't feel right. Not when it wasn't..."

"Yes, it was," he says, then frowns slightly, studying my face as though he's never seen me before. His eyes linger over my lips, and I recall the touch of his fingers, just as he shakes his head, like he's coming out of a trance. "Am I permitted to know your name?" he asks.

It seems only fair, considering how generous he's been. "Remi Fox," I say, surprised by how quiet my voice is.

"That's pretty." He pauses, a smile touching at his lips. Then he opens his mouth, quickly closes it again, and says, "Can I maybe walk you to the library? I—I could buy you a cup of coffee on the way, if you like?"

I could be wrong, but it feels like he wants to do more than walk me to work and buy me coffee. Why did he stumble so much over asking if that's all he wants? And why ask in the first place? He doesn't know me, and even if he is more than generous, and has impeccable taste in suits, a clean-shaven square jaw, and eyes that feel like they can see right through me, I can't possibly accept. His suit might fit every contoured muscle on his gorgeously tall body, but there's no escaping the fact that this man must be in his mid-thirties... and I can't do this again.

"I—I really don't have time." Now I'm the one stumbling over her words.

"You're walking to work, anyway." He sounds more self-assured again now. "What harm can it do to have some company? Unless you think your boyfriend wouldn't like it..." He lets his voice fade and I shake my head at him.

"I don't have a boyfriend."

He smiles. "In that case..."

He might have me confused about his intentions, but I was right about one thing. He's not good at taking 'no' for an answer.

I take a step back, shaking my head at the same time. "I can't."

He frowns. "Are you turning me down because I damaged your car?"

"No." *I'm turning you down because I don't know where walking to work and buying me coffee is going to lead.*

It might be nowhere, but if he wants it to be somewhere, that can't happen.

Not after the last time.

It's just not possible.

He stares at me for a moment, but I'm not about to explain any of that. It would be rude and ungracious, but it would also be far too personal, so I just give him a smile and turn, walking away as fast as I can.

Chapter Four

Gabe

Her smile has haunted me all day.

Just like Remi herself.

There's something arresting about her... something different. Perhaps that's why − for the first time in my life − I drove into another car. I've never even come close to having an accident before, and yet, there I was, so damn distracted by a beautiful woman, I forgot to pay attention to the fact that I was about to crash into her car.

That's what made it my fault.

I left it far too late to swerve and brake, because I was too busy staring at her.

I had to claim responsibility for what happened, because being captivated by a woman's face isn't a good enough excuse for not focusing on what's happening on the road, and paying for the damage to her car seemed like an easier option than admitting to any of that on an insurance claim.

I can't even begin to imagine how I would have phrased that.

I think anyone who saw her would understand the distraction, though, and I'm just grateful she wasn't injured, and that the damage to her car wasn't as bad as it might have been.

I may have temporarily lost my mind, but I swerved enough that the fender took the brunt of the impact. Even then, it came off better than I'd expected.

It was a relief to know I hadn't done any serious damage, and when she got out of her car, I thought about asking why she'd pulled out like that, and then stopped so abruptly. Except something very confusing happened in my head… and my chest… and my cock. And just about everywhere else, too. There was no denying how beautiful she was. I'd already noticed that, right before hitting her car. This was something far more than that.

It was like she'd cast a spell over me, and while I know how ludicrous that sounds, I can't think of any other way to describe the sensations that were going on inside me. I certainly didn't have any control. The only thing that mattered as she stood staring at her crumpled car, was that she was okay. My work, my non-existent social life, my best friend's wedding, and everything else that had been occupying my mind could be damned as far as I was concerned. I had this overwhelming need, or urge, or longing, to protect her, and nothing was going to get in the way of that. I didn't even know her name, but I had to know she was okay.

When she said she was, her voice kinda tickled my skin. I'd never felt anything like that before. Alongside all the other strange sensations going on inside me, I wasn't sure what to make of it… so I asked her again. And every time she spoke, the same thing happened.

I don't know how she did that, but I liked it. I wanted to listen to her, to sit and talk, and gaze into those bright blue eyes… and lose myself.

Yep… I know I just said lose myself, and that's not something I've ever considered before, but that's what I wanted. That's how it felt. Like losing myself in her would be the best place to be.

The weirdest thing about all that – aside from the thought itself, which was alien to me – was that she's nothing like the kind of woman I usually go for.

Fiery redheads are a real thing for me. They always have been. Failing that, I like blondes. The blonder the better. Ideally, I prefer women with long hair, and even longer legs. And I like them to dress provocatively. Cover everything that needs covering, by all means, but I'm not into guessing what's on offer. I like it on display. That way, we both know where we stand. I like my women tall, too. That's hardly surprising. I'm six foot three, and I don't remember the last time I even looked at a woman who was under around five foot nine in her bare feet. In twenty years or more of admiring the opposite sex, I've worked out what I like… and that's it. It's simple, really.

Or it was, until this morning, when I was mesmerized by a beautiful brunette, with sleek, shoulder-length hair that she tucked behind her ears whenever it got in the way. I noticed that about her straight away, along with her stunning blue eyes. The contrast between hair and eyes was unusual and enough to grab anyone's attention, as was her perfectly clear skin, which seemed to be unadorned by even a hint of makeup. It was only when she tilted her head to look up at me that I realized the disparity in our heights. She can't have been over five foot four, and yet rather than dismissing her as I might have done any other woman of her height and coloring, I only wanted her more. It was a struggle to hide my feelings, to bury the burning need inside me, to pull her into my arms and hold her… to kiss her. Hard. But I managed it, continuing our conversation while taking in the way she was dressed. There was nothing on display, and yet that seemed so much more alluring than if she'd revealed herself to me. Her clothes were simple, yet stylish and sophisticated. Her dark gray coat only partially concealed pale gray pants that fitted her figure perfectly, as did the light sweater she wore on top, with a single string of pearls around her neck.

As for her age, that was something of a mystery, but based on her clothes, I'd have said she was around twenty-eight, although there was something in her eyes, and that natural shyness she seemed to possess, that made me wonder if perhaps she was a little younger. Even at twenty-eight, she was young. Too young for a man of thirty-six?

Hell, no.

In my view, there's no such thing as 'too young', as long as a woman is legal.

Besides, I've only just turned thirty-six.

And in any case, what does it matter? She said 'no'.

She turned me down.

Dammit.

Why does that bother me? Other than the obvious facts that she'd made my skin tingle, my breath hitch, my brain freeze? Why did it matter? Why does it still matter, even now?

It wasn't like I'd propositioned her. Hell, I'd faltered over asking her to let me walk her to work, and maybe grab a coffee along the way. I've never felt more nervous in my life. I've never wanted anyone to say 'yes' more, either.

I won't deny that, if she had, and I'd managed to find my balls somewhere along Main Street, I'd probably have asked her to have dinner with me by the time we got to the library. She wasn't to know that, though, was she? At face value, it was a simple offer to keep her company while she walked to work. Nothing more, nothing less. And in reality, that's all it was, too. I wanted to spend time with her. Once I'd ruled out her having a boyfriend in the background, I wanted it even more.

Except she didn't want me.

And I'm surprised by how much that hurts.

It's physical, like a stabbing in my chest. It's been there all day, and no matter how hard I try, I can't seem to shift it.

I also can't shift the memory of how soft her lips felt against my fingers when I touched them. All I wanted was to stop her from taking the blame for the accident... or to let me accept it. I couldn't kiss her into silence, so placing my fingers over her lips seemed like the quickest and easiest way of achieving that. It worked, too. She stopped talking. The problem was, the jolt of electricity that rocked through my body when I touched her was like nothing I'd ever felt, and I had to pull my hand back almost immediately.

I was intrigued, though. Her lips had felt so tender, so I took a chance and touched them again at the very first opportunity. I needed to feel that softness, although I kept the contact much lighter the second time, knowing the effect it would have on me. I was better prepared for it, and didn't want it to end. It's an experience I'd like to re-live again... and again... and again.

Somehow, I've made it through the day, although I don't know how. In a way, I'm relieved it's Friday. At least I won't have to come to the office tomorrow and pretend to work, or face Ryan and the strange looks he keeps giving me. I can't blame him for that. I haven't been myself all day.

"Are you sure you're okay?" It was only lunchtime and that had to be the fifth time he'd asked that question. "I know you said the accident wasn't bad, but..."

"I'm fine." I did my best to shut him down, but I could tell he was concerned.

I'd been drifting around the office, unable to settle to anything all morning. Given how busy we are right now, that wasn't helpful.

To put his mind at rest, I spent most of the afternoon staring at my computer screen. I wasn't achieving anything, but I figured he'd worry less if he saw me doing that, than if I was gazing out the window, looking vacant.

"Have you got any plans for the weekend?" I look up to see Ryan standing in the doorway to my office, almost filling the frame. We're of quite similar builds and heights, although our coloring is very different. My hair is a reddish brown, while his is dark, as are his eyes. Mine are a bright green. So bright they often draw attention… usually of the female variety, and in the past, I've used that to my advantage, as a means of starting conversations with redheads or blondes who've caught my bright green eye. Oddly enough, the idea of doing that now feels foreign to me, like that was another life, lived by a different man.

How can that be, though? It was only last night I jerked off, thinking about all the women from my past, lining up to fuck me. I might have felt uneasy straight afterwards, but that was because I needed the reality of at least one woman. I was feeling lonely and in need of sex, but I don't recall a single moment of regret about the past. So why is it, less than twenty-four hours later, I'm feeling unsure about myself, and all the things I've done before?

This can't have anything to do with Remi. She turned me down, so there's no point in dwelling on what might have been… is there?

"Ahem." Ryan's fake cough brings me out of my trance and I look up. "Are you sure you're okay?" he asks.

I wonder about lying to him. I could easily say I'm fine again, but I doubt it would carry any conviction when I can't even answer a straight question about my weekend plans. He'd see right through me, so there's no point in trying to hide it. "N—No. Not really."

He steps into the room, walking up to my desk. "Do you wanna go to the hospital? I'll take you, if…"

"There's nothing physically wrong with me." At least I don't think there is. That pain in my chest hasn't really subsided all day, but I don't think that's anything a doctor will be able to fix. I think only Remi can heal that particular wound.

"Are you sure? Sometimes things don't appear until a few hours after an accident. It might be best to get a doctor to check you over."

"No. Really. It's nothing like that."

"Then what's the matter?"

"I don't know how to say this…"

"Say what?"

I sigh, letting my breath out slowly. "I think I've met someone."

He frowns. "I'm assuming we're talking about a woman?"

"Yes."

"But you only *think* you've met her. You don't know?"

"I know I met her. I remember it happening. What I'm not so sure about is what it means."

"What does it normally mean?"

"For me? Sex." That's the truth. Meeting a woman in the past has always been about sex, and nothing else. Except this time that's not true. Well… it is. Obviously. But there's more to it.

"Exactly," he says. "So, what's the problem?"

"I don't know." I do. It's that she's different from anyone I've ever met, and I don't know how to handle that. I don't even know what to make of it… or her. I shrug my shoulders. "She turned me down, so…"

He shakes his head, smiling. "That's unusual."

I smile back. "It's been known to happen."

He doesn't look convinced. "When did you meet her?"

"This morning. She's the woman who was driving the other car."

"The car you ran into?"

"Yeah."

His smile widens. "I know you're a fast worker, but are you seriously telling me that, having run this poor woman off the road, you immediately…"

"I didn't run her off the road." I only explained the basics of the accident to him this morning, after I arrived at the office, without going into too much detail. My mind wasn't in a fit state for detail. "It wasn't like that. It was an accident for which I took the blame."

"Because you saw it as a way to get her into bed?"

"No. Because I felt responsible for what happened." And for her.

"Well, I guess you're gonna have to see her again when her car's fixed. You're paying for it, aren't you?"

"Yeah, I am."

"In which case, you can try again, can't you?"

I suppose I can, although I don't know when that will be. It could be next week, or if Levi can't get the parts, it could be after the holidays. The thought of waiting that long feels like torture. But what can I do?

"Are you guys doing anything over the weekend?" I ask, just to change the subject, even though I know I still haven't answered his original question.

"The chairs are supposed to be delivered tomorrow. They haven't given us a time, though, so we could be waiting in for most of the day for all we know. If they arrive early enough, I think Peony wants to go to the Christmas Fair."

"And you don't?"

He shrugs. "I don't mind. It'll probably be fun."

I nod my head. "I was thinking of taking a look myself." My idea at the time had been to meet new people, but now I'm wondering whether I might run into Remi, and the thought of that makes a visit to the fair seem even more appealing.

What are my other alternatives?

Waiting for her car to be fixed, stalking her at the library, or hanging out on Main Street in the hope she'll come by.

All in all, going to the Christmas Fair seems a much better idea… and less likely to get me arrested than at least two of my other options.

"We might see you there," he says, turning away and heading for the door. "But if not, have a good weekend, and get some rest, will you?"

"I'll do my best."

He leaves, and I shut down my computer, locking the office as I leave, since I'm the last one here.

The drive home takes no time, and as I get to the corner of Cedar Street, I glance toward the library, just to see if there's any sign of Remi. If she's there, I could stop by and offer her a ride home… except the place is already closed up and in darkness.

I've missed her.

It doesn't seem to be my day, and I head home, parking outside.

I don't think I've ever felt this despondent or unsure of myself. It's really out of character for me, and as I sit in the living room, staring at the darkened Christmas tree, I wonder whether that feeling of losing my mind might not be so temporary after all.

I don't feel any better this morning than I did last night. I'd like to blame the lack of sleep, but it's more than that. It's like there's a cloud hanging over me that I can't seem to shift.

Having got up early, bored with lying in bed staring at the ceiling, I've showered, dressed, done the laundry and tidied the house. It's not ten-thirty yet, and I know the Christmas Fair doesn't start until eleven, but I can't see the harm in going a little early. It's got to be preferable to moping around the house, although as I pull on my coat, I tell myself I'm only doing this so I can avoid the crowds that are more likely to come out later on. Deep down, I know the reality is that I'll probably stay there all day, just in the hope of seeing Remi.

There's no use trying to kid myself.

So I won't bother. I'll be thrilled if she's there, and crushed if she isn't.

Why pretend otherwise?

It's freezing outside, and I fasten my coat, pulling up the collar as I make my way down the sidewalk to the corner of Main Street. It seems busy, not just with people, but with cars, and I stop for a moment, waiting to cross. Someone turns into Cedar Street and I step back, my heart flipping over in my chest when I catch sight of Remi on the other side of the street.

It's definitely her. I may have only met her once, but I'd know her anywhere.

She's outside the florist's shop, trying to drag a Christmas tree along the sidewalk, while struggling with a couple of bags… and I mean struggling.

I check the traffic, and dodging around a car that's waiting to turn into the hotel car park, I run across the road, straight up to her.

"Hi."

She looks up, frowning, although her face quickly clears when she recognizes me. Thank God. At least I didn't have to remind her who I am.

"Hello."

"Can I help?" I nod toward the Christmas tree and she smiles.

"I'd love to be able to say I can manage, but it's obvious I'd be lying."

I smile back. "Here… let me take it."

She steps away and I lift the tree, raising it onto my shoulder and balancing it there. "It's heavy… be careful," she says.

"It's fine. Give me your bags." I hold out my free hand.

"No... really."

I keep my hand where it is and tilt my head, raising my eyebrows. After a second or two, she holds them out and I take them from her.

"Where are we going?"

"Maple Street."

I feel like a heel. "Of course. I should have realized. You were turning out of there yesterday, weren't you?"

"Yes." She blushes, which is about the cutest thing I've ever seen.

"Were you gonna drag this thing all the way there?"

"I was gonna try."

"Well... having damaged your car and rendered it useless for the next few days, the least I can do is carry your Christmas tree home."

"Thank you," she whispers, and we set off down Main Street.

"At least you've accepted the accident was my fault," I say, gazing down at her. She looks even prettier than yesterday, if that were possible. Today, she's hidden her hair beneath a cream-colored woolen hat, and although she's wearing a matching scarf, her face is completely visible, her cheeks pinked by the frosty breeze. Her coat is buttoned up, coming down to her mid-thighs, beneath which I can see a gray winter skirt, or maybe a dress, and flat black boots. Again, there's that polished edge to her, which I really like... a lot.

"I haven't done any such thing," she replies, although she's clearly not affronted by my remark. She's smiling. "I was just thanking you for helping."

I lean in to her, careful not to drop the tree. "Any time."

She tilts her head, her eyes lingering over my face for a moment, studying my lips before they drop to my shoulder, where the tree is resting.

"That's not too heavy, is it?"

"Not at all." *It feels as light as a feather, especially when you're smiling at me.*

We have to stop to let a woman with a stroller and two young children pass, and then we set off again.

"Did I hear you say to Levi that you only moved here in May?" I ask, desperate to keep the conversation flowing.

"Yes."

"You've been here longer than me, then."

She raises her eyebrows. "Why? When did you move here?"

"July."

A smile tugs at her lips and I long to lean in and kiss them, first in the corners, to feel that smile forming, and then more fully, our tongues meeting in a slow caress.

"It takes some getting used to, doesn't it?" she says.

I have to smile myself. "I'm glad it's not just me."

She giggles unexpectedly, and my cock hardens in an instant. What a sound. There's nothing like it on this earth... at least, nothing I've ever heard before.

"What do you do?" she asks. "Was there a reason you moved to Hart's Creek? I remember you said you worked for a property company, but does that mean you're in construction?"

I love that she's interested, and that she remembered what I do, and I smile down at her.

"Construction? No. That's not what I do at all."

"Really?"

I slow my pace, looking down at her more closely. "Why are you surprised by that?"

"Because of the way you're built, I guess." She blushes. Once again... real cute. "I'm sorry."

"Hey... don't apologize." *I like that you're looking.* "I've never built anything in my life. My background is on the business side, not the practical one."

She nods. "You said who you work for, but I can't remember now."

"Andrews and Son Properties. Ryan Andrews is my oldest friend."

"And he has a son, does he?"

"Not yet. Ryan is the son. It was his father's company. Ryan took it over when his father died."

"And you work for him?"

"I do."

"You don't find that… awkward?" She struggles for a word, finding one eventually. It's the one people usually use when they ask about my relationship with Ryan, and how it functions.

"Not at all. He never treats me like an employee, and I never forget he's my boss. It's simple, really."

She frowns. "It doesn't sound very simple."

"It is. Honestly. It's about trust."

"And you trust each other?"

"Implicitly."

She nods her head. "So, why did you move here? It doesn't seem like the most obvious place for a construction company to be based."

"We're not really a construction company. Our game is buying land and working out how best to utilize it."

"I see… kind of." She smiles. "Even so, I can't imagine Hart's Creek is the center of the universe when it comes to property development."

"It's not. Until the spring, we were based in Boston. That's where I'm from… and so is Ryan."

"Are you going back there, then?"

I want to ask how she'd feel if I did, but I'm a little worried about her answer. Besides, we're getting along okay just talking, so I may as well give her a straight answer.

"No."

There. That's about as straight as answers go, and I study her face for a second or two, hoping for a response. She looks up at me, her eyes meeting mine, and after a moment, she just nods her head. I don't know what that means, but it can't be bad, can it? Okay, so she didn't say 'great', or even 'good', but she didn't say 'that's a shame', either.

"What made your friend choose Hart's Creek?" she says as we cross the street.

"He fell in love."

She stops walking as she steps onto the sidewalk, looking up at me. "Seriously? He fell in love with Hart's Creek?"

"No," I say, smiling down at her. "He fell in love with someone who lives here. He came up here earlier in the year to buy the apple orchard and fell for the lady who owns it."

"Is this the apple orchard just outside the town?"

I nod my head. "It is."

"And he fell for the lady who owns it? Just like that?"

"He did."

"How did she feel about that?"

"They're getting married next weekend, so I guess she was okay with it."

Her eyes widen, and her mouth opens slightly. "They're getting married?"

"Yeah."

"Did he buy the farm?"

"No." We turn into Maple Street. "He didn't want the land anywhere near as much as he wanted Peony. So he gave up the idea of buying anything, moved his business up here, and is busy making a life for the two of them."

"In what way?"

"In all kinds of ways. They've just converted one of the barns into a wedding venue."

"Oh, yes. I heard something about that. My colleagues at work were talking about it a while ago."

"In a good way?" I ask, intrigued by the local response.

"I think so. To be honest, I don't always pay attention. If I did, none of us would get any work done."

"I see. It's like that, is it?"

She rolls her eyes. "Most of the time."

She stops outside a single-story house, and I copy her, looking up at it. "Is this you?" I ask, and she nods.

I feel a little disappointed that we've reached our destination already, but things don't have to end here… not as far as I'm concerned.

"Where would you like me to put your tree?"

She turns, looking up at it, and then tilts her head. "Can you carry it inside for me?"

"Sure."

We start up the sloped driveway and I wait while she unlocks the door, and then follow her inside.

The lobby is long and narrow, with four doors coming off of it. It may be a little dark, but the decor is light, the walls being just off white, and the floor a pale wood.

"Which way?" I ask, unable to turn because of the tree I'm still carrying over my shoulder.

"In here."

She opens the door to the left… the only one on this side, and leads me into her living room. It stretches from the front of the house, all the way to the back, with a fireplace in the middle of the longest wall. They're painted a light shade of blue, and the floor is that same pale wood as in the lobby. There are two darker blue couches on either side of the unlit hearth, with a low table between them. It looks homely, but is nowhere near as homely as the area at the back of the room. There's a window which takes up most of the rear wall, but on either side of it are some bookcases, and in front of them are two chairs, covered in the same dark blue fabric as the couches.

"What a beautiful room," I breathe, taking it all in.

"Thank you. I took a while to decorate it, but it was worth it in the end."

"You did this?"

She nods her head, looking pleased with herself, and rightly so. "I'm taking a break from decorating until after the holidays, and then I'll probably start in the bedroom."

I put down the bags and lower the tree to the floor, letting it rest on its wooden stand. It's an inch or so shorter than me, although its branches are tied up at the moment, so I can't see how wide it is.

"Where do you want this?" I ask, looking around.

"How about by the window?"

There's plenty of space there and I abandon the bags and lift the tree again, putting it down in the center of the window at the front of the room.

"That's perfect." I turn to see Remi gazing at the tree, and then at me, a light smile etched on her lips. "I felt really guilty having the only house in the street that wasn't decorated, so I thought I'd better put that right."

"Putting it right would have been a lot easier if I hadn't crashed my car into yours."

She shakes her head. "I still don't accept that version of events, but I'm really grateful for your help."

Then don't dismiss me again… please…

I don't know whether to ask if she needs my help with anything else, or whether to cut to the chase and ask her to have lunch with me. Or dinner. Either would be great. Or should I tell her the truth, and admit she's gotten under my skin, and that I can't stop thinking about her?

I don't think that's the best idea in the world, but I can't just leave her... not now.

What should I say, though? How can I convince her to let me stay a while longer?

"Would you like a coffee?" she asks, surprising me, and I nod my head, unable to speak at all.

Chapter Five

Remi

He's really easy to talk to.

To be honest, I thought that yesterday, even if I did practically run away from him. He was kind and considerate from the moment he stepped out of his car. Most people would have been angry, but he wasn't. He was lovely. He still is lovely. There's no denying that. Although one of the things I didn't realize about him while we were standing in the street and at the auto repair shop, was how deep his voice is. I'm going to put that down to shock, rather than spectacular inattentiveness on my part. Or maybe it was because I was focusing too much on his motives and his age to notice that his voice has a musical depth to it that sings across my skin whenever he speaks.

Does that mean I've forgotten his age and his motives?

No.

Okay, so I accepted his offer to carry my tree, but that was because any fool could see there was no way I was going to get it and my bags back here. The tree may not be the biggest in the world, but I'd bitten off more than I could chew. Just the weight of it was enough to floor me, let alone its size and sheer unwieldiness. I don't know what I thought I was doing, and I'm glad Gabe came along to save the day.

That doesn't mean a thing, though.

Even if he is kind and considerate, and gorgeous, and funny. None of it means a thing. Just like that tumbling feeling I keep getting in my stomach when he looks at me. That doesn't mean anything, either.

He's staring at me now, and while my stomach is doing backflips, I remember I just offered him a coffee, and he just accepted with a nod of his head, which means I need to pull myself together and go make some.

"The kitchen's this way," I say, leaving the room and heading toward the back of the house.

I'm not sure why I told him that. It was an invitation to follow me, and he has, but I could just as easily have left him in the living room and come to make the coffee by myself. Instead of which, I open the door and he joins me in my country-style kitchen.

"This is a nice big room," he says, looking around.

"It'll probably be the last one I get around to changing."

"Why? Do you like it the way it is?"

"No, but kitchens are expensive. I blew my savings on the deposit for this place, and buying my car, which is one of the reasons I'm taking my time over decorating."

"So it's not just because you have better things to do?"

"No."

He nods his head, glancing around the room again. "This isn't your style, then?"

"No. Why do you ask?"

I look at the wooden cabinet doors, the brightly colored square tiles, and red linoleum flooring, all of it jarring. I know why it's not my style, but I'm intrigued by what a comparative stranger might have to say on the subject.

"Because there's a lot going on in here, and that doesn't seem like you."

"You're saying I'm plain?"

He shakes his head. "No."

"Simple, then?"

"No. I'm saying you're cultured."

"Cultured?"

"Yes. The way you dress, the decor in your living room… that little reading nook at the back. It's all very tasteful."

I hadn't been expecting that. It feels like a compliment, so I nod my head, knowing I'm blushing, and whisper, "Thank you."

I'm getting really warm, but that's not just because Gabe is standing right in front of me… although I think that might have something to do with it. The main reason is because I'm still wearing my coat, hat and scarf. Before I can even think about making coffee, I need to be wearing less, so I unwrap my scarf and pull off my hat, quickly straightening my hair, and then I unfasten my coat, shrugging it off and laying everything over the back of one of the four chairs surrounding my circular kitchen table, which nestles in a corner at the back of the room.

Gabe is still wearing a pea coat, which looks good on him, even though he's turned down the collar now, and although he hasn't bothered with a scarf and hat, he must be warm, too.

"Why don't you take your coat off?" I suggest and he smiles and does as I've said, laying his coat over the chair next to mine, turning to reveal he's wearing dark jeans and a pale gray sweater, which he pulls down a little at the front as he stares at me.

"Do you need any help with the coffee?" he asks.

"No, thanks. I'm fine."

I wander back to the sink, filling the coffeepot, adding some grounds to the machine and switching it on. When I turn back around, I find Gabe leaning against the countertop on the other side of the room, his arms folded, and his eyes fixed on me. My stomach does that same toppling over thing it was doing before, but I do my best to ignore it, and eventually he drags his eyes away, looking around the room again.

"You inherited this kitchen from the people who lived here before you?"

"In a way. The house was rented, so I don't know when it was last decorated."

"In the seventies, maybe?" he says with a smile.

"I thought that."

"If this was their taste in kitchens, what did they do with the rest of the place?"

"They went overboard with ditzy floral prints."

"And that's not who you are?" he says, sounding a little less sure of himself now.

"I like flowers, and I like floral prints, but there's only so many of them that should be put into one space at any given time."

He laughs, making my skin tingle.

The coffee machine beeps, letting me know it's ready, and I turn around, trying to calm myself, and let my skin and the rest of my body cool down. It's still too hot in here… or is that just me?

I grab two cups from the cabinet above my head, pouring out the coffee and then turn back to Gabe.

"Do you take milk and sugar?"

"No, thanks."

I don't, either, so there's nothing else to do but hand him one of the cups, and rather than just stand here looking at each other, I lead him back into the living room.

He follows without a word, and once we get inside, he stops by the bags he carried back for me, glancing down into them.

"You've been buying a lot of lights and decorations," he says.

"Yeah. I don't own any, and like I say, I felt embarrassed about having the saddest looking house in the street. The problem I have now is where to start."

He looks up at me again. "You mean you've never decorated a house for the holidays before?"

"Not on my own, no."

"Is it something your boyfriends have done in the past?"

What is it with Gabe and boyfriends? He said something about me having one yesterday, when he offered to walk me to work, but boyfriends? Plural? He's got to be kidding. One was enough for me. Still, I suppose he's gifted me the perfect opportunity to put him straight. I'm not about to tell him my life story, but I can at least reveal something… something that'll make him realize I'm a lot younger than he is, and that whatever his motives, this won't work.

"No. When I was younger, my dad always took care of it, and for the last few years, I've been at college. I lived in a house with two friends, and we did it between us. Alex was particularly good at organizing things, and I didn't mind being bossed around."

He shakes his head, which surprises me. "This Alex dude sounds like a control freak."

I smile. "Alex was a girl, and it wasn't like that. She was just better at planning than Sofia and me. She bought the decorations, decided when we were gonna put them up, and told us both what to do. If she hadn't, we'd never have done it. We were both too busy."

"With your boyfriends?"

There he goes again with the multiple boyfriends. "No. With our studies. We almost always had our heads buried in books."

He's staring at me again, and I can't help being struck by the sparkling green tint of his eyes. It's hypnotizing.

"So you shared with two girls?"

"Yes."

"And you left college…?"

"In May."

He bites on his bottom lip, looking me up and down, like he's thinking. He takes so long over it, I even bend my head to look myself. There's nothing wrong with my dress. It's the same one I put on this morning… dark gray, knitted, with a belt at the waist. I've still got my boots on, but there doesn't seem to be anything wrong with them, either. They're definitely on the right feet, and I look back up at him again, bemused.

He coughs, then shakes his head. "Sorry," he murmurs. "I got distracted."

"What by?"

"You."

"Me?"

"Yes." He sighs, looking down at the bags again. "Would you think I was bossing you around if I offered to stay and help with putting up your decorations?"

"Not if it means you're willing to climb a ladder, no."

What am I saying? I was supposed to be putting him straight, getting him to realize that, even if he makes my skin tingle and my stomach flip over, he's way too old for me. What I wasn't supposed to do was to be so entranced by his admission that he'd been distracted by me, that I'd invite him to stay. Although, I have to admit, I've been dreading having to climb the ladder myself.

"I'll happily go up a ladder for you," he says with a smile, taking a long sip of his coffee before his eye catches the bags by our feet and we both bend at the same time, banging our heads. "God, I'm sorry." Gabe speaks first, although I feel like I should be the one apologizing… again.

"It wasn't your fault."

He smiles. "We're back there again, are we?"

"It looks like it."

He studies my forehead for a moment. "Are you sure you're okay?"

"I'm fine."

He reaches out, nudging my hair aside to get a better view, just the tip of his finger brushing over my skin. My breath catches in my throat and I struggle not to choke as he leans in a little closer, nodding his head.

"I think you'll survive."

I have no doubt I'll survive the bang on my head. As for everything else, I'm less clear about that. The effect he's having on me isn't what I expected, or wanted, and I take a step back.

"Shall we look at the decorations?"

"Sure."

He waits for me to crouch first, then copies me, and between us we empty the bags of boxed-up lights and baubles, spreading them out onto the floor, separating them into things for outside and things for inside.

"I bought two sets of lights for the front of the house, and the clips to go with them," I say, looking up at him. "I wasn't sure how many I'd need."

He picks up one of the boxes, turning it over. "Where do you want them to go?"

"Just along the roofline."

He nods. "One box will be enough, but I'm sure we can find something to do with the other one."

I don't want it to look too garish, but I can't say that. For all I know, his house may be completely festooned with lights. "I guess we could trail some through the shrubs under the window."

"Hmm... I think that'll look good."

I smile, relieved he's agreed with me, and we both stand up. "I could do that while you're risking life and limb up the ladder."

He chuckles. "Your house is only one story high. It's not exactly like climbing Mount Washington."

I have to laugh, despite myself. "It would feel like it to me. I hate heights... but that's probably because I'm so short."

"You make that sound like a bad thing."

"It has its disadvantages."

"Such as?"

"Getting things down from shelves... especially at the grocery store. I've lost count of the number of times I've had to ask for help."

"Maybe I should come with you," he says. It's hard to tell whether he's joking or being serious, but before I can answer him, another thought flits into my head.

"Oh... oh, dear."

"What?" he asks.

"I've just realized I was gonna go grocery shopping later today, but I can't, can I?"

"Because you don't have a car?" I nod my head. "That's fine. I'll take you."

"You can't do that."

"Yeah, I can. It's my fault you don't have a car, and besides, I can reach things from the top shelves for you."

I shake my head, even though I'm smiling. "I guess we'd better get on with putting up some of these lights first."

He nods, swallowing down the last of his coffee. I take his cup, and he follows me to the kitchen, putting his coat back on, while I slot the cups into the dishwasher.

"Where's your ladder?" he asks.

"It's in the garage." I hand him my keys, finding the correct one. "The door can be a little stiff in cold weather, so..."

"I'm sure I'll manage."

I don't doubt he will, with shoulders like that.

"I'll just put on my coat, and I'll bring out the lights."

"Okay."

He disappears into the hall, while I shrug on my coat, doing up the buttons, and then wrap my scarf around my neck. I don't bother with my hat, but wander to the living room, grabbing the lights before I join Gabe out front.

He's already set up the ladder, leaning it against the front of the house, and is standing at the bottom, looking at it.

"I know we said you'd fix the lights under the window while I did this, but I think it might be safer if you could hold the ladder for me. I hadn't realized how much of a slope there is to your driveway."

He has a point. "Of course." The last thing I need is for him to fall and break something. I already feel bad enough about yesterday's accident, without adding anything else to my conscience.

He unfastens the first box, while I blow on my hands, trying to warm them.

"Do you have any gloves?" he asks.

"Sure, but I won't be able to help with the lights if I'm wearing them."

"I'll take care of the lights. You go find your gloves."

My fingers are freezing already and I'm not about to say 'no' to his offer. Instead, I run back into the house, straight to my bedroom, which overlooks the front yard. I can see Gabe through the window, unraveling the lights and fastening the clips to the cable, and I smile to myself. I remember doing this last year with Alex and Sofia, and how much of a mess we got into. Still, I can't stand around here daydreaming. I find my gloves in the bottom drawer of my dresser, pulling them on as I walk back outside.

Gabe is still fastening clips, but with my thick woolen gloves on, I can't help. Instead, I stand and watch him, noticing how careful he is to space the clips evenly. He glances up and obviously notices me watching.

"I used to do this with my dad. He liked to make sure we got it right before going up the ladder."

"Didn't he like heights?" I ask.

"He didn't mind, but his theory was that it's easier to reset them when you're on the ground."

"He was probably right. Shall we check they work first, too?"

He nods his head, fixing the last of the clips, and carries them over to the garage, where there's a power supply fixed to the outside wall. He lifts the flap, plugging them in and they light up, brilliant and white.

"Well, that's a relief," he says with a smile, unplugging them and getting to his feet again.

He's ready to climb the ladder now, and I hold it while he makes his way up with ease, the lights in one hand, while he holds on with the other. I do my best not to focus on his butt, even if it's almost impossible, and I have to say, it's an admirable sight.

He makes quick work of fixing the clips, coming back down the ladder so we can move it along to the right and he can repeat the process. Each time he does, he asks if I'm okay, and each time I tell him, "Yes." I like that he asks. I like the look in his eyes when he stares down at me, too.

But it seems Gabe is a very likable kind of guy.

Within no time at all, the lights are done, and once he's put the ladder away in the garage, we work together to arrange the second string through the shrubs beneath my bedroom window. In a way, I wish I'd bought a third string now, so we could replicate this on the opposite side, to make it look more symmetrical, but the lawn goes right up to the wall over there, so there's nothing to attach any lights to, other than the window itself, and I don't want to do that.

"There's another power supply down the side of the house," I tell him, and he disappears for a moment, the lights sparkling to life once he's plugged them in.

We both step back, admiring our handiwork.

"Once you've got your tree lit up in the window on the other side, it'll look a lot better," he says, and I realize he's right. That will balance things out.

"Yeah, I think it will."

He stares down at me. "You look freezing."

"I am. I've lost all sense of feeling in my nose."

He smiles. "We can't have that. Shall we go inside?"

I nod my head and lead him back into the house, relishing the warmth the moment we've closed the door.

I turn to face him, looking up into those lovely emerald green eyes, and I'm about to thank him, when he says, "Before we get too comfortable, shall we go back to my place and get my car? Then I can drive you to the grocery store."

I'd been looking forward to a hot cup of coffee, lighting the fire and decorating the Christmas tree, but he has a point. "I guess it makes sense to get it over and done with."

He smiles. "Do you need to make a list?"

"No. I already have one on my phone."

"That sounds very organized."

"Not especially. I just make a note of things when I run out of them."

"Like I say... very organized. Do you wanna grab your purse?"

I shouldn't have needed reminding, but then I shouldn't be staring into his eyes like this... at least not so much of the time. I nod my head and rush to the living room, collecting my purse and reminding myself that he's not for me.

He's really not for me...

"If you need to go again before your car's fixed, just let me know," Gabe says, helping me unload the last of the groceries into the kitchen cabinets.

"I think I've bought enough to last a month."

When we got to the store, I realized the impracticalities of not having a car, or knowing when I would have one, and bought a lot more than I normally would, hitting up my credit card, rather than using my bank account to pay for it. It seemed sensible. After all, I can't keep taking up Gabe's time. I'm sure he's got better things to do, although his house is already decorated for the holidays… and is very tastefully done, I have to say. There are lights around the roofline, and through the tree on the front lawn, but that was all I could see. His car was parked out front, and rather than wasting time going inside, he helped me into the passenger seat, and we set off straight away.

He made the shopping fun, too, and I'm surprised by how much I'm enjoying his company.

"Would you like to stay for lunch?" I ask, wanting to prolong his stay.

"I'd love to."

He seems enthusiastic, and as time's already moving on, I open the refrigerator. It's really full, and I turn to face him again.

"How do you feel about cheese and tomato sandwiches?"

"I feel fine about them."

"Okay." I take out what I need, making more coffee, before I fix our sandwiches.

"Would you like me to put these timers on the sockets outside?" he asks, picking them up from the countertop. We bought them at the grocery store just now. It was Gabe's suggestion, and I have to say, it was a good one. My other choices would have been to leave the outside lights on all day and all night, or to turn them on and off myself. This is so much simpler.

"Would you mind?"

"Not at all. When do you want them set for?"

I tip my head, giving it some thought, and he smiles at me. "What's wrong?" I ask.

"Nothing," he says, although he doesn't stop staring. That ought to feel unnerving, but it doesn't. I like looking at him, too, and we take a moment, before I glance down and see the timers in his hands, and remember he's waiting for an answer.

"I think they could switch on at five in the afternoon, and probably turn off at…?" I'm not sure what to say. I haven't stayed up late enough to check what my neighbors are doing.

"I've got mine set to switch off at two in the morning," he says, and I nod my head.

"That sounds okay."

He gives me a smile, and without another word, heads out the door. He's not wearing his coat, so I hope he won't be long. It's still freezing outside, and I waste no time making our sandwiches and pouring the coffee.

He comes back, rubbing his hands together.

"Man, it's cold out there."

"You should've put your coat on."

He comes over, just as I'm cutting the sandwiches and putting them onto plates, and I turn, handing one to him.

"Where shall we eat?" he asks.

"In the living room?"

He nods his head and waits, letting me lead the way, even though he knows where it is.

We sit together on the same couch… the one facing the front of the house, the bare Christmas tree blocking the view. It makes the room darker than usual, but I know once it's decorated, and the lights are on, that won't be so noticeable.

"I guess that's our next job," I say, and he smiles, finishing his mouthful.

"Decorating the tree?"

"Yes. Unless… unless you've got somewhere else you need to be."

"No. I'm having a great time."

I smile and so does he, and we both get back to eating.

To be honest, the coffee is more welcome than the food. I think we both need warming up, and once we're finished, I take the plates.

"I'll bring back the scissors to cut the string," I say, nodding to the tree as I leave the room, and when I return, I find Gabe already going through the decorations I bought this morning.

"You've gone with silver?" he says, holding up the boxes of baubles.

"Yeah. I thought it would fit in with the color scheme in here."

He nods his head. "I agree. Although I guess the first job is the dreaded lights."

"Yeah… I hate doing them, but there's no alternative."

"Other than buying a pre-lit, artificial tree."

"I guess. Except I love the smell of pine you get with a real one."

"So do I."

With that in mind, I quickly cut through the strings that have been binding the branches together, and they fall down in all their glory, filling the space.

"It looks so much bigger in here than it did outside the shop." I gaze at it, worried now that I haven't bought enough decorations… or lights, for that matter.

"It's a lovely tree," Gabe says, admiring it as he pulls the lights from their box.

"Are there going to be enough?" I ask and he studies the tree again.

"I'm sure it'll be fine."

"Shall I get a chair?"

He turns, frowning down at me. "What for?"

"To stand on."

He shakes his head. "I can reach the top, don't worry."

I smile. "I suppose I'm so used to being short, I've got no conception of what it feels like to be tall... to be able to reach things."

He chuckles. "Let me show you." He holds out the lights and I take them from him, feeling confused as he steps behind me. Then I feel his hands on my waist and before I know it, he's lifted me, like I weigh nothing, putting me up on his right shoulder, and holding me there. I can't help squealing, and then giggling as he walks effortlessly to the tree. "Okay," he says. "It's your turn to feel tall."

I reach out, placing the lights into the uppermost branches of the tree.

"The view from up here is spectacular," I say, and he laughs, which makes both of us shake, and he lowers me to the floor.

"It's probably not a good idea to make me laugh when I'm holding you like that," he says.

"No. And I think it's almost certainly gonna be quicker if you do the lights yourself."

He tilts his head to the left and then the right. "Quicker, yes... but a lot less fun."

I can't disagree with him, but before I can say a word, he takes the lights from me and turns, threading them through the branches and making it look easy. By the time he gets to the bottom, I'm able to join in, and then I plug them in at the socket and they light up perfectly.

"That looks great," I say, and he nods his head.

"Not bad at all."

We each take a box of baubles, hanging them on the branches as evenly as we can and occasionally nudging into each other when we aim for the same branch.

"I got there first."

"No. I did."

We end up laughing a lot, and by the time we're finished, I have to admit I don't want him to leave.

The problem is… finding a reason for him to stay. We've cleared away all the boxes, and he's even helped me to light the fire, fetching some logs from outside the back door, where they're kept in a wooden store. He filled the basket, carrying it back in, and once that was done, I lit some candles. I actually lit quite a lot of candles, but that's because I like them. It made Gabe laugh, but as I explained to him, I prefer candles to electric lights. The thing is, we've unintentionally made it look really romantic in here. It feels romantic too, and I'd love for Gabe to stay… just a little longer.

He's probably got plans for tonight, though, and I'm surprised by how much I hate the thought of him having a date lined up.

Because even if I've spent the day telling myself he's not for me, I honestly think he might be. He makes me feel more comfortable than anyone I've ever met. With him, I can be myself… and regardless of how old he is, that's got to be a good thing, hasn't it?

I can't hold his age against him because of something that someone else did. To do that would be wrong. It would also be cutting off my nose to spite my face, and even I'm not that dumb.

"I—I don't suppose you'd like to stay for dinner?" I whisper, turning to face him.

He's closer than I thought and I look up into his eyes, the light of the candles flickering in them, making them sparkle.

"I—I can't," he says, stammering just like I did. My disappointment is overwhelming, and I step away, although he moves closer, gazing down at me. "I'm sorry, Remi. I wish I could stay, but I can't."

"It doesn't matter." It does. I'm surprised by how much. But what can I say? "I'm grateful for your help today."

He sighs, pushing his fingers back through his hair, and I take another step away. This time he doesn't close the gap, and I can't help feeling sad about that.

"You're welcome. I've enjoyed it."

Just not enough to stay.

Chapter Six

Gabe

I had to leave then.

I didn't want to, but I had to.

I was in serious danger of kissing Remi. Standing there, surrounded by candles, with the light from the fire and the Christmas tree we'd decorated together, it would have been so easy, too. And so romantic. She was looking up at me, her eyes piercing mine, and the need for her was overwhelming.

I'd been fighting it all day, sometimes with more success than others.

Lifting her up to put the lights on the tree was probably the most noticeable of all. I don't know what possessed me to do that, but by the time I'd thought it through, I already had my hands on her waist. It would have looked odd to pull them away. Besides, I wanted to hold her, even if it was only part of the fun we were having. It was fun, too. It made her giggle, and that made me laugh, which unfortunately meant I had to put her down again, before I dropped her. I could have kissed her then, though. I could have bent my head and crushed my lips to hers. It would have been easy enough… and natural, too.

Just like when we were in the kitchen and she took off her coat.

God… did I want to kiss her then.

Seeing her in that dress… the way it hugged her figure, hinting at what lay beneath. That was almost too much for me, and I struggled not to take her in my arms.

I didn't, though, because she seemed a little uneasy, and I reasoned I had time. She'd offered me a coffee and didn't seem in any hurry to kick me out. Kissing could wait… at least a little while.

The problem was it was then that I realized Remi wasn't the twenty-eight-year-old sophisticated woman of the world I'd assumed her to be.

She only graduated in May, and that being the case, she can't be more than twenty-two or possibly just twenty-three.

And that piece of knowledge changed everything.

Because I've known since the moment I first set eyes on her that if I ever got the chance to let my lips touch hers, I wouldn't be able to stop. A kiss wouldn't be enough. Neither would two, or three, or more. I'd want to peel her out of her clothes and lay her body beneath mine. I'd want to explore her with my tongue and my fingers, and I'd want to fuck her. Hard.

But the knowledge that she's thirteen or fourteen years younger than me came as a bit of a shock…

Enough of a shock that, when she offered dinner, and I thought about what I'd want that to lead to, I knew I had to put some distance between us.

At least, I think I did.

I let out a sigh, turning over in bed, the early morning light cracking around the drapes. I've been lying here all night, thinking things through… getting nowhere.

Did I get it spectacularly wrong last night?

I thought I was looking out for her when I left. It felt like I was protecting her from the man I know I am. But I can't deny, she looked a little disappointed when I said I couldn't stay.

Should I have found a way to control my feelings for her?

Feelings?

I sit up in bed, staring at the wall.

Feelings?

I don't do feelings.

I never have.

"Lust is a feeling," I say out loud, trying to reason with myself.

That's true enough. Except I know this is different. Sure I want to fuck her, but this is more than that, and I lie back down again, my head hitting the pillow, my view changing to one of the ceiling.

This is more than lust.

I'm not willing to admit what it might be, but I know lust well enough, and this isn't it.

This is more... a lot more.

I throw back the covers and get out of bed, walking straight to the bathroom, and into the shower, turning on the water. It's adjusted to my favorite setting of just below scalding, and I stand beneath the jets, trying not to think about her full lips, pressed to mine, her naked body in my arms, pushing her back against the wall, holding her there and touching every inch of her, tasting her...

"Stop it!"

How can I, though?

I want her, and while I'm very familiar with that feeling, too, it's never been like this. There's never been this burning, aching need.

I brace my arms against the wall, struggling... fighting the reality of what I know to be true.

It wasn't Remi I was protecting last night when I left her standing there.

It was me.

I turn around, my back against the cool tiles, admitting defeat… letting my barriers down, their protection no longer needed.

"I love her," I whisper, the words sounding strange on my lips. Strange, but true.

Don't ask me how I know that, but I do.

Just like I know I'll make this work… somehow.

Because I have to.

The alternative is too painful to contemplate.

Even so, Remi isn't the kind of woman I can rush things with. Hell… she's not the kind of woman I'd normally even look at, but I don't care about that anymore. That's the past. That's the man I used to be. The man I am now is someone completely different.

I quickly wash and shampoo my hair, getting out of the shower and wrapping a towel around my hips before wandering back into my bedroom. The bed's a mess, which isn't surprising. I didn't sleep last night, although I don't feel as tired as I might have expected. In fact, I feel great. If this is what love does for you, I wonder why I haven't tried it before.

Because you've never met the right woman before, you idiot.

I want to see Remi, to tell her how I feel, to hold her and kiss her, and… what on earth is wrong with me? That won't work with Remi. She needs a man who'll take it slow, who'll take the time to get to know her, and give her what she wants and needs.

Okay. So, should I explain why I walked out on her last night?

I nod my head to the empty room.

I owe her that much, and I rush to my dressing room, grabbing jeans and a button-down shirt, along with some underwear.

I'm back in my bedroom in no time, sitting on my bed, realization dawning.

I can't explain, can I?

What would I say?

How can I tell her why I left without telling her how I feel?

I've already established that's the opposite of taking it slow. So how am I supposed to explain?

My shoulders drop.

This is complicated. It's way more complicated than I thought.

How do guys do this?

I grab my phone from the nightstand, surprised to see it's already nine-fifteen. As well as making you feel great, it seems love also makes you lose track of time.

I connect a call to Ryan and he answers on the second ring.

"It's not too early, is it?" I ask, without bothering to say 'hello'.

"No. Is everything okay?"

"Sure. I'm just at a bit of a loose end and thought I might come over."

"Okay." I'm not sure he's convinced by my lame excuse for going to see him, but I'm not about to elaborate. I'm just hoping that when I get there, I can somehow get his advice, without being too obvious about it.

Because otherwise I'm lost... hopelessly lost.

"How's it going?" I ask, sitting at the table with Ryan and Peony opposite, all of us clutching cups of coffee.

"The chairs arrived," Peony says with a smile. "So at least it feels like we can get married now."

"We were getting married anyway." Ryan's growly voice makes me smile, and he leans in and kisses her, the two of them gazing at each other for a moment.

I've seen their obvious affection on many occasions now, but never felt jealous of it before. That's because I've never craved what Ryan's got. I've always thought it weird that he could want just one woman... and now I'd give anything to have the one woman I want.

"Are you okay?" Peony asks, surprising me.

"Sure. I'm fine." Even I don't believe me. My voice is too high, my reply too fast, and Ryan puts down his cup, leaning his elbows on the table and staring at me.

"Say that again, but with a little more conviction this time."

"I am fine."

I just don't enjoy being scrutinized like this.

"Then why don't I believe you?" He narrows his eyes. "Has this got anything to do with the accident?"

I may as well give up pretending. He always could see right through me, and in any case, I came here for his advice, so why not just ask for it?

"Not with the accident itself, but with Remi."

"And who exactly is Remi?" he asks.

"You remember… the woman I told you about? The one whose car I hit."

"I remember you telling me you'd met a woman, but you didn't mention any names. Are you still fretting because she turned you down?"

"No. I spent the day with her yesterday, and…"

"You spent the day with her? I thought you were gonna wait until her car was fixed."

"I was, but then I saw her yesterday morning, struggling to drag a Christmas tree along Main Street, all by herself. I offered to help, and we got talking, and before I knew it…"

"You were in bed?"

"No. I said I spent the day with her, that's all."

"You mean you didn't talk her into anything?"

"No." I glance at Peony, noticing the blush on her cheeks. "Would you stop making me sound like a player in front of your fiancée?"

"Why? It's the truth."

I'm tempted to remind him he wasn't too dissimilar himself before he fell in love. Except I can't do that to him, or to Peony.

He might not have told her about his past, and even if he has, I doubt she wants it raked up less than a week before their wedding. Besides which, I'm not in the mood for thinking about who we used to be.

"Maybe it was the truth, but it's not anymore."

"What's changed?" he asks, staring at me with a smile twitching at his lips, like he already knows the answer to that question.

"I have."

"What you mean is, you're in love," he says, grinning like the cat that got the cream.

I shake my head, even though I'm smiling. "No comment."

"We both know that's just another way of saying 'yes'."

That may be the case, but the only person I'm going to say the actual words to, other than myself, is Remi, so he can fish as much as he likes.

"Leave him alone." Peony leaps to my defense before I can utter a sound, nudging her elbow into Ryan and giving me a smile. "Tell us what happened yesterday."

"I already did, really. Remi and I spent the day together, decorating her house for the holidays. I took her grocery shopping because she doesn't have a car right now..."

"Not since you drove into it," Ryan says, smirking, and I glare at him before looking back at Peony.

"And then she invited me to stay for dinner."

"It sounds lovely."

"I declined."

They both sit forward, mirroring each other's actions. "You declined?" Ryan's the one to speak first.

"Yes."

"Dinner?" he says and I nod my head. "Why?"

I sigh. "At the time, I thought it was to protect her from me."

Peony frowns. "I'm sorry. Why would she need protecting from you?"

"Because your future husband is right. I'm a player... or I was. It didn't feel right to stay, knowing what I wanted."

"Which was?" she asks, and I tilt my head, raising my eyebrows until she blushes and sits back a little. "Oh. I see. And you couldn't control yourself, just for one night?"

"At the time, I wasn't sure I could, no. Don't misunderstand, I wouldn't have forced her to do anything she didn't want, but I knew I wanted to kiss her, and I wasn't sure how she'd react to that, or the fact that I wanted a lot more."

"Seriously? I can't believe this," Ryan says, and Peony turns, glaring at him.

"Excuse me? Gabe's a good-looking guy, Ryan, but women aren't obliged to throw themselves underneath him, just because he wants them," she says, sounding offended.

"I know, baby." He takes her hand in his. "That's not what I'm saying."

I sit forward, coming to his rescue. "No. I get what he means. I wasn't assuming she'd want me at all, or that she'd throw herself underneath me." Although I like the sound of that. "But we'd spent the day together and for me, that's unusual. Ryan knows that. He gets that I'd normally devote that much time to anyone." Peony shakes her head and I shrug my shoulders. "I'm not gonna apologize for who I am... or who I was. I'm just telling you how it is."

"Okay," she says. "But having given her so much of your valuable time, why didn't you hang around to find out if she was interested? She might have been."

"Maybe. But she's young. I get the feeling she's inexperienced, too, and I didn't wanna spoil things by being me."

"Define 'young'," Ryan says, releasing Peony's hand and leaning closer, his eyes boring into mine.

"I don't know exactly. She told me graduated last May, so…"

"So she's legal," he says, letting out a sigh and sitting back again.

"Of course she's legal." I shake my head at him and he smiles.

"This is alien territory for you, isn't it?"

"Yes, it is."

"Why?" Peony says, her brow furrowing in confusion as she looks from Ryan to me. "All you have to do is wait. Surely you've done that before."

I shake my head. "Nope."

"Never?" She's surprised, and it shows.

"Not once. It's a weird feeling."

"Having to wait?"

"No. Wanting to."

She smiles, forgiving me for being such an ass… at least a little. Ryan joins in, nodding his head at the same time. "You thought you were protecting her from you, but you were really protecting yourself, weren't you?"

I hate that he's worked it out so easily. It took me all night, goddammit.

"I was."

"And do you still wanna do that?"

"No."

"You wanna go for the whole nine yards?"

"Every inch of them." He grins, like he gets it, which I guess he does, better than most. "The problem is, I don't know how. What am I supposed to do?"

His smile fades and he tilts his head, opening his mouth to speak, although Peony gets there first. "Why do you need to do anything?" she asks and we both turn to face her as she looks at us, like we're the ones not making sense.

"Of course he has to do something, baby," Ryan says.

"I know." She nods her head, rolling her eyes at the same time, like she can't believe how dense we both are. "I get that he can't just sit around at home waiting for something to happen. What I mean is, why does it have to be so planned? What needs to be so organized about it all?" She turns to me. "Just ask her to dinner and take it from there."

I smile. "You make it sound so easy."

"Because it is. You said Remi invited you to have dinner with her. She's probably confused about why you said 'no', especially as you'd had such a nice day together, so why not return the compliment and invite her to go out with you? Maybe you can explain why you declined."

"I don't think I could. Not yet."

"You're gonna have to tell her something, or at best, she'll think you don't care."

"And at worst?"

"She'll think you're an asshole."

I hadn't thought about that, and I'm suddenly filled with fear. What if Peony's right? What if I've given Remi completely the wrong impression?

Oh, hell…

"She wouldn't think that, would she?"

"I don't know. I've never met her, so I can't judge how she'd think. All I can say is, I can remember being twenty-two. I can remember being inexperienced, too, and if a man I'd only just met spent the day with me and I plucked up the courage to ask him to stay for dinner, I think I'd be offended if he turned me down. Either that, or I'd assume he had somewhere better to be… or someone better to be with."

Oh, God… this just gets worse.

"I—I never thought about that," I say, pushing back the chair as I get up. "I have to go see her, to explain."

Neither of them tries to talk me out of it, or stop me, and I head for the door.

"Call me later, if you need to talk," Ryan says, and I wave over my shoulder, rushing out onto the porch and down the steps.

I make quick work of getting back to the town, turning left onto Maple Street, and stopping outside Remi's house.

The lights aren't lit, but they probably wouldn't be at this time of day. The Christmas tree is in darkness, too, and as I approach the front door, I wonder if she's even home.

My worse fears come true when my knock goes unanswered.

I don't have her number. She gave it to Levi at the auto repair shop, but I didn't think to make a note of it myself. So I can't even call her. All I can do is go home, feeling like a loser.

Sleep seems to be evading me these days.

Is that a 'love' thing? Or is it just because I spent yesterday afternoon wondering where Remi was… or, more precisely, who she was with? It might seem unlikely to me that she'd have spent the day with me on Saturday, and invited me to stay for dinner, only to spend Sunday with another man, but I know so little about her. And if Peony was right, and Remi believed I might have abandoned her in favor of another woman on Saturday evening, why shouldn't she enjoy herself with someone else?

The thought of that was enough to make sleep impossible, and this morning, I've decided to call on her before I go to work. I'm going crazy right now, not knowing what's happening between us. It might be that the answer to that is 'nothing'. I hope not, but I have to know now… one way or the other.

I can't wait until lunchtime or the end of the day, either. It's now or never, as far as I'm concerned.

The parking lot at the library is almost deserted, which isn't surprising for this time of the morning, and I pull up next to a vintage Chevy, making my way through the wide double doors, into the warmth of the historic building.

There's no sign of Remi, but there's an older woman standing behind the counter and I walk straight up to her, waiting for a second until she raises her head with a smile, before I say, "Is Remi here?"

She frowns, putting her finger to her lips, which makes me realize I just spoke in a normal tone of voice, in the hallowed sanctuary of a library.

I nod my head.

"Sorry," I say in a whisper. "Is Remi here?"

The woman turns her head and I copy her, smiling as Remi appears from the book racks, with three large volumes in her arms. She's wearing smart navy blue pants and a pale pink v-neck sweater, and I step away from the counter just as she stops by a trolley and looks up. As she does, I know… I know beyond any doubt that my heart is hers. This is love, pure and simple. Except it's not that simple, and if the thoughts rushing through my mind are anything to go by, it's not even remotely pure, either.

She seems to be rooted to the spot, so I stride over, taking the books from her and putting them onto the trolley before I grab her hand and pull her down one of the aisles, out of sight of the woman at the counter.

"Can I see you?" I ask, the whispered words falling from my mouth. That's not perhaps how I meant to start this conversation, but I need to know we're not over before we've even begun.

"What about?" She frowns up at me.

"No… I mean, can I take you out somewhere? For dinner, maybe?"

She tilts her head now, that frown still etched on her forehead. "Why?"

I hadn't expected that. "Because I want to. Don't you?"

Her brow clears a little, although she still looks confused. "Yes. I'm just surprised you do."

"Really?"

"You left in such a hurry on Saturday, I assumed you had a date, or at least somewhere better to be."

So Peony was right.

I shake my head. "That wasn't it at all."

She sighs, and raises her hand, like she's going to tuck her hair behind her ear. I beat her to it, reaching out and gently pushing the hair from her face, my fingers dusting over her cheek. She gasps, which feels promising, and I stare into her bright blue eyes.

"Why did you leave?" she whispers.

"Because I had to."

"Yes, but why?"

"Because I wanted to kiss you." She steps back, blinking hard, clearly shocked by my admission. "And I was afraid you might react like that if I did."

She shakes her head, and then tentatively touches my arm, moving closer again at the same time. "I'm sorry, Gabe."

"It's okay." It's not, but what can I say?

"You don't understand. I didn't mean to react like that."

What's she saying? "You didn't?"

"No. I'm just surprised, that's all."

"Surprised by what?"

She smiles, lighting up my world. Can it be that all is not lost? "That you'd want to kiss me."

"You're kidding… right?"

"No."

I step closer to her, so we're almost touching. "I want to kiss you, Remi. More than I can put into words."

"And you left because you thought I might not respond well?"

"Partly."

Her frown returns, and she leans back, looking up at me. "Only partly? What was the other reason?"

I have to be honest. There's no going back now. "I want to do more than kiss you."

She swallows hard, her breath faltering. "You do?"

"Yes. A lot more." She licks her bottom lip, but I know from the look in her eyes that she's way too innocent to have done that on purpose, and I lean a little closer. "I didn't realize I might have offended you."

"When? How?"

"By walking out on you like that. I—I drove by your place yesterday morning to apologize, but you weren't there."

"No. I went for a walk. I hadn't slept very well."

"Oh? Was there a reason for that?" She nods her head, her eyes never leaving mine. "Was it anything to do with me?" She nods again, struggling to speak, it seems. "I'm sorry," I whisper. "I was trying to do the right thing, but I think I got it wrong. Will you let me make it up to you by taking you to dinner?"

"Yes... yes, please."

Her enthusiasm is adorable, and I chuckle. "I'll book us a table at the French restaurant across the street, shall I?"

"Okay."

"I'll call for you at seven."

She nods her head, excited by the prospect, and I take a half step back, before the temptation to kiss her becomes too much.

"You've been quiet all day."

Ryan sticks his head around my open door at just before five-thirty. I know the time without checking because I've been watching the clock all day to make sure I don't leave late.

"I've been busy," I reply, looking up at him and leaning back in my seat.

"Anything I need to know about?"

I shake my head. "Just routine. I chased up the planning department in Vermont, although I haven't heard anything back. Other than that, I've just been going over the latest bids."

After Adrian bought the troublesome piece of land in Vermont, Ryan made a new rule that all future bids had to be approved by either him or me… and although we shared the load at the beginning, the task seems to be falling to me of late. I don't mind that. Mostly, it's just a question of scanning through documents and double-checking figures. It's not hard work at all.

He moves closer, so he's right in front of my desk, and lowers his voice. "Any word about Remi?"

I smile up at him.

"Yeah. I'm taking her for dinner tonight."

He grins, nodding his head. "Remember not to rush things."

"I won't forget, don't worry."

I've been repeating that in my head ever since this morning, when I booked the table. Whatever else I do tonight, I've got to take it slow.

"Good luck," he says, walking backwards to the door. "And get the hell out of here. You don't want to be late. It doesn't look good."

He disappears before I can say anything in reply, but he has a point. There's nothing here that won't keep until tomorrow, and I shut down my computer, switching off the lights as I head out the door.

When I get home, I shower and spend a while debating what to wear. A suit and tie feels too smart, but jeans feel too casual.

I don't think I've ever put this much thought or effort into such a simple decision, but it matters to me that I create the right impression. I don't want Remi to think I don't care about my appearance… especially not when she takes so much care over hers.

In the end, I choose dark gray pants and a matching jacket, with a white button-down shirt and no tie. It feels like the best compromise between smart and casual.

Once I'm ready, I drive to her house, parking outside and sucking in a deep breath before getting out of the car. I've taken women to dinner before, but it's never felt like a date. Not like this. In the past, I've always thought about what comes later, the dinner itself being the precursor to the main event. The women I've been with have usually felt the same way, and sometimes we've barely made it through our appetizers before adjourning to somewhere more comfortable. On one occasion, I recall, we didn't even order. We just went straight back to my place.

That won't be happening tonight, though, because everything about this is different.

I'm nervous for one thing. That's new to me. As is my excitement, which is bubbling beneath the surface in anticipation of seeing Remi, and has nothing to do with what might happen later.

I knock on the door, barely hiding my gasp when she opens it, and it's hard not to feel like I'm seventeen again as a smile forms on her lips.

"I just need to grab my shawl," she says, filling the gap caused by my inability to speak.

I nod my head, waiting while she turns, giving me a chance to see how her navy blue dress hugs every contour of her body. Coupled with the high-heeled pumps she's wearing, my thirty-six-year-old imagination goes into overdrive, and it's all I can do not to follow her inside, kick the door closed, slam her up against the wall, and fuck her.

No! Take it slow… take it slow.

I repeat the mantra over and over in my head, reminding myself that, although she's dressed like a sophisticated woman who knows her way around, the truth is almost certainly very far from that.

She returns, a light gray shawl wrapped around her shoulders, and I offer my hand, which she takes, pausing to lock her front door before she lets me lead her to my car.

"How was your day?" I ask, once we're both settled inside, and she looks across at me, watching as I turn the car and start the brief journey to the restaurant.

"Quiet. But Mondays usually are."

"I wish mine were."

She smiles. "Have you been busy?"

"Fairly. Although I'm not complaining. It's made the day go quickly."

"Did you want it to go quickly, then?"

"Of course. I've been looking forward to tonight, ever since I left you this morning."

"So have I," she whispers, and I glance at her. She's still staring at me, which is nice. I don't want her to stop, and I'd like to keep gazing at her, too… except I need to park my car.

There's a space right outside the restaurant, and I reverse into it, getting out and helping Remi. It's cold, so as much as I want to take my time, it seems better to get her somewhere warm, and I lead her into the restaurant.

It's not that busy tonight, which is fine with me. I'm not in the mood for crowds, although I can't fail to notice that every male head is turned toward Remi as we enter, and are shown to our table near the back. I'm reminded of how the men reacted when Macie walked into that bar in Boston. Except this feels so different. Then, I was just one of many admirers, wondering what she'd do next. Now, I'm torn between feelings of pride and protectiveness. Remi's mine… or I want her to be, and I don't like the attention these guys are giving her.

It's a weird sensation, but there it is.

I can't help it.

The waiter leaves us with menus, and Remi studies hers, while I study her. She's wearing a little makeup tonight, her lips shining in the candlelight. It makes that need to kiss her almost impossible to bear, and when she glances up at me, she tilts her head.

"What's wrong?"

"Nothing."

"Tell me."

I suck in a breath, deciding to be honest. "I was just thinking how much I want to kiss you." She smiles, a blush creeping up her cheeks, and I groan.

"Did you just make a noise?"

"Yes."

She frowns slightly. "Why?"

"Because this is torture."

Her frown deepens. "It is?"

"Yes."

She leans back. "Why is it torture, Gabe? Don't you want to be here?"

"More than anything. And it's torture because nothing's changed since this morning."

"This morning?"

"Yes. Don't you remember what I said?"

"You mean about wanting to do more than kiss me?" she says, lowering her voice to a barely audible whisper.

"I do. I want to do everything my very vivid imagination will allow, but I'm trying to control myself here... so before I go insane, shall we choose what we're gonna eat?"

"You expect me to eat? After that?"

I chuckle. "I promise to behave. As long as you promise not to tempt me too much."

"I didn't realize I was."

"We're in the same room, Remi. I'm gonna be tempted."

She smiles. "Would you like me to leave?"

"Hell, no."

She lets her eyes linger on my lips for a second or two, then lowers her head to the menu. I do the same, studying what's on offer, although I'd rather look at her.

"The mushroom soup sounds good," I say, glancing up at her again.

"I was just thinking the same thing." She looks over my shoulder, through the window behind me. "I feel like it's the kind of weather for something like that."

"Me too."

She focuses on me again, and I notice how her eyes keep dropping to my lips. It makes me wonder if she wants my kisses as much as I want hers, but after a moment or two, she lowers her gaze to the menu again, and I copy her.

The main course is easy for me, and I put down my menu within moments. Remi glances up at me, tilting her head. "I love ribeye," I explain. "It's a simple decision."

"I see." She goes back to looking at the menu for a second, then raises her head again. "I really want to have the risotto with asparagus and peas, but I'd rather have it without the basil oil."

"I'm sure they'll do it, if we ask."

I get the waiter's attention and he comes over. "Yes, sir?"

"Is it possible to have the risotto without the basil oil?"

"Of course." He smiles down at me.

"In that case, we're ready to order." He nods his head. "We'd both like the mushroom soup to start."

"Very good. And for your entrées?"

"The lady will have the risotto, without the basil oil, and I'll take the ribeye."

"How would you like that?"

"Rare, please."

He's not writing anything down, but I'm not worried. He seems to know what he's doing.

"And to drink?" he says.

I look at Remi. "Wine?" I say.

"Yes. But just a glass. You choose."

"Okay. In that case, a glass of Chenin Blanc for the lady and I'll have the Pinot Noir."

"Excellent choices."

He would say that, but I smile up at him anyway as he takes our menus and leaves. Then I pour us both some water from the bottle on the table and watch Remi sip hers, mesmerized.

"Why didn't you want the basil oil?" I ask to distract myself from thoughts of kissing her. "Don't you like it?"

"I do… but I sometimes find it a little overpowering, and asparagus is one of my favorite things in the world. I want to be able to taste it, rather than the basil."

I smile. "I can understand that."

She puts down her glass and lets her hands drop into her lap. "Can I ask you something?"

"Sure."

"Why do you say basil differently?"

I can't help grinning. I wasn't expecting that, but the answer's an easy one. "My mom is from England. She's always said 'bah-sil', not 'bay-sil'. I guess it's stuck, although I can try to change, if you want me to."

She shakes her head. "No… please don't. There's nothing about you I'd want to change."

She blushes, but I reach out, putting my hand half-way across the table and after just a second, she raises hers and I take it.

"That's good."

"Because you're not gonna change?" she says.

"No. Because there's nothing about you I'd wanna change, either."

She smiles, dipping her head, and I cough. "You're doing it again."

"Doing what?"

"Tempting me."

"Sorry."

"Don't apologize."

She sighs, looking at our clasped hands, and then sits up. "Tell me about your parents."

Again, she's hit me with something unexpected, but I don't mind in the slightest. This feels like she wants to get to know me, and I like that.

"What do you wanna know?"

"Is your dad American?"

"Yes. He's from Boston."

"How did he meet your mom?"

"He went to London for a case."

"A case?" she says, frowning. "What is he? A lawyer?"

I smile. "No. He's a pediatrician. There was a kid with an unusual condition and my dad was called in to help. I don't know all the details, but my mom was one of the nurses at the hospital, and they met on his first day there. It was love at first sight."

"For both of them?"

"Yes. Dad stayed in London for about two weeks, and after he came back here, they called each other all the time, and then Mom came for a visit. He went back there a couple of times, but it wasn't long before they got bored with all the traveling and decided Mom would have to move."

"Why her and not your dad?"

"Dad was older. He had the more established career. His parents were older, too, and more likely to need him around before Mom's parents would. They always intended going back to England one day…" I let my voice fade, remembering how that decision came about.

"But they didn't?" she asks.

"No, they did. My dad's parents died about six months apart, and then Mom's dad got sick, too. It all happened in quick succession, one thing after another."

"That must have been hard for them."

"It was. They didn't want to go like that… not in such a hurry, but my grandmother in England wasn't coping well, and they needed to be there. I'd just turned thirty and was living my own life. It wasn't like they had anything to stay here for."

"Do you see them at all?" she asks, sounding concerned.

"Of course I do. They visit when they can and I go over there, too."

"Do they still work?"

"No. My father inherited from his parents, and he retired when he and Mom left the States. My mom's father died about six months after they got to the UK. Her mother passed about a year later, and they decided to live in the house where my mom and been brought up. They liked the life they'd built over there, and the house itself is lovely. It's in the Cotswolds."

"The Cotswolds? What's that?"

I think about how to explain it. "It's what the British call an area of outstanding natural beauty and when you see it, you'll understand why."

I've just realized I said 'when', not 'if'. Judging by the surprised look on Remi's face, she noticed that, too, although a smile settles on her lips, so I have to assume she doesn't mind.

The meal was fantastic.

I particularly enjoyed the mushroom soup, although the ribeye was great, too. Remi didn't talk at all while she ate her risotto, and apologized afterwards, explaining it had been so good she couldn't focus on anything else. That made me smile, and we held hands over coffee, neither of us wanting dessert.

Once I'd paid, we stood, and I helped her with her shawl, letting my hands rest on her shoulders for a second or two. She leaned back in to me then, which felt fabulous… and promising.

The entire evening has been promising, although it's over now, and as I park outside her house, the lights twinkling prettily along the roofline, I wish it didn't have to end yet.

Neither of us says a word, and I get out, helping her from the car and seeing her right to her door, where she pulls her keys from her purse, putting them in the lock before she turns and looks up at me.

"Would you like to come inside?"

I didn't expect her to offer, and now she has, I'll admit I'm torn. The natural answer would be a resounding 'yes'. I don't want to leave, and I don't think she wants me to, either. But I'm supposed to be taking it slow.

"I don't think that's a good idea," I reply and her face falls, making me regret my words.

"Why not?"

"Because I still want to kiss you."

"Is there a reason you shouldn't?" she asks, with breathtaking innocence.

She has to have remembered that I want to do more than kiss her. We've talked about it more than once.

I can't believe she's forgotten, but I'm not arrogant enough to think she's suggesting anything more, either. I said I wanted to kiss her, and she's right, there's no reason we shouldn't. Just as long as I can keep control…

I take a step closer, pulling her into my arms as I clasp her cheek with one hand and dip my head. I keep it gentle, just brushing my lips across hers. She feels so good, I repeat the movement, over and over.

Take it slow… take it slow…

She sighs, tilting her head.

Oh, fuck… take it slow, for Christ's sake.

I feel her hands inside my jacket, sliding around my waist, and I hold her tight against me. She has to be able to feel my arousal, but I don't care. She's over twenty-one – and she feels amazing.

I can't do this for much longer, though… not without going crazy.

I pull back, gazing down into her beautiful face, my lips barely an inch from hers. She's breathing hard, and I'm so tempted to do all that again…

Except I can't. Not now. Not yet.

"Can I see you tomorrow?" I ask.

"Yes," she says, without even thinking, but then a slight frown forms on her face. "We can't go out for dinner every night, though. I'll gain too much weight."

I shake my head, smiling. It's tempting to tell her I won't care, but I'm too busy thinking about spending 'every night' with her. God… what a thought.

"We could go for drinks instead. If I pick you up at eight, we could walk to Dawson's bar from here."

"That sounds perfect," she says with a smile, her eyes sparkling, and as I gaze into them, I wonder if I'm gonna keep falling in love with her over and over, every day, for the rest of our lives.

Chapter Seven

>>>—<<<

Remi

Last night was just magical.

By the time we got to the restaurant, I'd forgotten all about Gabe's age, or my objections to it. In fact, I'd forgotten about any of that by the time he came into the library in the morning.

I was surprised to see him there. I'd convinced myself he'd run out on me on Saturday night because he had a date... or at the very least, somewhere else to be. Somewhere that didn't involve me. I didn't want to be hurt, or even bothered by that, but after he'd gone, I moped around the house for a while, then I made myself something to eat and pushed it around the plate, unable to face it.

I was being silly, and I knew it. So what if he'd said he was distracted by me? That didn't mean anything. It didn't matter if he'd held me in his arms and put me on his shoulder, did it? He was just helping me with my Christmas tree lights. Everything else was in my imagination. It wasn't his fault he'd gotten under my skin. He couldn't help the fact that he'd made me forget my objections to the age gap between us, or that even though he'd been gone for less than an hour, I missed him.

So much.

I couldn't sleep that night, wondering who he was with, no matter how often I told myself it was none of my business, even as images of him with another woman kept filtering into my head. I had no right to be jealous, and yet I was.

That's why I went for a walk on Sunday… to clear my head.

It didn't work, and when I got home, I just moped around some more.

I was actually relieved to go to work yesterday morning, just so I'd have something to do.

Seeing Gabe standing at the counter in the library was the last thing I'd expected. Hearing him ask me to have dinner with him was even more bizarre… at least it was in my head. I think that's why I had to swallow my pride, and my natural shyness, and ask him why he'd left me.

His answer was the biggest shock of all.

He'd wanted to kiss me. He'd wanted to do more than kiss me.

I hadn't seen that coming at all, but I was so relieved he hadn't been with someone else, that when he asked why I hadn't slept, and if it had anything to do with him, I had to tell him the truth. That's to say, I had to nod my head, because speaking was beyond me. His eyes lit up then, and I wanted him to kiss me more than anything.

Age didn't feel at all important. Neither did the past.

He was so sweet, so kind, and I enjoyed listening to his stories over dinner last night. His family sound so different from mine and although his parents live thousands of miles away, I could tell how close Gabe is to them, and how much he loves and misses them.

It felt like he wanted me to get to know him… and I wanted that, too.

Was that why I invited him in when we got back to my place?

Probably.

I didn't want our night to end, and I definitely wanted to spend more time with him. But was it just about that? Or did I have other things in mind?

Was that what made me ask if there was a reason he shouldn't kiss me?

That was the most brazen thing I've ever done, and I don't know how I'd have reacted if he'd declined.

Except he didn't, and I loved every single second of what followed.

I've been kissed before, but never like that. Nothing like that. I marveled at the sensation of his lips on mine, so soft and gentle, his hand cupping my cheek, like he didn't want to let me go... and his arousal pressing into me, like he wanted me to know what I was doing to him, and what 'more' might entail. I wished there was some way of letting him know what he was doing to me, but there wasn't. How could I explain the tingling of my skin, the heated need inside me, the burning desire for him to stay? How could I ask?

I couldn't.

But at least we're seeing each other again tonight. He said he wanted to, and I wasn't about to say 'no'.

We're going to Dawson's Bar, so I don't have to get as dressed up as yesterday, although I still want to look nice for Gabe, and I stand in front of my closet in nothing but my underwear and a smile, trying to decide what to wear. The smile is because it's less than thirty minutes until I'm due to see him again, and that's enough to make anyone smile, even if they have had a dreadful day at work.

Maybe that's overstating things...

The day itself wasn't dreadful. It was just the piece of news I got at the end. Although I refuse to let that spoil my evening with

Gabe, and I pull out a pair of black pants and a cream-colored cowl neck sweater, which I know looks good.

Before I get dressed, I put on a little makeup, like I did last night, and then pull on my clothes, adding my flat black boots. I'd wear heels, but we're going to be walking and it's icy out there tonight. I nearly fell on my way home, and while I expect Gabe will hold my hand, I don't want to take any chances.

The doorbell rings just as I'm fastening my boots and I rush to open it, staring out at him. He looks gorgeous… but I think he always does. Last night, he wore a suit and shirt, with no tie. Tonight, he's got on dark jeans, a pale blue sweater and his pea jacket. It's the one he was wearing on Saturday, when he helped with my tree and I can't help smiling. I like the way he dresses, although I'm not sure I'm brave enough to say so.

"You look beautiful," he says, smiling at me with a sparkle in his eyes.

I can tell he means it, although I can't help smiling as I recall how dumbstruck he was last night when I opened the door to him. I was wearing my figure-hugging blue dress which I bought for a Christmas party in my last year at college, my friends having convinced me it looked amazing. That was their word, not mine, and that was why I wore it last night for my first date with Gabe.

"Thank you."

I grab my coat from the hook behind the door and he steps inside to help me put it on, watching while I wrap my scarf around my neck.

"Ready?" he says, holding out his hand and I take it, picking up my purse before we leave the house.

"How was your day?" I ask once we're on the sidewalk.

"Not bad… apart from missing you." I look up at him. He's staring down at me with a smile on his lips and I have to smile back. "What about you?"

"I missed you too."

His smile widens. "That's good to know… but what I meant was, how was your day?"

I blush and he leans in, kissing my forehead as we walk, just to put me at ease, I think.

"My day was okay, except for the end."

He frowns now. "What happened at the end?"

"I got some bad news."

He slows our pace so he can look at me properly while we're still walking, or meandering, toward the end of the road. "Oh?"

"It wasn't anything disastrous," I say, hoping to put his mind at rest. "It's just that I've found out I won't be working over the holidays."

He looks even more confused, although at least he's smiling again. "And that's a problem?"

It is for me. Work is the only thing that keeps me sane, even if Camilla and Audrey drive me crazy. I love what I do, and the prospect of staying home for days on end, just staring at the wall, isn't something I'm looking forward to.

I shrug my shoulders. "I suppose it's just that I wasn't expecting it. No-one told me until today that I'd have to use all my vacation allowance before the end of the year."

"How much time are we talking about?"

"Two weeks."

His smile widens. "Which means you'll be stopping when?"

"This Friday. I'll have the week off before Christmas, plus the days between then and New Year, and go back on January second, I think it is. I've got the dates on my calendar, but that sounds right."

He nods his head. "Yeah, it does."

"How do you know?"

"Because that's when I'm due to go back to work." He leans a little closer. "And before you ask, I'm stopping on Friday, too."

I look up at him, tilting my head, unable to believe I'm hearing this. "You are?"

"Yes. Do you remember I told you Ryan's getting married this weekend?"

"Yes. But what's that got to do with it?"

"Everything. He's decided that, as he wants to go on his honeymoon over the holidays, he's gonna close the office for two weeks."

"That's a bit drastic, isn't it?"

"I don't know. It's been a busy year. I think Ryan felt we could all use a break. He's keeping the Boston office open, so I'll have to be available in case of emergencies."

"He trusts you to take care of things in his absence?" I ask.

"He does, although I don't think I'll have very much to do. Christmas is usually pretty quiet for us, anyway."

Suddenly, the thought of having a few days off work doesn't seem so onerous... although I can't jump to conclusions. He might already have plans.

"Will you have to go to Boston at all over the holidays, do you think?"

"I doubt it. If anything happens – which is highly unlikely – I imagine I'll be able to handle it over the phone, and I'm not scheduled to go there again until the second week of January."

"Scheduled?"

"Yes. I have to go there a couple of times a month, just to check up on things."

"A couple of times a month?" He nods. "Do you stay over?"

"I used to, but I think I'll try to get there and back in a day now."

"Why?"

He leans his head closer to mine. "Do you really need me to explain?"

I don't think so, although I hope I haven't misunderstood.

"Do you miss it?" I ask.

"Miss what?"

"Boston. The life you had there."

He kisses the side of my head, just gently. "Not anymore."

I'm not sure that gesture can be misunderstood, but before I can comment, we arrive at Dawson's. The bar seems busy for a Tuesday, and while I contemplate spending a lot more time with Gabe, he orders our drinks and then finds us a quiet table, where we sit opposite each other, cradling glasses of white wine.

Having discussed his family last night, I wonder if he might want to ask about mine, and rather than spoil a perfect evening, I lean forward slightly and start the conversation before he can.

"If your friend is getting married in a barn, won't they get cold?"

He chuckles. "I asked that question, but they've installed heaters, which Ryan informs me are very efficient."

"And what about things like catering? Are they handling all that themselves, or…?"

He shakes his head. "Peony's done a deal with Archer Steel."

"Who's he?"

"The guy who owns the restaurant where we ate last night. He's gonna supply all the food, not just for their wedding, but for all the future ones as well, if the bride and groom want it. Obviously if people want to use someone else, they can, but Peony's recommending Archer's services, and he's doing her a special rate in return."

"So people will get to eat the same fabulous food we had last night?"

"They will. Peony's got a similar arrangement with the lady who owns the flower shop, too. It might have sounded like a pipe dream when Ryan first mentioned it, but it's all come together really well."

"Is Dawson supplying the alcohol?" I ask, sipping at my wine.

"No." Gabe leans forward, lowering his voice. "I think Archer's organizing that, too."

"Oh?"

He tilts his head. "Things are a little strained between Dawson and Peony."

"Were they together, or something?"

He smiles. "No. It's nothing like that. Dawson used to be married, and his wife and Peony's ex-boyfriend had an affair and left town together."

I glance over at Dawson, who's working behind the bar. He's a bear of a man, probably around the same age as Gabe, with dark hair and an even darker scowl.

"That's not Peony's fault, though."

"It's not Dawson's either, but he didn't take it well, and Peony feels awkward about the situation. From what Ryan's said, she hasn't plucked up the courage to come in here, or even face Dawson since it happened."

I can't think how to answer that. It seems unfortunate, but it's none of my business, really, and I take another sip of wine, studying Gabe while he does the same, his eyes lingering on my lips, which ought to make me blush, but actually just makes me smile.

It seems strange that I objected to his age when I first met him. Strange, and unreasonable. He doesn't seem so much older than me now. In fact, he seems perfect... in every way.

"Man, it's cold out here," Gabe says, buttoning up his coat. I've already done mine before we left the bar, but I pull my scarf a little tighter around my neck. "Here... take my hand. It's icy."

It is, although I don't need an excuse to hold his hand, and we make our way along the sidewalk to the corner of Maple Street.

There's a really festive spirit in the air tonight, or maybe it's just that I'm looking forward to the holidays so much more than I was before.

"There's something I meant to ask you earlier, only we got sidetracked," Gabe says, looking down at me.

"Oh?"

"Yeah… I was wondering if you've got any plans for the holidays? Are you going to see your family, or anything like that?"

Not if I can help it, although I might have to put in an appearance if invited.

"Not that I know of," I say out loud, and he smiles.

"In that case, can we spend some time together?"

I can't help the grin from forming on my lips. "I'd like that."

He nods, not taking his eyes from mine. "So would I."

We reach my house far too quickly and walk to the front door, where I pull out my keys, putting them into the lock, just like I did last night. I look up at him, wondering what he'll say if I ask him to come in, and whether I'm brave enough to suggest it again.

"I feel like I've done nothing but talk about myself," he says before I get the chance.

"I know. I liked it."

He shakes his head, raising his right hand and tucking my hair behind my ear, which makes me smile. "The thing is, I still don't know anything about you."

I'm relieved about that. I may have stories, but they're nowhere near as nice as his have been.

"You know I like candles, and asparagus, and white wine… and you."

His eyes widen and he blushes, which is surprising. It's also endearing and I understand the temptation now… the one he was talking about last night.

"I like you too, Remi. A lot. But I'm guessing there's more to you than candles and asparagus and white wine."

"And you," I remind him.

"And me." He takes a deep breath, moving closer. "I guess we're just gonna have to go out some more, so I can find out all about you."

I like the sound of going out some more. I'm less keen on revealing my innermost secrets, but I can't say that. "Where do you want to go?"

He frowns. "I'm not sure. I've got a crazy day at work tomorrow. There are some planners in Vermont I've gotta chase up for about the hundredth time, and…" He waves his hand. "I won't bore you with all the other mundane things I've got to do. The point is, I don't want to make any definite plans and then have to cancel."

"Why don't you call me when you know what you're doing?"

"Because I don't have your number?" he says, the corners of his lips twisting up into a smile.

"No, you don't, but that's easily rectified."

"I guess it is." He reaches into his coat pocket and pulls out his phone, unlocking it before he hands it to me. "Put your number on there, and I'll call you as soon as I know what time I'll be finished. We'll set something up."

I add my number to his contacts list, handing the phone back to him, and once he's put it away, he looks down into my eyes.

"Do you want…?" I ask, but he raises his hand, placing his fingers over my lips. The touch is even more electrifying than when he did this the first time, and I feel that familiar tingle brush across my skin.

"Don't ask me to come in," he says, moving his hand to cup my cheek.

"Why not?"

"Because I won't be able to say 'no'. Not tonight."

"I see," I say and decide to take a chance. "But what if I don't want you to?"

He frowns, letting his hand drop to his side. "You don't want me to come in? You mean, that wasn't what you were gonna ask?"

"Yes, it was. What I meant was, what if I don't want you to say 'no'?"

He stares at me for a moment, then raises both hands, clasping my face, and dipping his head, his lips grazing over mine as a low growl leaves his lips. He keeps it gentle, but oh, so sensual, and steps closer, so our bodies are touching. I can feel his arousal press against me, just like it did last night, and I want him more than ever. I'm lost in him... lost in his kisses and his sighs, and I grab his arms, just for something to cling to, my body igniting to his touch.

He pulls back eventually, and I gaze up into his fiery eyes, wanting more.

"Goodnight," he whispers.

What? No. You can't go now.

"Y—You don't want to stay a while?"

He smiles. "More than anything, baby. But I'm trying to do the right thing."

He just called me 'baby'. It doesn't get any more 'right' than that. Although I know what he means, and as much as I wish he'd stay, I'm grateful to him for leaving.

Yeah... I get how confused that sounds, but that just about sums up how I feel. Not that I'm complaining. It's a nice kind of confused...

"You'll call me tomorrow?" I say, and he smiles.

"I will."

He steps away, giving me a wave as he walks backwards down the path. "Sleep well."

"I will now."

I can't stop smiling as I watch him walk away, then turn to go inside.

What will tomorrow bring? It's hard to tell, but I've got a feeling Gabe might want to hear my story, and even though I'm reluctant to tell it, I think I owe him that much.

I owe him the truth, if nothing else.

Chapter Eight

Gabe

What a night.

That went so much better than I'd expected, and after our evening at the restaurant, I had fairly high hopes.

It surpassed even those, though.

Okay, so all we did was talk about me again, at least for the most part. But Remi seemed interested. She asked questions and wanted to know the answers. That felt good. It proved she wants to get to know me, just like I want to get to know her.

I told her whatever she wanted to know, including the fact that I'd missed her, and I won't be going back to Boston in the future for any longer than is strictly necessary. She knows why, too. I didn't need to spell it out for her. It was obvious I'd rather be here… with her.

I like the fact that we don't have to be explicit all the time. We can hint at things with either words or gestures, and we understand each other. Just like I knew at the end of the evening that she was going to ask me to go inside with her. It would have been so easy to say 'yes', and I really wanted to. She wanted me to as well. She said so. There was nothing implicit in that.

Nothing at all. I hadn't expected such an admission, but hearing the words on her lips made me want her even more. I wanted to hear my name in a wild, pleasure-filled scream… for her to beg for more, while I fucked her, harder and harder. But I knew it was too soon. She might have invited me in. She may even have had a sparkle in her eyes when she did so, but I had to do the right thing.

I had to wait… just a little longer.

Because I know that once this starts, it won't stop. Not even for a second. And I need to be sure she's ready for that.

I finish breakfast, trying not to think about the kiss we shared last night. She felt so good, her body pressed against mine, and although we haven't made any plans for tonight, I know it'll take all my willpower to hold back.

I'll do it, though. Because she's worth it.

Once I've cleared away, I head out the door, glancing across at the library as I reach the end of the road. The lights are on, but unfortunately, I don't have time to stop today. Like I told Remi last night, I've got a busy day ahead of me. First and foremost, I've got to chase up the planning department in Vermont. They still haven't replied to the email I sent on Monday and Ryan is getting impatient. He wants it tied up before Christmas, so the construction work can begin in the New Year, but as it stands, it could be Easter before we get started.

I park by the office and make my way inside, grateful for the warmth. It's freezing today, and the forecast is for snow, which sounds wonderful but has all kinds of practical issues in our business. We might not do any construction ourselves, but we manage projects all the time, and snow causes havoc with deadlines.

Still, it's not here yet, and I've got other things to do… like getting finished in time to see Remi tonight.

"Hello."

I stop in the doorway to my office, surprised to see Ryan standing by the window, his arms folded across his chest.

"Have you been waiting for me?"

"Yes. But don't worry. You're not late."

"I wasn't worried." And I couldn't care less if I'm late… not that I am, but Ryan knows as well as I do that I always make up any time I might lose.

He smiles, coming over as I take off my jacket. "Don't get comfortable."

I pause, my jacket still in my hand. "Why not?"

"Because you won't be here for long."

"Why? Where am I going?"

Please don't say 'Boston'. That's the last thing I need.

"Vermont," he replies, which is marginally worse, and I dump my jacket on my desk, staring across it at him.

"Why?"

"Because I've had a call from the planners up there."

"You have?" Why the hell did they call Ryan and not me? Unless it's just a case of self-importance… of someone up there wanting to talk to the boss, and not his deputy.

"Yes," he says, rolling his eyes. "I don't know why it's taken them this long to get in touch, but there's a problem."

Why am I not surprised? This project has been a nightmare ever since Adrian bought the land.

"What kind of problem?"

"The kind that needs someone to go up there and deal with it."

"And that someone has to be me?"

"It does." He smiles. "I'm sorry, but with the wedding so close, I can't leave town."

And you think I can?

"I thought everything was organized, now the chairs have arrived."

"It is, but I still need to be here." He stares at me, like he's willing me to understand, even though he's not telling me anything, and I let my shoulders drop. This is one of the few times when he's made me feel like an employee and not his best friend.

"Do you have any idea what I'm gonna be walking into?"

"The woman who called me was Selena Oaks. She's the one you'll be meeting. She's been in charge of the project ever since we put in the first application."

"Am I allowed to tell her she's no good at her job?"

"I wouldn't advise it."

"That's a shame. So, what did she say?"

"That they've realized there's going to be an access problem."

"They only just discovered this? What have they been doing all these months?"

"I don't know," he says with a shrug of his shoulders. "But it's got something to do with a stream."

"There isn't a stream on the property, other than the one that runs alongside it."

He holds up his hands. "I know, but for some reason that's causing a problem and they're holding up the application until someone goes up there to iron it out."

"Why can't we send someone from the surveying team? They'll be better qualified than I am."

"I am sending someone from the surveying team. Bailey's coming with you."

"Fucking hell, Ryan. What are you trying to do to me?"

He smiles. "I know she flirts with you, but she's the best surveyor we've got."

"Then why don't you promote her and put her in charge of the department?"

"Because John is in charge of the department and although he's not as good as Bailey, he's got more organizational skills."

"Can't John come with me?" He might be as boring as watching paint dry, but anything would be better than Bailey.

"No." He pulls a face, shaking his head. "John drew up the original plans, and I want a fresh pair of eyes on this. Can't you just deal with her for one day? I need someone up there, other than Bailey, who's got the authority to make a decision, and I trust you to do that for me. Okay?" He sounds exasperated and I suck in a breath. Maybe I'm not just an employee, after all.

"Okay."

"Thanks, Gabe. I appreciate it." He lets out a sigh, like he's relieved. "Does this spoil your plans with Remi?" he asks, grinning at me.

"I didn't have any plans with Remi."

His smile falls, and he steps closer. "You've been seeing her though, right?"

"Yes. But how did you know?"

"Because you haven't stopped smiling since the weekend." I nod my head, shrugging my jacket back on. "How's it going?" he asks.

"I'm taking it slow."

He smiles, nodding his head. "Good for you. Bailey will be here in a minute, and the two of you will need to head off straight away if you're gonna get back tonight."

"We're gonna get back tonight, come hell or high water." His smile widens. "Is Selena Oaks meeting us at the site?" I ask, and he shakes his head.

"No. She suggested you go there first and then join her at her office."

"Great... so we'll be up there even longer."

"If you and Bailey can work out a solution while you're at the site, it shouldn't take long to get Selena to agree to it. The access is the only thing holding up the application now. That's what she said to me."

"Okay. I'll see what I can do."

He nods his head, leaving the room, and I pull my phone from my pocket, looking up Remi's number. I don't know how she's going to react to the news that I might not even make it back from Vermont in time to see her tonight, but I guess there's only one way to find out.

"Hey, Gabe." I'm about to connect my call when Bailey comes straight into my office without knocking.

She walks over, sitting on the edge of my desk, her perfume following close behind. Tall, blonde, with a perfect hourglass figure and the longest legs in the world, there's no denying Bailey matches the description of everything I ever wanted in a woman... before I met Remi. As usual, she's showing off her assets in the best way possible. Her short black skirt reveals slender, toned thighs, and beneath the matching jacket, she's wearing a white blouse that's so low cut it does nothing to conceal her ample cleavage. The four-inch black heels are particularly impractical for field work, but I don't think that's what she had in mind when she got dressed this morning. She's usually office-based, and like Ryan said, she loves to flirt... especially with me. Although she ought to be perfect for me, I've never shown any interest in her, because while I'm not a man for rules, or for following them, I also never mix business with pleasure. I'd never risk what Ryan and his father have created by screwing around at work. So Bailey has always been strictly off limits.

Except that's never stopped her from trying.

"Hi. I've just got a call to make," I say, giving my phone a nod.

"Don't mind me." She smiles up at me, then checks her watch. "But don't you think we should get going? You can make your call in the car, can't you?"

Not with you there, no.

She has a point about leaving, though. If we don't get started now, there's no way we'll make it back in time for me to even call Remi tonight, let alone see her.

There's bound to be an opportunity to call her later, and it's not as though she was expecting to hear from me first thing this morning, so it'll be fine.

I pocket my phone and grab the file that relates to the Vermont project.

"Is there anything else we need?" I ask Bailey, and she tilts her head, licking her lips.

"Just you, Gabe... just you."

For Christ's sake.

I shake my head and head for the door, wondering how I'm going to survive the day.

The journey up here has been just as tortuous as I expected, mostly because Bailey didn't stop talking. I switched off after about the first five miles and focused on the road... not that she seemed to notice.

She may be beautiful, with a figure a lot of men would fall over themselves to appreciate more closely, but I'm not sure I could put up with her for more than a few hours. Her voice alone would drive me crazy, and I smile to myself, thinking about what Remi's soft tones do to me. They whisper over my skin, making my body tingle and my cock throb. I've never known a woman whose voice alone could do that... until now.

"What's making you smile?" Bailey asks as I take the next corner.

"Nothing."

Nothing I'm going to tell you about, anyway.

She turns in her seat, letting her already short skirt ride up even further, and while that might have tempted me to break a few rules in the past, I ignore the sight of her smooth thighs and think about Remi's sense of style instead. I know she'll probably be wearing tailored pants and a sweater today, and that she'll look a hundred times better than Bailey ever could.

"You need to take the next left," she says from beside me. "Then we go over the bridge, and we're there."

The bridge is the one that crosses the stream, which seems to be causing all the difficulties, and as I get to it, I slow down.

"Where's the access due to be?" I ask her.

"Right here."

I check there are no other vehicles coming, and stop the car. "You mean it's directly by the bridge? Here on the right?"

"Yes."

"In that case, I think I can see what the problem is."

"You can? I can't."

"It's obvious, isn't it? Anyone driving over that bridge won't be able to see vehicles coming out of the exit, and vice versa. It's an accident waiting to happen." I turn to face her. "Was it John's idea to put the access here?"

"I guess. He's been in charge of this project since the beginning. He's the only one with any background in residential developments."

"In which case, he ought to know better."

I pull the car forward so it's far enough away from the bridge to be safe, and then park at the side of the road, getting out. Bailey follows and comes around the car, both of us looking out across the plot of land.

"It's bigger than I thought," she says.

I have to agree with her. Even though I knew the dimensions, seeing the area laid out before me, it's significantly larger than I'd expected. Formed in the shape of a square, it occupies the corner between the bridge and the next intersection, with that road creating the left-hand boundary.

"Hmm… it is."

She giggles and I turn to face her. "I wasn't talking about the plot, Gabe," she says, letting her eyes drop to my groin.

I shake my head. "Are you gonna be okay in those heels?" I ask, refusing to rise to her bait.

"Why? Are you offering to carry me?"

"No. But it might have been more sensible if you'd worn flatter shoes."

"Maybe. But I didn't know I was coming up here, did I?"

Good… I've annoyed her. That should stop her flirting. At least for a while.

She flips around and wanders down the road, pulling a sheet of paper from the file I gave her earlier.

"Are you coming?" she growls over her shoulder and although I'd rather stay at the car and call Remi, I'm here to do a job, and the sooner it's done, the quicker I can go home again.

"Where are we going?" I ask, catching up to Bailey, who's positively strutting now.

"Down this side road. I don't think it's gonna be wise to situate the access anywhere along here." She turns, walking backwards, which is a feat in those heels. "It's either gonna be too close to the bridge, or too close to the intersection."

"I agree."

"In which case, putting something down this side road seems the best answer. I just wanna check there's nothing down there that would present an obstacle."

I nod my head as she flips back around again, and I follow her.

Despite the flirting, I have to admit, she's good at her job. She's worked for Ryan for quite a while now. I ought to know. She's spent a lot of that time flirting with me. I believe her to be thirty-two years-old, which makes her ten years older than Remi… or thereabouts, and I have to smile, thinking about the way I seem to keep making comparisons. I'm not really, because there is no comparison, but what surprises me is that Bailey is someone who I would have always thought of as my 'ideal woman', and yet, when I compare her with Remi, she comes up short... every single time.

"Here," she says, breaking me out of my thoughts.

We're already in the side road, and I look to my right and left, noting that the visibility in both directions is great, and there's nothing opposite to impact an access road from going in here.

"It's perfect. Why on earth didn't John put the access here in the first place?"

"I couldn't possibly comment."

I think I've done more than annoy her, but that's probably for the best. "Can you adjust the plans?"

"I can. But only in rough form. I can't re-draw them while we're in the middle of nowhere."

"Hopefully that won't be necessary. As long as we can show where the new access is going to be, it should be fine."

She makes a note on the plans, then folds everything away and puts it all back in the file.

That's the first part of the day over and done with. Now all we need to do is meet with Selena Oaks and I can get home to Remi.

I thought Bailey had long legs, but Selena Oaks puts her to shame.

Not only that, but she's a redhead, with a figure that must make men drool, wherever she goes.

Regardless of that, her tight gray skirt, and open-necked blouse, she's doing nothing for me, although a month ago – or even a week ago – I'd have been first in line.

As it is, I just want her to sign off on our plans so we can get out of here.

I think Bailey feels the same... but probably for different reasons. She's done nothing but glare at Selena since we arrived.

As it was, our journey from the site was broken by Bailey insisting we stop for lunch. I could hardly say 'no', and I found a diner, where fortunately she was still sufficiently mad at me that she didn't flirt too much over our burgers.

The delay meant we didn't get here until just before two, and although we didn't have a specific appointment with Selena, I was disappointed to find she was in a meeting. Leaving wasn't an option, so we waited, and waited, until nearly forty-five minutes later, she finally came out to greet us… in all her red-haired glory.

"So you're happy?" I ask for the third time. "If we move the access, you'll sign off on the plans?"

She looks down at the documents that are laid out on her desk, then gets up and walks around it, coming to this side. I half expect her to say something, but instead she turns and leans over, giving me a perfect view of her shapely ass as she rests her elbows on the table and points to the place where Bailey's drawn in the new access road.

"You're sure there's nothing opposite to cause any difficulties?"

"Positive," Bailey says, getting up too, and bending over, in exactly the same way as Selena. I'm not sure whether I'm supposed to sit here and admire, or choose between them. Of course, if this meeting had taken place last week, or the week before, I'd probably have suggested they could share. But that thought leaves me cold now. Those days are gone. I'm not that man anymore, and I'm not in the mood for this, either.

I just want to go home.

I want Remi.

"We checked it," I say, standing up and walking to the end of the table. "There's nothing there at all."

Selena straightens, puffing out her ample chest, which causes the buttons on her blouse to strain.

"In that case, we don't have any further objections."

Hallelujah.

"So we can break ground in the New Year?"

"Sure," she says, like we haven't been waiting months for this moment. "I'll send everything through, so you've got it before the holidays."

It doesn't matter that we're not working next week. As long as I've got the permissions on my desk by the time we come back in January, I'm happy.

I pack up our things and for once Bailey's helpful, folding the plans and putting them away.

"Thank you for getting this done," I say, turning to Selena.

"Are you staying over somewhere?" she asks, giving me a sparkling smile.

"No. We're heading straight back to Hart's Creek."

"I can't interest you in dinner?"

My many years of experience tell me she's talking about a lot more than dinner, but I'm not interested.

"No, thanks. We've got a long journey, and the weather doesn't look great."

She looks crestfallen, confirming my suspicions, and I hold out my hand. It's the only part of me she's gonna get to touch.

She takes it, giving me a firm shake, and holding on for a lot longer than is necessary before I pull away.

"It's been lovely meeting you, and if you ever change your mind about dinner, you know where I am."

Could she be any more obvious?

"Thanks."

I can't be rude. She's done us an enormous favor today, although it's not one that entitles her to anything more than my professional gratitude.

Bailey joins me at the door with a smug look on her face, clutching the file, and we head out.

It's already getting dark, and I check the time, cursing under my breath when I see it's half past four. Where did that afternoon go?

My car is across the other side of the parking lot, and Bailey pulls her jacket around her, although I doubt it's giving her much protection from the brisk wind, or the snowflakes that are starting to fall.

Dammit.

"It's snowing," she says, stating the obvious.

"I noticed."

She looks up at me as we pick up the pace. "I know we weren't planning to stay up here, but given the weather, do you think we should?"

"No."

She switches the file to her other hand, resting the one closest to me on my arm. "Why not, Gabe?"

"Because I wanna get home."

"But what harm can it do? We could get a room for the night, order in something to eat…" She blinks rapidly, brushing her hand down my arm now, and I stop walking, meaning she has to as well.

"Just cut it out, will you, Bailey?"

"Cut what out?"

"Flirting with me. I'm sick of it." She opens her mouth, taking a step closer, but I move back, keeping some distance between us. "I mean it, Bailey. I'm not interested."

"But, Gabe. You know that's not true. You know…"

"Which part of 'I'm not interested' are you not hearing?" I raise my voice, her eyes widening in surprise. "Keep this up, Bailey, and I'll fire you."

"You'll what?" She stares up at me in shock.

"You heard what I said. I'll fire you."

"For flirting?"

"For inappropriate behavior. You've been doing this for years, even though I've given you no reason to think I welcome your attention." She opens her mouth, but I hold up my hand and she closes it again. "I'll admit I'm partly to blame for letting things slide for so long. But it ends now. Okay? No more."

Her eyes spark with anger, but she holds it in, clearly valuing her job above anything else.

"Fine," she says, turning and striding toward my car.

I follow her, resolving to call Ryan later. I'll have to fill him in on today's events, and not just those surrounding the planning consent. He'll need to know what I've said to Bailey, too.

He's always thought of her flirting as a bit of a joke, and to an extent, so have I. But the joke has to stop.

I'll make sure of it.

Chapter Nine

Remi

I'm exhausted.

Perhaps that's because I spent a lot of last night dreaming about Gabe. I think I slept, but I woke this morning feeling restless… probably because we hadn't made any plans for tonight, and I was desperate to see him again.

It's pathetic, I know, but it's true.

I'm hooked.

I thought I might have heard from him by lunchtime, but I hadn't… although I got a call from Alex. She timed it perfectly, my phone ringing not long after I'd fixed myself a coffee in the staff room, and I answered straight away.

"How are you?" she said.

"I'm great. How are you?"

"The same." There was something about her voice that made me wonder. She sounded excited.

"Has something happened?" I asked.

"Yes. I'm getting married."

"You're what?"

The words fell from my lips before I could stop them, and for a second I felt guilty for sounding so incredulous. Before I could apologize, though, Alex started laughing.

"I know, I know… it's been a whirlwind. Even I'll admit that."

"Who is he?"

"His name's Jacques."

"That's sounds French."

"Because it is," she said with a sigh that spoke volumes.

"You're not moving to France, are you?" I asked.

"No. He lives here. I met him at work, and he's just… perfect."

"So, when's the wedding?"

"We haven't worked that out yet. To be honest, it's the venue that's giving us trouble at the moment."

"Why is the venue such a problem? Can't you agree on what you want?" That didn't sound to me like the recipe for a happy future, if they couldn't even see eye to eye over where to get married.

"It's not that. It's just that Jacques has a lot of family in France. They want us to hold the ceremony over there, and it makes sense when there's only my mom and dad, plus an aunt and uncle or two over here. The problem is, it'll all be in French, and I'd kinda like to understand my vows when I'm making them." I can't help laughing.

"So, what are you gonna do?"

"We're gonna go over there for the holidays and talk it through with his family, so we can make a decision, and then start the planning in earnest."

"Have you told Sofia yet?"

"No. She and Tate are on vacation."

"They are?"

"Yes. I only found out because I tried calling her and didn't get an answer, so I checked her social media page and found about twenty pictures of the two of them on a white sandy beach somewhere."

"That sounds romantic."

"It looked romantic." She stopped talking for a second and then said, "You know, it wouldn't surprise me if Tate proposed while they're away."

"Seriously?"

"Yeah. They've been together for quite a while now."

"I suppose…"

"Which just leaves you," she said, and I could hear the smile in her voice as I blushed, thinking about Gabe. I wasn't sure what to say, though, and after a few moments, Alex filled the gap. "Is there something you're not telling me?"

"There might be." I couldn't help smiling as I spoke.

"Have you met someone?" she asked.

"I have."

She giggled. "Wouldn't it be crazy if we all got married in the same year?"

"It would be insane. I only met Gabe on Friday morning."

"So? Jacques only started working here at the beginning of November… and we're engaged."

She sounded so happy, I had to smile. "I'm really pleased for you, Alex."

"Thanks. Maybe in the New Year, when Sofia's back from wherever she is, and I'm back from France, we'll set up a video call between the three of us."

"That'd be great. It's been too long."

"And it sounds like we all have a lot to catch up on," she said, and we both laughed, although we had to end the call then, because her boss wanted to go through something with her.

I was pleased for her, although I still had a nagging feeling in the pit of my stomach. I hadn't heard from Gabe. Not even a message, and as I finished my coffee and swallowed down my lunch, that was starting to bother me.

I didn't have long to dwell, though, because time was moving on and Wednesday afternoons are always busier than most. We have a children's story hour between three and four, and although it's chaos, I love it. It was my idea, and one that Audrey and Camilla were reluctant to get on board with at the beginning. Even they enjoy it now, though, and while it's mayhem when everyone first arrives, we all love the way the kids respond to the stories I tell them. They sit around on the floor in the back corner of the library, their necks craned, their mouths open, and their eyes alight, as I transport them to another world.

There's always a lot of tidying up to do afterwards, which takes a while, and has to be done on top of everything else we need to do at the end of the working day.

By the time we're finished, it's time to go home, and I'm beyond exhausted.

I lock up the library and head for home, wishing I had my car.

It's absolutely freezing, and really icy underfoot, too.

Levi called this morning, while I was getting ready for work, making me jump out of my skin, because I hoped it was Gabe. It wasn't, but at least I know when I'm getting my car back.

"It won't be until Friday," he said, sounding contrite.

"That's okay." I'd half expected it to be next week, having heard nothing from him since taking it into the repair shop.

"I'll have it ready by eight-thirty, so come down any time after that."

"I'll try to get down before I start work. Thanks."

I hung up, feeling relieved. At least I'd be able to go grocery shopping without putting Gabe to any inconvenience, although I smiled then, recalling our visit to the store on Saturday. I've never enjoyed buying groceries that much in my life, and the thought of doing it by myself seemed dull by comparison. I consoled myself that I might be able to persuade Gabe to stay for dinner on Friday or Saturday, and that I could plan what to cook and what to buy.

Now, of course, I'm feeling less sure.

He said he was busy, so that seems the most obvious explanation for his silence… even if I'm struggling to believe anyone could be so busy, they couldn't find five minutes to make a call or send a text message.

In which case, is he just unreliable? He didn't come across like that, but as I said to Alex at lunchtime, I've only known him for a few days, so am I qualified to say?

Or could it be that he's found someone else to distract him?

I shake my head, unwilling to let that thought make a home there. He wouldn't do that…

Would he?

"Of course not," I mutter under my breath.

I might not know Gabe very well, but there was no mistaking his kisses. He said he wouldn't be able to say 'no' to me. He wanted to see me over the holidays… to spend more time together. Those aren't the actions of a man who'd go back on his word, or one who'd have spent his day – or even a part of his day – with another woman.

I smile at my own folly as I cross the road, getting to Dawson's Bar, my smile widening as I recall our evening there. It reminds me that he wants to learn more about me, and while that thought fills me with fear, I've reconciled myself to the fact that I'll have to tell him about my life at some time, and it may as well be now.

I look up, frowning, and wishing I'd thought to take Gabe's number when I gave him mine, just as I slip on a patch of ice, twisting my left ankle and tumbling to the ground, lying there in pain and humiliation.

"Hey… are you okay?"

The owner of a deep male voice is right beside me and I look up into a pair of dark brown eyes, set in a very handsome, young face.

"I—I don't know."

"Can you stand?"

"I don't know that, either."

He smiles, dimples forming in his cheeks, as he holds out his hands. "Let's see what happens when you try." I take his hands and he pulls me up with ease. "Where does it hurt?" he asks.

"Just my ankle. I twisted it when I fell."

"Try putting your weight on it," he says, still holding my hands.

I do as he says, wincing slightly at the increased pain. "That hurts."

"I can take you home, if you like. My car isn't far away."

I shake my head. "No, it's fine."

"Okay… but you're not gonna get very far like that. You need to rest for a while. I was just heading to Dawson's, so why don't you come with me?"

I try leaning on my foot a little harder, but the pain seems even worse this time, and seeing I have little alternative, I nod my head, reasoning to myself that it seems fairly busy in the bar tonight, and that the man who's still holding on to me is pleasant enough.

What harm can it do to sit for thirty minutes?

I turn, resting my weight on my uninjured ankle, and the man puts his arm around me. "Lean on me," he says, and I do, letting him guide me toward the doors.

Once we get inside, he stops, looking around, and then heads for one of the booths at the side, sitting me down. I'll admit, it's a relief, and I look up at him, taking in his clean-shaven features, chocolate brown eyes, and generous lips.

"Thank you."

He smiles. "You're welcome. Can I get you a drink?"

We can hardly sit in here and not have anything, can we? "I'll have a dry white wine, please."

He nods his dark head and turns away, walking to the bar, while I twist in my seat, holding out my leg and studying my ankle. It looks a little swollen... or I think it does. That could be my imagination, though, and I twist it one way, and then the other, noting that it only hurts now when I turn it to the left. Perhaps it's not as bad as all that, after all.

"How is it?" the man asks, returning with our drinks and putting them on the table. He removes his coat, hooking it up on the post at the end of the booth, revealing rippling muscles that are barely contained within stonewashed jeans and a black t-shirt.

"I don't think it's too bad."

"Do you want me to take a look?" he asks, sitting opposite me.

"Are you a doctor?"

He smiles, shaking his head. "No. I'm a fitness instructor at the gym further down the street." I suppose that makes sense of his physique, which is impressive, to put it mildly. "We have to learn about strains and sprains as part of our training."

"Oh. I see."

He holds out his hand. "I'm Jesse, by the way."

"Remi." I take his hand, although we don't really shake. We just hold hands for a second or two before I pull away.

"So, do you want me to have a look at that ankle?" It feels silly to say 'no', so I nod my head and he shifts along his seat until he's in the corner. "Come around here," he says, and I get up, hobbling over to his side of the table and sitting beside him. He twists around, then smiles at me. "Put your leg up here."

"Where?"

"On my lap."

I do as he says, resting my calf across his thighs and he tilts his head, studying my foot. "I'm gonna take your shoe off. Let me know if it hurts."

"Okay."

He carefully removes my shoe, which only has a low heel, and puts it on the seat beside him, sucking in a breath.

"I think there's a slight swelling," he says. "But it doesn't look too bad, and taking your shoe off didn't seem to hurt."

"It didn't."

"Good." He smiles at me, still holding my foot. "I don't think I've seen you around here before."

"I've only lived here since the spring, which I've gathered by Hart's Creek standards, is no time at all."

He chuckles. "It is a bit like that, isn't it? I've been here a little longer than you, but not much."

"What do you make of it?" I ask.

"It's quiet, but I'm getting used to it." He puts his hand around my foot. "I'm just gonna manipulate it a little. Let me know if it hurts, won't you?"

I nod my head, watching as he turns my foot one way and then the other, mimicking the motions I was going through earlier on my own. It still hurts a little when he twists it to the left, but it's getting better all the time.

"That's really not too bad," I say, just as my phone rings. I pull it from my purse, seeing Gabe's name on the screen, and although I wouldn't normally do something like this, I look up at Jesse, with an apologetic smile. "Please excuse me. I've gotta take this."

"That's okay."

He keeps hold of my foot while I connect the call.

"Hello?"

"Hi, Remi."

"Where have you been?"

"It's a long story." He pauses. "What's all the noise in the background?"

"I'm at Dawson's bar."

"You are?"

"Yeah. I slipped on the ice outside and came in here with…"

"You slipped?" He interrupts before I can explain.

"Yes. It was my own fault. Although a very nice…"

"Are you okay?"

"I've hurt my ankle, but…"

"Stay exactly where you are. I'm coming to get you."

He hangs up before I can say anything else, and I stare at my phone for a moment before looking up at Jesse.

"Is everything okay?" he asks.

"Yes."

Except it's not.

It's very far from okay.

Who exactly does Gabe think he is?

He doesn't call me all day, and then when he does, he offers no explanation for his silence, interrupts when I'm trying to tell him what happened to me, and then goes all possessive about coming to rescue me.

'Stay exactly where you are'? Is he serious?

Does he think I can't look after myself?

I shake my head and take a deep breath, trying to control my anger, just as Jesse rubs my ankle, letting his fingers roam, so they're caressing my foot. His touch is very delicate and sends a shiver up my spine.

It's not a shiver of pleasure, though… it's one of dread.

I may be mad, but what's Gabe going to say when he finds me sitting here with another man? A man who's currently fondling my foot?

I imagine he'll be mad, too.

I try to pull my leg away, just as the door slams open and I look up to see Gabe standing there, out of breath.

Oh, God... he's here already...

Chapter Ten

Gabe

The ride back to Hart's Creek was mercifully silent, and once I'd dropped Bailey at the office to collect her car, the first thing I did was to call Remi. My conversation with Ryan could wait. As far as I was concerned, Remi was more important.

Hearing her voice made me smile, even if I was confused by the noise I could hear in the background. When she told me she was at Dawson's Bar, I'll admit my confusion deepened. She's always struck me as shy, and not the kind of person who'd go somewhere like that by herself. But I guessed she might have gone there with her work colleagues. It made sense in my exhausted head, until she told me she'd fallen over.

Then, all I wanted was to be with her, and once I'd hung up, I floored the gas, tearing back to town.

I've made it here in no time at all, and rather than heading around back to the parking lot, I leave my car out front, grateful there's a space right by the door, and rush inside, my heart constricting when I see her.

She's sitting in one of the booths, and our eyes lock... but that's not what really grabs my attention. What I'm focused on more than anything is the gorilla who's sitting beside her, holding her leg across his lap. He's caressing her foot, taking his time over it, and I feel my blood boil. Remi didn't mention him. But why would she?

And who the fuck does he think he is?

I stride over, trying to stay calm, to keep my focus on Remi and not the gorilla.

"Are you okay?" I ask the moment I get to her.

She's wide-eyed, startled by my presence it seems, and just for a second, I wonder if I read her all wrong... if there's more to her and to this situation than meets the eye. Except there can't be. She's not like that.

She hasn't answered, and just continues to stare up at me, biting on her lip... dammit.

"She's fine," the gorilla growls. "Who the hell are you?"

I look at him, tilting my head. He's handsome, I'll give him that. *Asshole.*

"I'm Remi's boyfriend. Who are you?"

He doesn't answer, but frowns, then turns to Remi. "You didn't say you had a boyfriend." As he's speaking, he releases her foot, pushing it from his lap and letting it fall to the floor, which makes her wince and I step forward, taking her hand.

"Are you okay, baby?"

She nods and I pull her to her feet. The gorilla shimmies to the edge of the seat and stands. He's enormous, but I don't care. I'm not interested in him. I'm not scared of him, either. My only concern is for Remi, and the fact that she hasn't said a word yet.

"Where's your shoe?" I ask her.

She nods toward the seat, but before I can lean in to get it, the gorilla does it for me, handing it over.

"Thanks," I mutter, then I kneel in front of Remi. "Try slipping it on." She does as I say, and I take care, helping her, making sure she's not in pain. "Okay?" I say, getting to my feet again and she nods, then turns to the gorilla.

"Thanks," she whispers.

He shrugs, although he doesn't reply, and I put my arm around Remi, ignoring the gorilla now, as I take her weight and lead her slowly outside.

We make it to my car before she stops and pulls away from me.

"What's wrong?" I ask, looking down into her upturned face. I can see the anger in her eyes, but I don't flinch from it... mainly because I don't understand it. Yet.

"You can't do this."

"Can't do what?"

"You can't treat me like a child and then walk into a bar and announce you're my boyfriend."

"Excuse me? Treat you like a child? When did I do that?"

"Just now. When you called, you told me to stay here... that you were coming to the rescue."

"I didn't say any such thing."

"You told me to stay here."

"Yes. You were hurt. I was scared. I wanted to help you."

She blushes and I move closer, although she steps back, keeping her weight on her good ankle. "Why did you call yourself my boyfriend?"

"Because it's the truth."

"Is it?" I don't like the sound of this, but even if my heart is racing and my skin is prickling with fear, I won't be defeated.

"Yes, it is. Or have our kisses meant nothing to you?"

She blinks, then tilts her head, her eyes softening.

"They've meant everything to me. I just didn't think they meant anything to you."

Is she serious? "Why not?"

"You said you'd call, and you didn't."

"I know, but only because Ryan sent me out of town first thing this morning."

"You could have called before you left, couldn't you?" she says, quite reasonably.

"I would have done, but the woman I was going with came into my office before I got the chance. I didn't feel like talking to you in front of her."

I thought Remi looked angry before, but that was nothing compared to her expression now. Her eyes are alight with rage. "Y—You went out of town with another woman?"

"Yes. She's one of the company's surveyors. Why? What's wrong?"

She shakes her head, letting out a loud sigh. "Why would anything be wrong, Gabe? I mean… you clearly had a problem with a man helping me when I slipped on the ice, but why on earth would I object to you spending the day with another woman?"

I nod my head. "Oh, I get it. You're jealous."

"No, I'm not." She raises her voice slightly and I think twice about the smile that was forming on my lips, although I lean in a little closer to her.

"Yes, you are. But it's okay, because I'm jealous of the gorilla you were sitting with in there."

"He's not a gorilla," she says, narrowing her eyes at me. "His name's Jesse and he's a fitness instructor."

"I guess that makes sense."

"What does that mean?"

"Most men aren't built like that, Remi, in case you haven't noticed."

She lowers her eyes, focusing on my shoulders, then my arms, and my chest, before she looks up at my face again. "I can't say I had." I want to laugh, but I daren't. She's still too mad for humor. "Tell me about the woman you were with today."

"I wasn't 'with' her. Not like that. I drove her up to Vermont, watched her do her job, sat through a meeting with her and brought her home again. That's it."

She sucks in a breath. "Fine, but you still haven't told me anything about her."

"Okay. If you want details… her name's Bailey. She's thirty-two years old, tall, blonde…"

Remi holds up her hand and I stop talking. "I've heard enough, thanks."

"No, you haven't. I was gonna say she's tall, blonde, and nowhere near as beautiful as you." I step closer and pull her into my arms. She's stiff and reluctant, but I do my best to ignore that and gaze down at her. "You've got nothing to be jealous of, baby."

"Really?"

"Yes." I shake my head. "I know I'm probably not handling this very well, but I've never been in a situation like this before."

"A situation like what?"

"Where I've had to explain myself."

Somehow, she leans back far enough to fold her arms across her chest between us. I'm not sure she could be any more defensive if she tried, but I refuse to let that defeat me, either.

"You don't have to do anything."

"I think I do. At the very least, I think I need to tell you what happened today."

"Do I want to hear it?" she says.

"I can't see why you wouldn't." She stares at me, a blush on her cheeks, a hint of something more than doubt sparkling in her eyes, and I shake my head. "Stop it."

"Stop what?"

"Looking at me like that."

"Why?"

"You know why. You know what you do to me. I'm either gonna tell you about my day, or I'm gonna kiss you so fu—, so hard, you'll be begging me to stop. You choose."

Her breath stutters and she stares up into my eyes. "T—Tell me about your day."

"Okay. It was horrible."

"Why?"

"Because Bailey spent most of it flirting with me."

Remi leans back again, the sparkle gone and doubt filling her eyes now. "She did?"

"Yeah. So did the woman we went to see in Vermont. She was the planning officer in charge of processing the application for the plot of land up there."

"What was her name?" Remi asks.

"Selena. She invited me to have dinner with her."

"Just you? Not… not Bailey?"

"Just me."

"What did you say?"

"I said 'no', of course. I had to be polite, because we need her on our side for now, but there was no way I wanted to have dinner – or anything else – with her."

"And Bailey?"

"I didn't want anything she was offering either."

"What was she offering?"

"She suggested we should stay the night up there."

"Are you serious?"

"Yes. It started snowing, and for some reason, she thought staying up there was a good idea. I didn't, and I told her I'd fire her if she didn't stop flirting with me."

Remi's eyes widen. "Really?"

"Yeah. It's not the first time she's done it, and while I've always found it slightly annoying in the past, it really got to me today."

"Why?"

I pull her closer, keeping a firm hold on her. "Not because I was torn, or tempted, or anything like that. It was because I don't want anything to come between us... not even your unfounded suspicions."

I hear her sigh and feel it against me, too. "So you told her you'd fire her?"

"Yes, if she doesn't stop it."

"Do you have that kind of authority?"

"Not really. It's not something I've ever had to think about before, but I'm fairly sure Ryan would agree with me in these circumstances. I'll talk to him tomorrow."

"And he'll back you?"

"If necessary. I hope it won't be, because she's good at her job, but..."

She tips her head to one side, frowning up at me, although she's a lot more relaxed now, her hands on my waist, tucked inside my jacket. "I don't think I like the idea of you working with someone who flirts with you all the time."

"I doubt she will anymore. She knows the consequences. And you've got nothing to worry about. There's no way I could be tempted by her, or anyone else. I promise." I raise my right hand, cupping her cheek and gazing into her eyes. "The only thing I've thought about all day is getting back here to you. I called you the moment I dropped Bailey at the office, because I was desperate to hear your voice. I missed you so much."

"You did?"

"Yeah."

She leans against me, her head on my chest. "I had a horrible thought earlier, when you didn't call."

"What was that?"

"That you might have been with another woman."

She looks up at me as I lean back. "I guess I was… just not in the way you thought." I kiss her forehead. "You've gotta trust me, Remi. I wouldn't hurt you. I wouldn't do anything to risk what we've got, or what I want us to have together."

She sighs. "I know. It was silly of me. I just hate the idea of other women flirting with you."

"I got that. But I don't like the idea of other men flirting with you, either."

"Jesse wasn't flirting," she says, like I'm the one being silly. "He was helping me. I'm sure he wasn't even interested in me like that."

I shake my head, smiling down at her. "He was, believe me."

"How do you know?"

"Because he'd be crazy not to flirt with you… and besides, you hurt your ankle, so what was he doing with your foot?" She frowns, like she doesn't understand, and I lean a little closer. "For some women, having their feet touched, or kissed, or licked, or fondled is a turn-on."

"It is?"

"Yes."

"I didn't realize."

"No, but the gorilla did. You can be sure of that. He knew exactly what he was doing."

"Is that why you turned into a caveman back there?" she asks, her lips twisting upward.

"Yes."

She smiles at last. Thank God. "I'm sorry," she whispers.

"What for? You didn't do anything wrong. And in any case, I'm the one who should be sorry. I should have been here, so I could be the one helping you. Or better still, I should have collected you from work. That way, you wouldn't have had to walk home in the first place. Instead of which I've been up in Vermont, enduring one of the worst days of my life."

"It can't have been that bad."

"Trust me, it was. Any day spent away from you is torture." Her smile widens. "Can we forget about flirtatious colleagues, and gorillas, and everyone else?"

"I think I'd like that."

"And can I kiss you?"

She nods her head, biting on her bottom lip. I don't think it's intentionally done, but it's too much for me, and I turn her around, pushing her back against the side of my car and holding her there with my body as I dip my head and kiss her hard, nipping at her bottom lip. She gasps, then moans, bringing her hands up onto my arms. I step closer still, grinding my hips, and I put my hands inside her coat, letting them roam down her sides, feeling the swell of her breasts and her narrow waist, before I move them around behind her, and rest them on her ass, pulling her onto me. I suck her lip into my mouth, then kiss it, and then explore her with my tongue. She responds with a tentative flicker against my lips before she copies me, delving deeper, and I change the angle of my head, a groan building in my throat and echoing around us.

This is so much more than last night, or the night before that.

But I need it to be.

I need her to understand how I feel, even if I can't tell her yet.

Chapter Eleven

Remi

Gabe breaks the kiss eventually, and I open my eyes to find him staring at me. That was very different to anything he's done before, and I'm struggling to breathe, or even to think as his lips twist up into a smile.

"Say something," he whispers, tucking my hair behind my ear.

"Wow."

He laughs. "That's something."

"It certainly was."

"Shall I take you home now?"

"Yes, please."

He steps back, opening the car door, and bends, lifting me into his arms before he deposits me on the passenger seat.

"Okay?"

"Yes, thank you."

He hands me the safety belt, and gives me a lingering smile, then closes the door, and I watch him walk around the front of the car, climbing in beside me.

"Do you need help?"

"What with?"

"Your seat belt."

I look down and realize I'm still holding it. "No, I'm fine." I snap it into place and he leans over, brushing his lips against mine.

"I know you are."

I feel like my body's on fire, but he seems so calm. How can that be? Why isn't he burning up like I am? How is he capable of starting the engine and driving? I can barely focus, or breathe, and yet he can do all these things, like he didn't just flip my world upside down.

It feels like nothing will ever be the same again, but as he pulls up outside my house, I turn to look at it, surprised to see it's just the same as it was when I left this morning.

Without a word, Gabe gets out of the car and comes around, opening my door and unfastening my safety belt.

"Where are your keys?" he asks.

"In my pocket." I delve inside, pulling them out, and he smiles at me.

"Good."

With that, he lifts me into his arms, kicking the door closed, and walks up the path to the front door. He waits while I open it, then carries me through to the living room, where he sits me on the couch that faces the front of the house. The room is in darkness, but Gabe quickly rectifies that, switching on the Christmas tree lights.

"I'll just close the door, then I'll be back," he says, leaving the room, although he's back within moments, kneeling in front of me to pull off my shoes, taking extra care of the left one. "Let's get you more comfortable." He lifts me into the corner of the couch, then raises my legs, putting a pillow under my injured ankle. "How's that?"

"It's perfect." I smile up at him and he leans over, resting one hand on the back of the couch, and the other on the arm behind me as he kisses me. I wonder if he'll keep it brief, but he doesn't. He lingers, his tongue finding mine in a gentle, nuzzling caress.

After a while, he pulls back, looking down at me, a smile on his lips as he tilts his head. "I probably should have taken off your coat before we got you settled."

He has a point, but it doesn't take long to remove it, and he takes his off, too, putting them both over the back of the couch.

"I'd offer to cook you dinner, but…" I look up at him, feeling inadequate.

He smiles. "You don't have to cook. I'll do it."

"Really?"

"Yes. I can cook, you know. You sit here and rest while I look after you, like any good boyfriend should."

I giggle, and he bends forward, kissing me again. I could get used to this, but he doesn't give me a chance. Instead, he stands, smiling down at me one last time before he leaves the room.

It's a little chilly in here, but I can't get up to light the fire, so I grab the throw from beneath our coats and lay it over my legs, smiling to myself. I like the idea of Gabe being my boyfriend, and of being his girlfriend, and I realize now how silly I was earlier. My reaction when he said he'd spent the day with another woman was so juvenile, but at least he didn't mind, or call me a child… because that's what I was being. A silly child.

"Are you cold?" Gabe comes back in, carrying a cup, and immediately spots the throw over my legs.

"I was, but I'm okay now."

"Do you want me to light the fire?"

"No, it's okay."

He puts the cup on the table. "I made you a coffee."

"Thank you."

He steps back. "Dinner will be about twenty minutes."

"What are we having?" I've got plenty of food after our visit to the grocery store, but I'm not sure what he'll make out of it.

"It's a surprise," he says, with a grin, and leaves again.

I pick up the cup, sipping my coffee, thinking how domesticated this feels. It's like Gabe belongs here already, and although I know he'll leave later, I wish he wouldn't. I wish he'd stay.

I feel myself blush, just for thinking that. But I can't help it. When he kisses me, it's like he ignites something inside me. It happens every time, and I'm craving more… and more. I might not know very much about what 'more' entails, but I really want to find out. I close my eyes, thinking about that kiss outside the bar, about how his hands wandered, coming to rest on my ass. He swiveled his hips into me then, and I could feel how hard he was. That's something else that happens every time… and I like it.

"Remi?"

I open my eyes to find Gabe staring down at me, a bowl in his hand.

"I wasn't asleep."

He grins. "If you were, you were clearly dreaming."

"Why do you say that?"

"You had a smile on your face." I blush and he tilts his head. "What were you dreaming about?"

"Nothing. Like I say, I wasn't asleep."

"Okay. What were you thinking about?"

"You."

He grins, sitting on the edge of the couch, and I move back to make room for him. "It's good to know I can inspire such a beautiful smile." I don't know how to reply to that, but I'm saved the trouble, as he hands me the bowl. "I made stir-fry. You bought so many vegetables the other day, it made sense to use some of them." I look down at the sparkling array of colorful vegetables in a nest of noodles. The smells are incredible, and I smile up at him.

"Thank you."

"I'll just get mine."

He goes, returning within seconds with a second bowl and cup, sitting at the end of the couch. Without taking our eyes from each other, we both eat, and I have to say, the smells didn't do justice to his cooking. It tastes fantastic, and I tell him so.

"You can cook dinner for me anytime you like."

"I hope so."

The atmosphere between us is charged with something I've never felt before, but I like it and I nestle back against the arm of the couch, unable to stop staring at him.

"What were you doing in Vermont?" I ask, swallowing down a slice of pepper.

"The planning commission up there discovered some last-minute problems on one of our more troublesome projects. We had to change the access onto the land and someone had to be there to handle the negotiations and sign off on it."

"And that someone had to be you?"

"Yes. Ryan said something about not wanting to leave town because the wedding's so close, although everything's ready now, so I'm not sure what that was about."

"Maybe he had some other reason for wanting to stay in town," I suggest and Gabe shrugs, swirling some noodles around his fork and swallowing them down.

"How was your day?" he asks. "Other than falling on the ice, I mean."

I notice he doesn't mention Jesse, and I won't either. It seems wise to stick to our agreement and forget about him… and everyone else.

"It was fine. I had a call from Alex at lunchtime."

"Alex…" He tilts his head and then smiles. "She's your friend from college, right?"

"Yes. She called to tell me she's engaged."

"Wow. Was that something you knew about?"

"Not at all. I didn't even know she was seeing anyone. She only met her fiancé a few weeks ago."

He twists in his seat a little, putting down his fork and staring at me. "And you don't think it's possible for two people to fall in love that fast?"

"No… I do." But I've just remembered something Alex said…

"Then why do you sound so bewildered by the whole thing?"

"Because Jacques is from France, and they're talking about getting married over there. I didn't think about it at the time, but I guess that means there's a chance I won't be able to go."

"Why not?" he says, frowning. "Don't you think she'll invite you?"

"I imagine she will. All three of us have stayed quite close, but… it's France."

"Yeah… a country in Europe. It's not Mars, Remi."

"Maybe not, but I've never been abroad. I've never flown anywhere, let alone somewhere they don't speak English."

"Your other friend will be going too, won't she?"

"Sofia? I would have thought so, but she lives in Arizona, so it's not like we could go together."

"Your friend lives in Arizona, and you've never flown there to visit her?"

"No. Just like I haven't been to see Alex in Austin. Although you have to remember, we only left college in the spring, and we've all been busy."

He nods his head and smiles. "It sounds like it… certainly in Alex's case. But if you want to go to your friend's wedding, I'll take you."

I drop my fork and stare at him. "Y—You will?"

"Of course. I don't like the idea of you going by yourself. Not if it makes you this nervous. More to the point, I don't want to be away from you for any longer than I have to. So, if you want me to, I'll come with you." He lets out a half laugh. "Of course, you'd have to tell your friends about me."

"Oh, I already told Alex…" I stop talking as his smile becomes a radiant grin.

"You did?"

"Yeah. I didn't go into too much detail, because at the time I was feeling a little confused."

"You were?"

I nod my head. "I hadn't heard from you, and I didn't know what was going on."

"I see. And if you hadn't been feeling confused, what would you have said?" It feels like he's teasing, and I have to smile.

"I don't know. But Alex and I agreed we'll have a video call with Sofia in the New Year, so I can fill in some of the gaps then."

"Hopefully, you'll have a lot more to tell them."

"Hopefully…"

We stare at each other for a moment or two, and then pick up our forks. Although I'll admit, I'm a lot less interested in eating, even though the stir-fry tastes so good.

After a minute or two, Gabe hesitates, his fork halfway to his mouth, noodles hanging from it, and he licks his lips, letting out a slow sigh.

"Is something wrong?" I ask.

He puts down his fork. "No. I was just thinking about weddings."

"What about them?"

He leans in. "I was wondering if you'd come with me to Ryan and Peony's?"

He can't mean that.

"But it's on Saturday."

"I know."

"How can I? I'm not invited."

"I'm inviting you as my guest," he says, like it's the most reasonable thing in the world.

"Are you allowed to do that?"

"I'm the best man. Ryan's my oldest friend. I think he'll cut me some slack." He moves a little closer. "I want you there, Remi." He shakes his head. "No… that's not right. I need you there."

How can I say 'no' to that?

"If you're sure it'll be okay."

"I'm positive."

I nod my head, and he smiles, picking up his fork again.

"Are you done?" Gabe asks, and I hand him my bowl.

"Thank you. That was delicious." It really was, and it was just what I needed, too.

He puts both bowls on the table and moves closer, leaning in. "Speaking of delicious…" he whispers, nipping at my bottom lip. He did this earlier, and just like then, it sends shockwaves around my body. I arch my back into him and he puts his arms around me, holding me close to his chest. A throaty, rumbling groan leaves his lips, reverberating into mine as our tongues clash and he rolls us somehow, so we're lying side by side along the length of the couch.

I can feel his arousal pressing into me again and I take a chance, flexing my hips, to let him know I like it.

I like his kisses, too, and everything else he's doing to me, as he puts his hand on my ass, pulling me closer and turning us, so I'm on my back, and he's on top of me.

I part my legs, creating a space for him to lie in, although he breaks the kiss, leaning up and looking down at me.

"Is your ankle okay?"

"I'd forgotten all about it."

He smiles. "Then maybe I should keep kissing you."

He dips his head, putting his words into actions, and I raise my arms, my hands drifting up to his shoulders, then clasping behind his neck. I'm struggling to breathe again, unable to believe anything could feel this good. To think, he's refused to come inside the house all week because he wanted more than kisses, and yet, here we are...

I lean back, and he tilts his head. "Is something wrong?"

"No. I just wondered... do you still want more?"

"If only you knew how much I wanna fu—" He smiles, looking a little sheepish, and I can't help the gasp that leaves my lips, as he lowers himself to his elbows, his lips almost touching mine. "We can go at your pace, baby."

"The thing is, I don't know what my pace is."

He chuckles. "We'll work it out."

"How? Obviously you've done all this before, but..." He closes the gap between us, silencing me with a kiss, his tongue darting into my mouth, lingering there for a while before he pulls back again. I lower my arms slightly, letting my hands rest on his biceps and feel his muscles flex through his shirtsleeves. "Can I ask a question?"

"You can ask anything you want."

"Okay." I stare up at him. "Without going into details, have there been many women? Before me, I mean?"

"Yes." I suck in a breath, surprised by his honesty. "Does that bother you?" he asks.

"A little. I don't know how I feel about you having had so many girlfriends."

"Who said anything about girlfriends?"

"You did. You just said..."

"I said there had been other women. I didn't say I'd ever thought of any of them as my girlfriend."

"Seriously?"

"Absolutely. This is the first time I've considered myself to be someone's boyfriend, too."

"But you went out with lots of women?"

"Yes. Does that still bother you?"

"I don't know. I guess you're a lot older than me, so…"

He chuckles, shaking his head. "Thanks."

"Sorry. I didn't mean it like that."

"I know. The age gap between us is quite big, though…"

"Don't remind me." I close my eyes, wishing I could take back my words, although it's too late now.

"Is that why you were so reluctant to start with?" he asks, and I open my eyes again.

"Reluctant to what?"

"To let me walk you back to your office… to have coffee with me… to start anything. Was it because of the difference in our ages? Because you knew I'd have a past?"

He's so close to hitting the nail on the head, except it wasn't his past that was concerning me then. It was mine. "I was thinking about the age gap, yes. But I wasn't thinking about your past."

"And you are now? Because if you are, you don't need to, baby." He sucks on my bottom lip, then traces a line of kisses along my jawline to my ear. "I can't change what happened before I met you, but I can leave it where it is, and enjoy the present… with you."

"The present?"

"And the future."

"You want a future? With me?"

"Oh, God… yes."

I've lost the power of speech for a moment, so I just nod and smile, my heart so light I can't control the flight it's taking, and he dips his head, kissing me harder than ever. I can't think straight anymore. My body is his and if he asked for more, I'd say 'yes'. A hundred times over, I'd say 'yes'.

Except I know he won't ask. Not because he doesn't want me, but because he's waiting, although the way I feel now, I don't think he'll be waiting very long.

He rolls us onto our sides again, facing each other, and as his lips meet mine, he wraps his leg around me, like he doesn't want to let me go.

And that suits me just fine.

Chapter Twelve

Gabe

How did we get here?

How did I get so lucky that I can call myself the boyfriend of someone as special as Remi?

I'm still not sure, although I know how close I came to screwing it up on Wednesday evening. I behaved like a caveman then, just like she said. Seeing Remi with that gorilla set off some very weird emotions... ones I've never experienced before. I wanted to protect her and claim her at the same time. She needed protecting, too. She couldn't see it for herself, but that guy was more than interested in her, and there was no way I was going to let him win.

I was jealous... but so was she when I told her I'd spent the day being flirted with. Oddly enough, I liked her reaction, and I think that's why I kissed her the way I did. I wanted her to realize she had nothing to fear, and although I wasn't taking it slow, I was beyond any such thing by then.

And I don't regret a single second of it.

How could I, when things since then have been so amazing?

I knew work was going to be crazy on Thursday, having lost a day on Wednesday, but I made time to take Remi to the library and arranged to pick her up in the evening before heading for the office. Despite a lengthy list of things to do, I made my way straight to Ryan's office, closing the door behind me.

He looked up, smiling. "I've had an email from Selena Oaks confirming she's approved the plans. She's gonna send all the official documents through next week, but at least we can start work in the New Year now." He nodded his head at me. "Well done."

"You should give me a fucking medal."

He frowned. "Was it that bad?"

"It was worse." I decided to cut to the chase. "I threatened to fire Bailey."

He sat back, his frown deepening. "You did what?"

"You heard me." I sat opposite him. "I'd had enough of her, man. She'd been driving me crazy all day."

"Flirting?" he said, even though I was sure he knew the answer already.

"Of course. No matter how many times I told her I wasn't interested, she wouldn't get the message."

"Does she ever?"

"No. But that doesn't make it right, does it? Why is it that when a woman says 'no', it means 'no', but when a man says 'no', a woman like Bailey can interpret that in any fucking way she chooses?"

"It's never bothered you like this before."

"I wasn't with Remi before."

His face softened then. "So that's the problem."

"It's not a problem. Not in that sense. I just didn't like the way Bailey was behaving, and the fact that she wouldn't take 'no' for an answer."

"So you threatened to fire her?"

"Yes. I get that it's not my role in the company to hire and fire, but I'd had enough. If you wanna make something…"

He held up his hand, and I stopped talking. "It's fine," he said, smiling. "I get it… and just so you know, I agree with you. She was out of line. She has been all along, and you're right, we should have done something about it before now. Do you want me to speak with her?"

"I don't think you'll need to."

"You think she understood?"

"Based on our silent ride home last night, it felt like it."

"Okay. Well… if she starts anything, let me know." He smiled. "At least Selena Oaks has signed off the plans now."

"Yeah. After she'd invited me to dinner."

He rolled his eyes. "Seriously? I take it you declined."

"Of course I did. I had to be polite about it, so I used the bad weather as an excuse."

"Very diplomatic."

"I thought so."

I got up then, aware of my busy schedule. "Thanks for handling everything yesterday," he said.

"That's okay." I turned to leave, but then remembered the other reason I needed to speak to him. "By the way, I hope it's okay, but I've invited Remi to your wedding."

He chuckled. "I was wondering when you'd tell me."

I frowned down at him. "How could I have told you before now? I only asked her last night."

"Really? Peony and I added her to the guest list on Sunday morning when you left the farm."

"You did?"

"Of course we did. She's your girlfriend."

"She wasn't my girlfriend on Sunday."

"It was only a matter of time before she was, though."

I laughed then and went to my office, where a pile of messages awaited my attention.

They kept me busy all day, along with a couple of bids that needed to be read through, but I made it to the library in time to collect Remi. I helped her to the car and drove us back to her place, asking how she'd managed, standing on her foot all day.

"I didn't. Audrey and Camilla took pity on me, and for once, they actually did some work. I spent my day sitting behind the counter."

"Good for you."

"Shall we cook together tonight?" she asked, as I parked in front of her house.

"Are you up to that?"

"I think so, and in any case, I haven't seen you all day."

I rested my hand on her thigh, turning off the engine. "Tell me about it. I've missed you so much."

"I've missed you, too."

I leaned over and kissed her, just briefly, and then got out of the car, helping her down from her seat, and holding her hand as we walked together up the path.

We cooked pasta, although I did more of the cooking than Remi. I didn't mind in the slightest. At least we were together, and once it was ready, we ate in the living room so she could put her foot up. Afterwards, I cleared away as quickly as I could, returning to her with two cups of coffee, and we lay together on the couch. We kissed for hours, until it was time for me to leave, and although I can't say I wasn't tempted to take things further, I held back.

I couldn't help smiling all the way home, which surprised me. Naturally, I'd rather have stayed with her, but we'd had a good evening. It feels like we could have a lot more, and I won't risk that by rushing things.

I'm just going to take it day by day. And see where we end up.

This morning, before I started work, I helped Remi collect her car. She didn't need my help. She was more than capable of dealing with it by herself, but I had to pay Levi, and I wanted to make sure Remi was okay to drive. Fortunately, it's her left ankle that she twisted, and her car has an automatic transmission, so that's worked out okay. Besides, her ankle is getting better every day. She said this morning it was just feeling a little stiff, with hardly any pain at all. Even so, I'll be taking extra care of her… because that's what boyfriends do.

At least that's what this boyfriend does, although I'll be able to do it a lot better once my best friend's wedding is over and done with. Then I'll be able to focus on my girlfriend, and building our relationship.

To be fair, I'd be with her tonight, if it wasn't for the fact that the wedding is tomorrow, and even though Ryan didn't want a bachelor party, I couldn't let the occasion go unmarked. He's coming to my place for dinner and is staying over, while Peony's friend Laurel and her daughter Addison are spending the night at the farm.

I haven't been able to see Remi since this morning, but Ryan isn't due here for another thirty minutes, so once I'm showered, I wrap a towel around my hips and sit on the edge of the bed, placing a call to her.

"Are you okay?" I ask the moment she answers.

"I'm glad it's the end of the week," she replies, sounding weary.

"I wish I could be with you."

"So do I."

I have to smile, even though my arms ache to hold her.

"You're gonna be okay getting to the wedding tomorrow, aren't you?" I ask.

She chuckles. "I don't think I'll get lost between here and the apple orchard."

"I know. But I'd rather come get you."

"I think you'll have more important things to do, don't you?"

"No. Nothing is more important than being with you... taking care of you."

I hear her sigh. "I—I..." She stops talking and I wonder for a second if she was about to say something momentous.

"You what?" I ask, desperate to know, although I'm not sure it's wise to push her. That's hardly taking it slow, is it?

"I—I feel the same way," she says. "I wanna be with you, too... all the time."

That may not have been the momentous thing I was thinking of, but it's pretty damn significant.

"Once the wedding's over, neither of us will be working for a couple of weeks. We can do whatever we like whenever we like."

"I'm looking forward to it already."

"So am I." I check the time. "I'm sorry, baby. Ryan's gonna be here soon. I'm not dressed yet and I'm gonna have to go."

"You're not dressed?" There's something in her voice that makes me smile.

"No. I've just showered." I hear her breathe deeply a couple of times. "Are you blushing?"

"Yes."

"And biting your lip, by any chance?" I ask.

"I might be."

"Then stop. Even thinking about your lips is too much for me at the moment."

"Why?"

Because I wanna see them wrapped around my cock. Because I wanna fuck your mouth so hard.

I can't say that out loud... not to Remi. It wouldn't be right.

"Because I can't kiss them, and I need to," I say instead, and she gasps. "I need you so much, baby."

"I need you, too."

I can't doubt the sincerity in her voice. No-one could. "I wish I didn't have to be here. Or if I did, I wish you could be here with me."

"So do I, but it's okay. I'll see you tomorrow."

"You can count on it."

"Have a good evening."

"I'll do my best." Although I know it won't be as good as any evening spent with her. Especially not now. "Sleep well, baby."

"You too."

We end our call with great reluctance, and I drop the phone onto the bed, removing the towel and running to my dressing room to grab some jeans and a button-down shirt.

I'm dressed in no time at all, and rush down the stairs, just as Ryan arrives, parking his car behind mine. He grabs his suit carrier from the back seat, along with the bag he's just picked up from the French restaurant in town, and walks up the path to greet me, a smile etched on his face.

"Shall I take this upstairs?" he says, nodding to his suit as he offers me the bag.

"Sure. You're in the bedroom at the back."

He smiles and runs up the stairs while I head for the kitchen, the smells from the bag already making my stomach rumble.

We talked through what we were going to cook and decided ordering in was a better idea. I believe Peony and her friend are cooking, but that's their choice. We're far too lazy, and after the week I've had, I'm too tired.

By the time Ryan returns, I've already set the table, and he comes in, sitting down and looking a little dejected.

"Hey… you're getting married tomorrow. You're supposed to be happy."

"I am," he says, checking the labels on the cartons I've spread out, and giving me the rack of lamb I ordered as I sit opposite him. It comes with ratatouille and gratin Dauphinois, and the heady hint of garlic is making my mouth water.

I open the wine while he delves into his carton of boeuf Bourguignon, dipping his head to catch the aroma before spooning it onto his plate, alongside the mashed potatoes and baby carrots.

"What's wrong?" I ask, pushing the cartons aside.

"I miss Peony," he says simply as we both start eating.

"Why?" He frowns at me, like I'm being dumb. "I mean, I get missing her, but you should be used to this. You spent a lot of time away from her at the beginning, when we were moving the offices up here and you had to be in Boston during the week."

"I know, but it's different... especially now."

"Why 'especially' now?"

He takes a sip of wine, tilting his head at me. "Because Peony's pregnant."

I drop my fork, which makes him chuckle. "Sh—She's pregnant?"

"Yeah." He looks so damn pleased with himself, I have to smile.

"Was this planned?"

"Yes, and no."

"Which is it? It can't be both."

"Yes, it can. She was on birth control, but we talked it through a while back and decided we wanted to start a family once we were married."

"Okay. You have remembered you're not actually married yet, haven't you?"

"I have. But Peony was due to see her doctor a couple of months back, and we agreed it wasn't worth her getting any more pills. We felt it was close enough to the wedding for her to stop taking them." He shakes his head, like he's remembering something. "I think we both imagined it would take a little longer than this to actually happen, though."

"When did you find out?" I ask.

"Peony realized she was late on Wednesday morning just before I left for work. I wanted to stay home, but there was too much to do at the office, so we agreed she'd get a test and call me once she'd done it... which was why I was a little stressed. I was waiting for her to call."

"And that's why you didn't want to leave town?"

He nods his head. "I know you didn't wanna go either, but I needed to be here, either way. Positive or negative, I knew she'd need me."

"It's okay. I get it now." Better than he thinks.

He sighs. "I've loved Peony since the first time I saw her, but this... this is so much more."

"In what way?" I ask. He's got me intrigued now.

"All kinds of ways, although the most noticeable is the need to protect her. It was always there, but it's multiplied now, maybe a million times over. If the last two days are anything to go by, I'm probably going to have a heart attack by the time the baby's born."

"Try not to."

He chuckles, sipping more wine and staring at the glass. "Peony's seriously pissed about one thing."

"What's that?"

"We ordered some fantastic wines for the wedding reception, and she can't drink any of them now."

I laugh and he joins in.

"I'm sure you'll make it up to her."

"I fully intend to." He puts down his glass, getting back to his food. "By the way, we're not telling anyone yet. Not even Laurel."

"Really? How is Peony gonna swing that?" He frowns, like he doesn't understand. "Surely Laurel will guess when Peony is sick over breakfast, won't she?"

He shakes his head. "Her morning sickness hasn't started yet. It's too early for that."

"Oh, right." I try to sound knowledgeable, even though I'm not. "If Peony isn't even telling her best friend, why are you telling me?"

"Because I thought you had a right to know why I sent you to Vermont and made your life a misery, and because I might need to be absent from the office from time to time, for doctor's appointments and things like that."

"Oh, I see. So, when will you make it public news?"

"Not until after the first scan."

"And when is that?"

He frowns at me. "Don't you know anything?"

I give up the pretense of knowledge. "No. And don't pretend you do, either. I'm pretty sure Peony will have had to tell you whatever you needed to know."

He shakes his head, surprising me. "No. I showed initiative and looked it up on the Internet."

We both laugh. "So, what was the answer?"

"To what?"

"When Peony will have her first scan?"

"It was a little vague, to be honest. Sometime between six and nine weeks seems to be the average, but it can be any time up to fourteen weeks."

"That's helpful."

"Not really... especially as Peony hasn't been able to get an appointment with her doctor until after the honeymoon."

"Aren't there two doctors here?"

"Yes, but Peony's adamant she wants to see Doctor Dodds and not Doctor Singleton."

"Why? What's wrong with Doctor Singleton?"

"He's older… much older, and his ideas are a little outdated, from what Peony tells me. She says she'd rather wait and see Doctor Dodds, and if there's one thing I've learned already, it's not to argue with a pregnant woman."

I can't help laughing. "It can't be that bad."

"Can't it? Believe me, you don't wanna go there."

"Don't I?"

A smile forms on his lips, and he raises his eyebrows. "You like the idea yourself, do you?"

"It's not something I've given any thought to. Why would I? I've never been in love before."

"Is that your way of admitting you are now?"

"No comment," I say, giving him a smile, which he returns. "Am I allowed to tell Remi your news?" I ask. "Only I don't like keeping things from her."

"Of course you can tell her."

I finish my lamb, pushing the plate aside and topping up the wine. "What are you gonna call the baby?"

"I don't know. We haven't even talked about names yet, and probably won't until we know what sex it is."

"No… I meant what will its last name be? If Peony's still gonna be 'Hart', and you're gonna be 'Andrews', what's your kid gonna be called?"

"Oh. Hart-Andrews."

"You've decided that already?"

"Yeah. We talked it through before Peony stopped taking her birth control pills."

"Man, that sounds organized."

He smiles. "Not organized. Committed."

Once upon a time, that word would have terrified me, but now it feels like the most natural thing in the world. I'm as committed to Remi as I could ever be, and it's difficult to remember how I was before I met her. I recall thinking how boring it would be to sleep with the same woman over and over, day in and day out, year in and year out. But now, I can't wait for that life to begin, and to leave my old life behind... for good.

The wedding might not be until two, but Ryan and I have been up since seven this morning.

I don't think he's nervous, or anything like that. I think he's impatient.

I know I am.

I can't wait to see Remi.

"Where are you going?" Ryan asks as I open the front door, a small overnight bag in my hand.

"I'm gonna put this in the trunk of my car."

"Are you going somewhere after the wedding?"

"Only to Remi's place." Unless she decides she wants to come back here.

"You're staying over, are you? I hadn't realized things had gone that far already. I thought you were taking it slow."

We're due to leave in a few minutes and he's been pacing the floor for the last half hour.

"They haven't. And I am."

"Really?" He glances down at the bag again. "Is that your idea of taking it slow? Or are you hoping things might progress a little further tonight?"

"Not necessarily. We're doing things at her pace." And although I told Remi we'd work it out, I'm still not entirely clear what that is. She said she needs me. I heard that loud and clear, but she might not have meant it in the same way I did. I've realized that since we talked last night. She might have meant she needed my company, or a hug, or just to see me. She might not have meant she has the same burning need that I do... to fuck, until neither of us can move, or speak, or breathe. "I'm just taking some clothes to change into, in case I want them later on."

He nods his head, although I get the feeling he doesn't believe me, and for a moment I wonder about leaving my bag behind. I've just told him the truth, though. When I packed these clothes, my sole thought was that I didn't want to spend the evening in a tux. Not when I could so easily change into something more comfortable. Why shouldn't I take them with me? I don't have an ulterior motive… no matter what Ryan thinks.

I dump the bag in the trunk of my car and he follows me out, clearly in a hurry to leave.

"You're sure it's gonna be okay for me to leave my car here?" he asks, nodding at his Mercedes.

"Absolutely." We moved the cars around earlier, so I can get mine out, and he stands next to it. "Can I take it you wanna go now?" I say, smiling up at him.

"You can. Is it too soon?"

"I don't know. Let me call Laurel."

Peony gave me her friend's number a few weeks ago, for just this purpose, and I step away so Ryan won't hear what she says, connecting a call to her.

"Hello?" She sounds a little nervous, but we've only met twice, so I guess that's hardly surprising.

"Hi. It's Gabe."

"Can I guess the groom is as impatient as the bride?"

"You can."

"In that case, you'll be relieved to hear all the guests are here, and the bride is hidden upstairs, so the coast is clear."

"Fabulous. We'll be on our way, then."

"See you in five," she says, sounding far more relaxed.

We both hang up at the same time, and I wander back to Ryan.

"Ready?" I say, smiling, and he nods his head.

"What do you think?"

I laugh, walking around to the driver's side, while he gets in next to me, and we set off.

The journey is silent, but I guess he's got things to think about... not just getting married, but impending fatherhood, too. For myself, I'm looking forward to seeing my girlfriend, and I'm relieved when I pull into the orchard and I see her car parked halfway up the track.

She's here... thank God.

I drive all the way up to the house, parking alongside Peony's truck. It's ancient and beaten up, and I can't help smiling.

"Does Peony know about her present yet?" I ask, turning to face him as I switch off the engine.

"No. It's supposed to be delivered at four-thirty this afternoon... so I'm just hoping that runs to time. Otherwise, I guess she'll just have to wait for her surprise until we get back from our honeymoon."

"Do you think she'll like it?"

He shrugs his shoulders. "Put it this way; I don't think she'll divorce me over it."

"I hope not... or you'll be looking at the shortest marriage in history."

He smiles, giving me a look that lets me know he thinks he's on fairly safe ground, and we both get out of the car, making our way to the barn.

Inside, it's much warmer than I'd expected. The seats are mostly filled already, and I glance around, my eyes alighting on Remi almost straight away.

Ryan wanders over to the celebrant, but I tug on his sleeve, making him stop and turn around.

"Is it okay if I abandon you for five minutes?"

"Can I assume you wanna see Remi?"

"You can."

"In that case, it's absolutely fine."

He smiles and I smile back, leaving him with the celebrant, while I walk down the aisle, stopping when I reach Remi, who's sitting one chair in, about halfway back.

She looks up, smiling when she realizes it's me, and I sit in the vacant seat beside her.

"Are you okay?" I ask.

"Yes."

"Sure?"

She nods her head, leaning in to me, and I put my arm around her, kissing the top of her head. She looks up, her eyes sparkling.

"Has anyone ever told you how good you look in a tux?"

"Not lately."

She smiles. "Well, you do."

"Thank you."

I glance down at her dress, which is cream-colored, with a matching jacket. I can't see the style of it properly when she's sitting, but it appears to be figure hugging, and although she's about to rest her head against me again, I place my finger beneath her chin, holding her steady for just a moment longer.

"You look stunning."

She smiles. "Thank you."

"I'm sorry I can't stay longer, but I've gotta get back to Ryan."

"That's okay. You're the best man... in every way."

I'd been about to get up, but I sit back, turning to face her, clasping her face with my hands and staring into her eyes, like nothing else exists, even though we're surrounded by people.

"You mean that?"

"Yes. I mean every single word."

Chapter Thirteen

Remi

I can't take my eyes off of Gabe. He's standing at the front of the barn now, and even though he's got his back to me and is talking to Ryan, all I can do is smile.

When he walked up to me just now, I practically slid off of my chair. He looks so good in a tux, which could be part of the reason I managed to swallow my nerves and my shyness, to tell him he's the best man. I didn't mean it in the wedding sense, but in the 'everything about you is perfect' sense, although I can't help wondering if he understood… if he got the message. Sure, he asked if I meant it, but did he really know what I was trying to say?

I thought the same thing last night after our phone call, and I can't help wishing I'd had the chance to explain that properly, too.

I'd told him I needed him, and I meant it. Only now I'm not sure if he might have thought I meant I needed him to look after me and care for me. That's what we'd been talking about, after all, and I won't deny, I like the sound of being cared for by Gabe. That wasn't what I meant at the time, though. What I meant was that the need for him to make love with me has become so overwhelming, I don't want to wait any longer.

I ache for him, body and soul. But I don't know how to put that into words.

That's why I keep dropping hints, in the hope he'll get it all by himself.

He turns around, giving me a smile, which I return, my body heating at the sparkle in his eyes, just as Ryan says something and Gabe laughs, facing the front again.

I take a moment to study the groom as the last of the seats fill up. He's the same height as Gabe, and roughly the same build, too, although he's got darker hair. He nudges into Gabe and whispers something, which makes Gabe's shoulders shake with laughter again, and I have to smile...

"Is this seat taken?" I look up to see a man gazing down at me. I'd say he's in his mid-thirties and is wearing a dark gray suit, white shirt and blue tie, none of which disguise his muscular physique. His smile is broad and his eyes are an electric blue, beneath a mop of blond hair.

"N—No."

He smiles and sits. "I'm Mitch Bradshaw. You've probably heard of me."

"I can't say I have."

He looks a little crestfallen and I wonder if I should have lied. Except I don't have a clue who he is... and I don't like him.

He takes a moment, twisting in his seat and looking me up and down, which makes me feel uncomfortable, especially as he takes his time over it, before smiling. "No. You're probably too young." That feels like a veiled insult, and I'm not about to ask what it is I'm too young for. It would only fuel his already enormous ego, although nothing seems to dull his smile. "In case you're wondering, I used to play pro football."

"I'm not very interested in sports."

His smile widens even further. "I'm sure you've got lots of other things to occupy that pretty head of yours."

Patronizing ass.

I wish I could change seats, but I'd have to ask him to let me out. And besides, this place is full to bursting now.

"How do you know the bride and groom?" I ask, feeling intrigued. I find it hard to believe Gabe's friends know anyone this obnoxious, but there must be some connection.

"My wife is the matron of honor," he says, leaning back in his seat. "And my daughter is the flower girl."

"That's nice." I'm surprised he's married… but only because I find it impossible to believe any woman could tolerate this man for more than a few minutes.

He shrugs his shoulders like he couldn't care less, and then leans in to me, making me feel even more uncomfortable than I already was. "How do you know them?"

"I don't. Not really. I'm here with my boyfriend. He's the best man."

He raises his head, looking forward at Gabe, who's still talking to Ryan. "That's your boyfriend?"

"Yes." And I've never been more pleased, or relieved, to be able to say that.

"Lucky guy," he whispers, turning back to me and studying my face. "I can't believe I've never seen you around town before."

"You probably don't frequent the library that much."

He chuckles. "The library? Why would I wanna go there?"

The answer ought to be obvious, but I guess it isn't to him, and I smile. "I don't know… but it's where I work."

"Oh, I see." He nods his head, but then frowns. "In that case, it makes even less sense."

"What does?"

"The fact that I've never set eyes on you before."

"Why?"

"Because my place is right opposite."

"You live opposite the library?"

"No. I work there."

"At the hotel?"

He laughs. "No. I own the gym."

That's not directly opposite, but it's close enough, I suppose. "I met someone else who works there the other day."

He looks a little concerned, leaning back and frowning at me. "Oh? Who was that?"

"A man called Jesse." Mitch's face clears, and he nods his head.

"Yeah. He works for me. How did you meet him?"

"I fell, and..."

"That must make you Remi," he says, interrupting me. "Jesse told me all about you."

I find that hard to believe. Jessie didn't know enough about me to tell. "He did?"

"Yeah..." He shakes his head, letting his eyes wander over my face, resting on my lips. "Although I've gotta say, his words didn't do you justice."

I'm not about to ask what words he's talking about... especially as I feel even more silly now for not realizing that Jesse was flirting with me.

Still, at least I've worked out that Mitch is, and I give him a nod of my head as the room falls silent and music starts to play.

The doors at the back of the barn open, letting in a cool breeze, and a little girl walks up the aisle between the two sets of chairs on either side. She's carrying a basket of rose petals and is dropping them on the floor in front of her. The dress she's wearing is white, with red polka dots, and her light blonde hair is tied up in a bun behind her head. She looks adorable, although I'm surprised when she walks straight past her father. I'd half expected her to pause or look up at him, either for praise or encouragement, but she doesn't do either, and just continues on her way toward the front of the barn.

She's followed by a tall woman with straight, shoulder-length blonde hair, who's wearing an elegant deep red, fitted, floor-length gown, with a white faux fur cape, which just covers her shoulders. She looks beautiful and I'm not alone in being captivated by her as she sweeps up the aisle.

"She looks like Mrs. Claus dressed like that," Mitch whispers, turning to face me as his wife passes us.

I hope to God she didn't hear him, although the woman in front of us clearly did and she turns around and gives him a glare, which he more than deserves.

I wonder for a moment if he's about to make a crass remark about being Santa, but he doesn't, and I realize he's just being cruel.

There's a hush, and then a collective intake of breath as the bride comes into view.

She's wearing a much longer cape than that worn by her matron of honor. It conceals her dress and has a hood, too, which she's wearing over her head, as she walks up the aisle, carrying a bouquet of red roses. I glance at Ryan to see he's mesmerized, just as I hear Mitch let out a low whistle. I find that distasteful, especially given the comments he made about his wife just moments ago, but I ignore him and return my attention to Peony as she continues toward her husband-to-be.

When she gets to him, she hands her bouquet to her matron of honor and turns to Ryan, lowering her hood to reveal her blonde hair, which is curly by nature, I'd say, but which she's tied up in a very stylish up-do, leaving a few strands framing her face. Without taking her eyes from his, she removes the cape altogether, and that collective intake of breath becomes an audible gasp, as her gown is revealed for the first time.

It's white, floor length, with long sleeves, a plunging back, fitted bodice, and a full skirt... reminiscent of something Grace Kelly might have worn in a movie from the '50s. When Peony turns to give her cape to her matron of honor, I get a glimpse of the scooped neckline and the simple string of pearls she has hanging around her delicate neck.

I've never seen a more beautiful bride, and Ryan obviously feels the same. He's spellbound, and the celebrant has to cough to get his attention, which makes Peony smile.

My heart skips a beat when I glance at Gabe and realize he's not focused on Peony at all, but is staring directly at me. I smile, unable to help it, and he smiles back, then tilts his head, his brow furrowing, like he's asking something. I don't know what that means, and I frown back at him, shaking my head just slightly.

He smiles, then mouths the word, "Okay?" at me. I get it now and I nod my head, even though I'm still uncomfortable having Mitch beside me.

He won't be there for long, though… because the ceremony is beginning.

"I have great pleasure in pronouncing you husband and wife." The celebrant smiles and then adds, "You may kiss your bride."

I don't think Ryan needed to be told. He was already leaning in, but now he clasps Peony's face between his hands and steps closer, kissing her. Hard. Everyone around me is applauding, and I sigh out my relief. At last I can get away from Mitch Whatever-his-name-is.

Ryan pulls back, whispering something to Peony, and she giggles, then he pats his pants pocket and she shakes her head, smiling up at him. I don't know what that means and I probably don't want to. What I do know is that a few people are standing, and with any luck, Mitch will soon move away. He'll want to be with his wife, or help with their daughter… surely.

"He'll learn," he says, nodding toward Ryan and Peony.

"Learn what?" What on earth does he mean by that?

"Excuse me." I glance up at the familiar sound of Gabe's voice, sighing out my relief at the sight of his extended hand, although he's looking down at Mitch. "Sorry to interrupt, but I need to steal my girlfriend."

I smile up at him and get to my feet, taking his hand, which forces Mitch to lean back and twist in his seat, so I can get past him and into the aisle.

"Of course," Mitch says, with a wave of his hand, looking up at me. "It was nice to meet you, Remi."

I can't say it was nice to meet him, so I just nod my head and let Gabe lead me toward the front of the barn.

"Let me introduce Mr. and Mrs. Andrews," he says as we get to the bride and groom, who are still in each other's arms. They turn to face us, and although they focus on me for a second, Ryan quickly turns to Gabe.

"I already I told you, Peony's keeping her name."

Gabe grins. "Yeah, you told me, but I thought you might wanna hear it, just once."

Ryan chuckles and shakes his head, looking back at Peony. "I don't need to hear it. I'm happy just to call Peony my wife. She doesn't have to be Mrs. Andrews as well."

Peony smiles up at him, and then lowers her gaze to me, her husband following suit.

"This is Remi," Gabe says, finally getting around to introducing me.

"You look beautiful," I say to Peony, and she smiles.

"Thank you. It's good to meet you at last."

"At last?" What can she mean by that? "I've only known Gabe for a few days."

Ryan laughs. "What my wife is trying not to say is that Gabe hasn't stopped talking about you since the two of you met, and it's good for us to put a face to the name he won't stop saying."

I look up at Gabe, aware I must be blushing, and I half expect him to say Ryan's only kidding. He stares down at me, stepping closer and just smiles. "I can't help it," he says, licking his lips. "You're the only thing I can think about, so naturally you're all I wanna talk about, too."

I can't believe he said that in front of his friends, but I'm not about to let an opportunity like this pass me by.

"Y—You're the only thing I think about, Gabe. Only I don't have anyone to talk to."

He moves closer still, looking down into my eyes. "Talk to me, then."

"About you?"

He tilts his head slightly. "About anything. You could start with why you looked so uncomfortable sitting beside Mitch Bradshaw."

"You know who is he?"

"Yeah, but what I don't understand is why his arrival made you look as though you'd rather spend an entire day in the dentist's chair."

"Because he was flirting with me," I whisper, hoping Peony and Ryan won't hear, even though they're still standing with us.

Gabe frowns. "Really?" He looks down at Peony. "I thought he and Laurel were really happy together."

"They are," she says, her brow furrowing, and I wish I'd kept quiet now. She glances around the room, her eyes settling on a spot in the far corner. "They look pretty damn happy."

I follow her gaze, my eyes alighting on Peony's matron of honor, who I now know to be called Laurel. She's got her back to me, but she's in her husband's arms. He's smiling down at her, talking, and as he does, he brings his hands around behind her, giving her ass a squeeze.

"I must have got it wrong," I say, turning back. "I must have misunderstood."

"It wouldn't be the first time," Gabe says, putting his arms around me now and pulling me close to him.

"Is this something we should know about?" Ryan asks with a smile.

"Let's just say Remi isn't the best judge of when a man is flirting with her, and when he isn't," Gabe says, looking up at his friend.

"Did you crash and burn, then?" Ryan asks, his smile widening.

"No. It wasn't me doing the flirting. And it's a long story that doesn't matter anymore."

It certainly doesn't. I already feel foolish enough without having any more of my misconceptions aired for public consumption.

"We'd better mingle with our guests," Peony says, looking up at Ryan, and I wonder if I've offended her... or at least offended her best friend.

"You're sure we can't sneak back to the farmhouse for a while?" he says with a mischievous grin.

"I'm positive." She pats him on his chest and rolls her eyes at me. "We'll catch up later," she says, with a friendly smile and I nod my head, feeling relieved. Whatever my mistakes, at least I haven't caused a problem with Gabe's oldest friend.

"I'm sorry," I say the moment they've gone. "I don't know what it is with me and misunderstandings."

He turns to face me, pulling me into his arms and kissing me just briefly.

"It's okay. There's no harm done, as long as you're okay."

"I'm fine."

I rest my hands on his chest, and he sucks in a breath. "Can I ask you something?"

"Sure."

"You remember last night, when we talked on the phone and you said you needed me?"

"Yes." My heart beats faster. *Please ask me what I meant… please…*

"Can I ask, did you mean need as in you wanted me to hold you, and care for you, and be there for you?"

"Yes." I can't lie. When he says it like that, I know that's what I meant.

He nods his head. "You know I will, don't you?"

"Will what?"

"Do all of that. You know I'll always be there for you."

I nod my head. "I do. But that wasn't the only thing I meant, Gabe."

He frowns. "It wasn't?"

"No."

I can't say the words, but his frown clears, the smile returning to his face, and he leans in so he can whisper, "Did you mean you need me?"

We both know what he's talking about, and I nod my head, resting it against his chest as he holds me tighter still.

Chapter Fourteen

Gabe

I didn't want to let go of Remi. I never do, but as she leaned against me, nodding her head, letting me know she needed me – and how – I wanted, more than ever, to just keep hold of her.

Unfortunately, being Ryan's best man meant I had duties to perform. It also meant I wasn't able to sit with Remi during the reception dinner. I could see her, though. When I stood to make my speech, I felt her eyes on me the entire time, even though I had to cast my own around the room from time to time. They still returned to her, over and over. Naturally enough. I'm hers, and it seems she's mine. That's what she meant when she said she needed me… and we both knew it.

Fortunately, Remi wasn't sitting at the same table as Mitch Bradshaw. She might have been wrong about him flirting, but I didn't like the idea of her having to sit with someone who made her feel uncomfortable.

The seating plan had been arranged in advance, and Mitch was with his daughter at the same table as Cooper White and his girlfriend, whose name I can't remember. They were joined by Dawson Pine, Doctor Dodds, and his sister, who I think is called Bronte.

Remi was sitting with Walker and Imogen Holt, Nate Newton and his girlfriend, Taylor, and the town sheriff, Brady Hanson. I know Ryan and Peony didn't plan this with the intention that Brady and Remi would hit it off especially well. They know how I feel about her, apart from anything else. And I'm not worried, either... not after the conversation we've just had.

Remi seemed to spend most of the meal talking to Taylor, which was hardly surprising. I think they're roughly the same age. Walker and Imogen only had eyes for each other. I know them by reputation, which is to say, I know Walker is a screenwriter of some repute, but I believe they got married not long after I arrived in town. Judging by the size of the bump Imogen kept resting her hand on, I'd say they were even quicker off the mark than Ryan and Peony... although no-one but me knows about that yet.

As for Brady and Nate, they talked among themselves, occasionally including Remi and Taylor in their conversation. I noticed Remi seemed much more at ease than she had with Mitch, and I'll admit that made me wonder whether she'd been right about him. Except she can't have been. He didn't take his eyes off of his wife for almost the entire afternoon, and I overheard him speak of a desire to strip her out of the dress she's wearing at the first opportunity.

I could empathize with that feeling. Especially having seen Remi's dress in all its glory. It's just as figure-hugging as I thought, and since the moment I first realized that, I've wanted nothing more than to peel her out of it.

Peony's new pick-up arrived on time, and although most people would have expected Ryan to want to make a fanfare out of it, he'd already decided he wanted to present his gift quietly, by themselves. My job was to keep everyone out of the way, so they could have a few minutes alone, and although some people were intrigued by that, most of them were so busy enjoying themselves, they barely noticed the absence of the two stars of the show.

As the day's gone on, I've grown more and more impatient for it to be over, so I can be alone with Remi, and I'm more than relieved when Ryan comes to find me to tell me their cab is finally here.

It's taking them to a hotel in Concord for the night. Then, tomorrow, they'll be going to Boston, where they'll catch a flight to the Maldives. Ryan has booked them a private island all to themselves for the next two weeks. It sounds idyllic, but I'm not at all jealous. I've got two weeks to spend with Remi, and with the way things are between us, I don't think we'll be spending a minute apart.

"Have you got everything you need?" I ask, escorting him to the door, where Peony is talking to Laurel.

"Yep. She's right here," he says and I have to smile as he turns to me, offering his hand. "Thanks for everything you've done today, Gabe."

"I didn't do that much."

"Yeah, you did." He shakes my hand, then pulls me in and gives me a hug. Ryan is the least tactile person I've ever known, and hugging isn't something we've ever done before, so I'm a little surprised. "Take care of Remi," he whispers. "She's good for you."

I lean back, nodding my head. "I know."

He smiles, releasing me, then turns, putting his arm around Peony's waist. She's changed out of her beautiful wedding gown into a floral wrap-around dress, and as he leans in and kisses her cheek, I notice Remi standing to one side and step over, pulling her into my arms. She smiles up, although we keep our attention on the happy couple.

"Two dresses in one day," Ryan says, shaking his head and looking down at Peony. "This is unprecedented."

She narrows her eyes at him, although she's struggling not to smile. "I'll be back in jeans before long, don't worry."

"I wasn't… and anyway, you won't be wearing jeans for the next two weeks."

"If it's as hot as I think it's gonna be, I won't be wearing anything at all."

Ryan holds her closer still. "I should hope not," he growls, and I step forward, ushering them out the door, although I keep hold of Remi's hand as I do.

"I think it's time you guys left."

Ryan grins at me. "So do I."

Peony's blushing, but I don't know why. She started this… kind of.

He helps her into the back of the cab as everyone stands around, waving them off, and before I know it, they're gone.

It feels like the months of planning have all boiled down to this one moment, and now it's over, it's a little deflating… except I can't feel anything other than euphoric, because I'm still holding Remi's hand.

I turn, looking down at her, and she smiles up at me.

"Are you okay?" she asks, like she's guessed there might be something anti-climactic about this.

"I'm fine, baby."

I pull her into my arms, her body tight against mine, and she lets out a slow sigh.

"What happens now?"

"I've just gotta make sure everyone leaves, then I can lock up and we can leave."

She nods her head as we turn and stroll back toward the barn. People are already heading off, some of them nodding to me as they do, even though I don't know their names.

"It was a lovely wedding," Remi says, looking up at me.

"It was."

"Peony looked beautiful."

"She did." I smile down at her.

"What did Ryan say when he first saw her?"

"Absolutely nothing. I don't think he was capable of speech."

She chuckles, leaning her head against my arm.

"Where are they going on their honeymoon?"

"They're going to a private island in the Maldives."

"Was that a secret? Or did Peony know?"

"It was going to be a secret, but once they found out Peony's pregnant, he felt he had to tell her, just in case it meant altering their plans."

"Peony's pregnant?"

"Yeah, but that really is a secret. No-one knows. Not even Laurel. So keep it to yourself."

"If it's a secret, why are you telling me?"

"Because I don't want to keep things from you. It feels wrong. That's what I told Ryan when I asked if I could tell you."

"You said that to him?"

"I did."

She smiles, looking up at me as we pass Laurel and Mitch Bradshaw. She's holding their daughter in her arms, and she stops, looking up at me.

"We're gonna head off, if that's okay? Addy's just about asleep on her feet."

"That's fine," I say, giving her a smile.

"I can hang on if you need me to," Mitch offers, and I feel Remi's hand tense in mine. "I'm sure Laurel could take Addy home if you need any help here."

He lets his eyes drop to Remi, and I release her hand, putting my arm around her. She nestles against me, like she belongs... which she does.

"That's fine, thanks," I say to Mitch, trying not to sound dismissive. "There really isn't much to do."

"You don't have to clear everything away?" he asks.

"No. Archer's people are taking care of the catering side of things, and Peony and Ryan told me to leave the tables and chairs as they are. They said they'd deal with it all when they get back."

Laurel turns to him. "You've gotta remember, Mitch, this is Peony's new business. I imagine she'll want to work out how everything fits together… including the clear up."

"Yeah," I say. "She said something like that herself."

Although I can't imagine Ryan's going to let her lift a finger herself… not in her condition. Still, I can't say that out loud.

Mitch nods his head, and they turn away, heading for a silver Lexus which is parked close to the house. Laurel deposits their daughter in the rear passenger seat, while Mitch stands and watches her. He doesn't move, or lift a finger to help, but the moment she stands up straight and closes the door, he pulls her into his arms, crushing his lips to hers. After about thirty seconds, he steps back, staring down at her, then he whispers something, and she nods her head. He walks away, which surprises me, and I watch him strut over to a bright red Camaro, which he climbs into, driving down the track, while his wife is still standing by her car, staring after him.

"Looks like I really got it wrong about him," Remi whispers, and I look down at her, smiling, although I'm not so sure. I'm not about to say anything, but that felt like it was being done for our benefit. Whether he was trying to tell me he's not a threat, or show Remi what she's missing, I can't be sure, but that was definitely for display purposes only.

"W—Would you like to come in?" Remi looks up at me, and I smile, reaching out and cupping her cheek with my hand. Now we're on her doorstep, everything feels so much more real than it did at the wedding, and I wonder if she's having second thoughts. I'm not, but it occurs to me that driving back here in separate cars has maybe given her the chance to change her mind. I'm worried that, now she's faced with the reality of what's about to happen, she might have decided she doesn't need me so much after all.

"Do you still want me to?"

She nods her head, resting her hand on my chest, letting her fingers play with the end of my tie, which I undid on the way over here, along with the top two buttons of my shirt. "Yes, I do."

"It's okay if you've had a change of heart. You know that, don't you? It took a lot longer to get everyone to leave than I thought it would, and it's late, and…"

"Have you gone back to finding excuses not to come in?"

I step closer, putting my other hand behind her back and pulling her close to me. "Not at all. I'm just saying…" I sigh, pulling her closer still. "We both know where this is going, don't we?"

"I—I think so."

"But if you're not ready yet, then it's okay."

"And if I am ready?"

I smile down at her. "Then lead the way, baby."

She gazes into my eyes for a moment, then steps back. I release her so she can open the door and wait while she crosses the threshold, following her and closing the door behind us.

There's enough light in here for me to see her and she turns to me, tilting her head, and letting her eyes wander to my lips, then downward to my tie. "I can't believe how good you look," she whispers.

"The feeling's mutual, babe." I rest my hands on her waist and lean down, letting my lips dust over hers. She gasps and I delve inwards, my tongue finding hers. I hear her purse drop to the floor, and I push her jacket from her shoulders, letting it fall too, before running my hands up and down her back. I deepen the kiss as she writhes against me, and then push her up against the wall, rocking my hips into hers and letting her feel my cock, hard against her hip.

Her moan fills the space around us, and I pull back.

"Is this what you meant when you said you needed me?" I have to be sure before we go any further.

"Yes," she whispers, her eyes alight with that very need, and without taking my eyes from hers, I reach around behind her, unzipping her dress. I pull it down off of her shoulders, revealing a delicate white lace bra, the sight of which makes my breath catch in my throat. I'm torn now between taking it off, or revealing the rest of her, and I decide on the latter, pushing her dress down over her hips and letting it pool at her ankles. The sight before me is one I know I'll never forget. I hadn't anticipated stockings and a garter belt, but that's what she's wearing, along with lace panties, all matching her bra, and I stare for just a moment, taking her in. "Do you wanna move this to the living room?" I ask.

"No... my bedroom," she says, heaving in a breath. "It... it's right behind you." She nods over my shoulder and I take her hand, waiting until she's stepped out of her clothes, before opening the door and leading her inside.

The drapes are open and the moon is bright enough to see her clearly, so I don't bother to close them, or turn on the lamps on either side of her bed. I don't have time to notice the decor she was talking about changing, and I couldn't care less about it, either. Instead, I lead her to the bed, stopping when we reach it and turning to face her.

She looks up at me, but without a word, I shrug off my jacket, throwing it into the corner of the room. Then I unfasten her bra, pulling it off and dropping it, lowering my gaze to her perfect breasts. I cup them, then bend my head and lick her hardened nipples, gently biting on them, which makes her squeal. She puts her hands on my shoulders, holding me still and moving closer, her back arched, like she wants more, which I know I do. I want everything…

I pull back, dropping to my knees and she stares down at me as I lower her panties, helping her to step out of them, so they don't snag on her four-inch heels. Then I lean in and kiss the tops of her thighs, one at a time, nudging her legs apart and focusing on the neat triangle of dark hair at their apex. It may not be that light in here, but I can see her lips are swollen, and I raise my hand, running my finger between her folds. She gasps at the contact, but so do I.

"You're so wet," I whisper, getting to my feet.

She stares up at me, breathing hard, and I bend my head, kissing her as I lift her and lower her to the bed, kneeling up as I do so. I kiss my way down her neck to her breasts, spending some time over her rigid nipples, before I move further downwards across her flat stomach to her rounded hips, and eventually, her pussy.

I push her legs apart, lying between them, and use my fingers to part her lips, licking from her entrance to her clit and back again.

"Oh… Oh, God…" she whispers as I repeat the process several times before focusing all my attention on her clit. I've never tasted anything so sweet, and I lap her up, flicking my tongue over her as she rocks her hips against me. Her body's shuddering, and I can tell she's close already, so I kneel up, because as much as I want to feel her come on my tongue, I need to be inside her for our first time. "W—Where are you going? Don't stop."

"I'm not going anywhere, and I've got no intention of stopping."

I stand, looking down at her. She's incredible, her legs parted wide, her pussy glistening, her stockings and garter belt framing her perfectly, and I waste no time stripping out of my clothes. My cock is straining, but I take a moment to grab a condom from my wallet. Remi watches as I roll it over my dick, her eyes wide, her lips parted in the most tempting way... but that will wait for another time. For now, I need to be inside her.

I kneel up on the bed, stroking my length as she sucks in a sharp breath, her eyes focused on mine.

"W—Will it hurt?" she whispers and I lean over her, balancing on one arm.

"If I'm right, then yes, it will."

She frowns. "Right about what?"

"About you being a virgin."

She tilts her head to one side. "How did you know?"

"I didn't. It was an educated guess."

"Because you've slept with a lot of virgins in the past?"

I shake my head. "On the contrary. This is a first for me."

"Really?"

"Yes. Really." And I'm dying here.

"H—How did you guess?" she asks, prolonging the agony.

"By watching you."

Her brow furrows. "I'm not sure how I feel about that."

"About being watched?"

"No, about giving myself away so easily."

I dip my head and kiss her. "You didn't. I just watch you very closely. All the time."

She smiles now and I rub my dick along her slick folds, back and forth a few times, until she's breathing hard, her legs parted wider still, wanting more. I pause at her entrance, waiting, and then nudge inside. She gasps and I release my dick, moving my hand up, placing one on either side of her head, and I gaze down into her eyes as I push all the way home.

She yelps in pain, and I drop to my elbows.

"Sorry, Remi. I'm so sorry. Forgive me, please. I thought it was better to get it over with as quickly as possible, but I guess I was wrong." I kiss her. "Like I said, I've never done that before, and…"

I feel one of her hands on my back, then the other on my ass, and I stop talking. "It's okay, Gabe. It doesn't hurt anymore."

"You're sure?"

"I'm positive. And you were probably right about getting it over with quickly."

I smile down at her, flexing my hips, and she closes her eyes, a slight moan escaping them. That's a sound I'm far more familiar with, and I raise myself up as she opens her eyes again, letting hers fix on mine.

"I wanna fu… I mean, I want you so much, baby," I whisper.

"I want you, too."

She's still got her hand on my ass, and she pulls me in. "You want more?" I ask and she nods her head, moaning even louder when I pull almost all the way out and then slide back into her again.

She bucks beneath me, her back arching, her hips rising and falling in time with the rhythm I quickly create, and I let my eyes trail downward to the place where we're joined. I'm stretching her. There's no getting away from that, but she feels so good… so tight.

"Look," I say, and she stares up at me. "Look at us."

She lowers her gaze, raising her head from the mattress for a better view as I take her a little harder, sucking in a breath. "We look good together," she whispers.

"We do."

"Gabe…?" She seems confused, and I feel her tighten around me. I know what's coming, even if she doesn't seem to, and she looks up at me, her brow furrowing.

"It's okay, baby," I murmur, pounding into her now.

She opens her mouth, but all that comes out is a breathless repetition of the word, "Yes," as she closes her eyes and tips over into ecstasy. Her body twists and flails. She tries to straighten her legs, then bends them up again, opening her eyes and crying out my name. I'd thought I'd be able to keep going a lot longer, but hearing that, and feeling her pulse around my cock, is more than I can take, and I thrust deep inside her, a deep-throated roar leaving my lips as I come harder than ever before.

Coming down from that euphoric high takes a while, and when I do, I realize I've collapsed onto her, and I quickly raise myself up again.

"Sorry. Are you okay?"

She nods her head, smiling, and I roll onto my side, keeping her with me, joined for now at least.

"Can I ask a question?" she says.

"Of course."

She nestles in to me. "Is there a reason you didn't take off my stockings or shoes?"

I can't help smiling. "Yes. It's because you look so damn sexy in them."

"I do?"

"Yes. You do. But we can take them off now, if you like."

"So we can go to sleep?" she says, biting on her bottom lip.

I lean in, kissing her, freeing her lip and then sucking it into my mouth, which makes her shudder in my arms.

"No," I whisper, leaning back again. "So we can do all that again. Between you being so tight, and the sight of you in those sexy heels, and then hearing you scream my name when you came, I didn't last as long as I'd have liked."

"Really?" She seems surprised and I can't help smiling.

"Yes, really. And with that in mind, I'd like a second chance to see if I can go for a lot longer… unless you're sore, of course."

She shakes her head, sucking in a breath, like she's as keen as I am. "I'm not sore at all." She tightens her internal muscles, like she's either checking or proving a point. Whichever it is, it feels great, and I grind my hips into hers. She gasps and I raise her top leg, giving myself better access to take her deeper, and leaning in to kiss her. Our tongues meet before our lips, flicking and fluttering, and I raise her leg higher still, the feeling of her soft stocking against my skin bringing me to my senses.

"Shit…" I mutter, leaning back and lowering her leg.

"What's wrong?"

"I need to go to the bathroom."

"Right this minute?" She looks disappointed, and I kiss the tip of her nose.

"Yes. I need to change condoms." She nods her head, and although the light in here is dim, I'd swear she's blushing. She's also biting on her bottom lip again, and that's more than I can handle. "Please stop doing that," I say, freeing it with my thumb before I give in to the temptation to kiss her again. "It was difficult enough before, but when you're lying there like that, looking like you do, resisting the urge to fu… to take you is almost impossible."

"Then don't," she says, blinking and gazing up at me.

I shake my head, pulling out of her, and grab her hands, rolling her onto her back and pinning her to the bed, leaning over her.

"I won't… when I get back."

She smiles and goes to bite her lip again, although she stops herself just in time, and I clamber off of the bed, rushing to the door. I already know where the bathroom is, and I hasten along the hall, taking no time at all to dispose of the condom, wash up, and get back to Remi.

I'm surprised, when I do, to find she's still lying in bed, in her stockings, garter belt, and heels.

"You didn't take them off, then?" I say, walking over to her, standing at the end of the bed, and gazing down at her perfect body.

"No. I thought I'd leave that to you."

For someone so inexperienced, she knows how to drive a guy wild, and I grab her ankles, pulling her closer, which makes her giggle.

She watches me as I raise her right leg, slipping off her shoe and dropping it to the floor, and although she raises the other leg, I keep hold of the first one, massaging, and then gently kissing the sole of her foot, through her stockings. She gasps, then moans as I lower it to the bed and repeat the process with her left leg.

She's breathing hard now, and I lean over, unfastening her stockings, teasing her by lowering them slowly down her legs, then pulling them off, and kissing her feet again, just like I did before, but skin-on-skin this time.

"I—I see what you mean," she whispers, struggling to speak.

"What about?"

"Feet," she says, letting out a sigh.

"Can I take it you liked that?"

"You can. And can I take it you like my feet?"

I smile. "I like every single part of you."

I gaze down at her, removing her garter belt, so she's completely naked… and utterly perfect.

"What happens now?" she asks, wide-eyed and expectant.

"First, I need to find another condom."

"And then?"

"Then I want to f… to make love to you."

It's so hard not to say what I feel… that I wanna fuck her from here to eternity. But she's such an innocent, I can't be sure how she'd react, and the last thing I want to do is offend her. As it is, she stutters in a breath, letting it out again, but before I can move, she sits up, surprising me.

"What's wrong?" I ask.

"Nothing. I—I just wanted to ask something."

"Okay." It's understandable that she'd be full of questions, and I don't mind answering them.

"What happens after you've made love to me?"

"That depends. There are all kinds of things we can do together. If you want to carry on, we can."

She shakes her head. "That wasn't what I meant. I was just wondering…" Her voice fades, and she looks down, letting out a sigh.

"Wondering what?"

She raises her head again. "Will you sleep with me? Will you stay the night?"

I smile, reaching out to cradle her cheek. "Of course I will, if that's what you want." She nods her head, like she's relieved, and I lean right over, kissing her. "You don't have to ask, baby. Sleeping with you will be a dream come true for me… and as for waking up beside you…" I kiss her again, and she sighs in to me, tilting her head when I deepen the kiss. "Condom," I whisper, needing to be inside her again, and she pulls back and nods her head, watching as I climb off the bed and find my wallet, pulling out another condom. She doesn't take her eyes off of me as I roll it over my dick, but I find I enjoy being the center of her attention, and once I'm finished, I climb back onto the bed pulling her down with me, her back to my front.

"I thought you were going to make love to me?" she says, sounding confused.

"I am."

"Like this?"

I raise her top leg, resting her foot on my thigh, and let my cock nudge against her entrance, then push inside her. "Yes," I say, kissing her neck as she sighs, arching her back. "Exactly like this."

I wrap my arms around her, my left across her breasts, so I can clasp one in my hand, and my right moving lower, my fingers finding her clit. I rub, gently to start with, and she twists her head around, looking up at me.

"That feels so good, Gabe."

"You feel so good."

I take her harder, circling over her clit, as I lean in and kiss her. It's like I've ignited something inside her, and she responds, her tongue darting into my mouth, her body bucking and twisting against mine. She's not coming yet, but she's hungry… and I like it.

No. I love it. Like I love her.

The words are poised on my lips, but I don't want to risk ruining the moment if she's not ready to hear them yet, and in any case, it's taking all my concentration not to come.

How is she doing this to me?

"Oh, f… oh, God…" I mutter, giving up the struggle, as she detonates around me, losing control, while I lose my mind and myself, deep inside her.

It takes even longer to calm this time, for both of us, but at least I'm not crushing her. I'm just holding her tight in my arms.

"I'm sorry," I whisper, once I've regained the power of speech.

"What for?" Her voice is dreamy, like she's on the verge of sleep.

"For what just happened. It wasn't meant to end so soon… again."

"I'm not complaining," she says, turning her head and looking up at me. Her eyes are kind of dreamy, too, which makes me smile. "I loved every second."

I love you. The words are there, so close to falling from my lips, but I hold them in, and gently pull out of her. She winces, and I hug her tighter. "Are you okay?"

"Hmm… I just miss you, that's all."

I can't help smiling, and I kiss her neck, which makes her shudder. "I miss you too, baby." It's true. I do. It's surprising how much, considering she's in my arms. "I need to go to the bathroom, but when I come back…"

She turns over, grabbing my arm. "I can't do that again, Gabe… not tonight."

"I know. I wasn't gonna suggest we did anything more tonight, other than fall asleep together. You're tired, and I'm not going anywhere."

A slow smile forms on her lips. "No, you're not." She lets out a satisfied sigh and lets go of me, and although I'd rather stay, the bathroom beckons.

It doesn't take me long to clean up, and I rush back, relieved to find Remi's still awake… just. For some reason, I want her to be aware of falling asleep with me. It matters. Maybe because it's our first night together… or maybe because I love her… so damn much.

Chapter Fifteen

Remi

I'm in that wonderful place between sleeping and wakefulness, where nothing feels quite real, and I turn onto my back, stretching my legs and savoring these last few minutes before I open my eyes and the day has to start…

Although it's Sunday, so I guess at least I don't have to worry about getting up and going to work. I can relax and take my time… oh, what a lovely thought.

I smile, unable to help myself, and then crack open my eyes.

The light from outside looks different… brighter, and I raise myself up onto my elbows to see four inches of snow covering the bush, and everything else beyond it.

"Oh, goodness."

I get up, wanting a better view, and stumble over a pair of black pants. Looking down, I see a man's shirt and shoes, socks and underwear…

Of course.

Gabe.

How could I have forgotten? And more importantly, where is he?

"Gabe?"

"Just coming."

It sounds like he's in the hall, but before I can get to the door, it opens and he comes in, my breath catching in my throat. He's carrying two cups, but it's not the fact that he's found his way around my kitchen that draws my attention. He's done that before, after all. No, it's him.

He's naked... and utterly glorious.

His hair is mussed up, and super sexy, and as I let my eyes wander south, I take in his broad shoulders, toned, muscular chest, tight abs and... oh, my God.

My mouth dries, my stomach churning as my eyes fix on his enormous erection, which seems to be getting bigger by the second.

"I see what you mean about the floral prints," he says, putting the cups on the nightstand and glancing at the walls, which are covered with pale pink flowers, before he steps up to me, taking my hands in his, a frown settling on his perfect face. "Hey... are you okay?"

I nod my head. "I'm just a bit taken-aback, that's all."

"By what? The snow? It can't be the decor in here. You've seen it before."

"It's nothing to do with the decor, or the snow. It's you."

"Me?" He frowns, looking confused.

"Yes."

"What about me?"

"You're... um..." I let my eyes dip to his arousal, surprised by the size of the bulbous head and thick, veined shaft. "You're a lot bigger than I imagined."

"Imagined?" he says with a smile. "You saw me last night, babe. There's no need to imagine anything."

"I know, but it was dark. You were an outline. I couldn't see you properly."

"And now you can, is that a problem?"

"No. But I think it's just as well I wasn't aware of quite how enormous you are before we did anything. At least I know we fit together now." I think I'd take some convincing otherwise.

"Of course we fit together," he whispers, leaning in and kissing me. He pulls my body against his, and I feel his arousal between us, throbbing and pulsing. I remember how good it felt inside me, and I want more, moaning into his mouth and grinding my hips against him, hoping he'll get the message.

He pulls back, looking down into my eyes.

"You're not sore?" he says, making it clear he's understood perfectly.

"No."

He grins. "In that case, I'd better get dressed and run out to my car."

"What for?"

"Because I want to take a shower with you, and I don't relish going to my car in nothing more than a towel."

I can't help chuckling. "Not in four inches of snow."

"Precisely."

I tip my head, feeling bemused. "Why do you need to go to your car at all?"

"Because I brought some clean clothes with me."

"You did?" I'm even more confused now. "Can I ask why? Were you expecting to stay the night?"

He takes my hand, leading me to the bed and sitting us both on the edge. "Not at all, baby," he says, turning to face me. "I just thought we might come back here after the wedding, and that I might wanna change out of my tux so I could be more comfortable. I wasn't making assumptions, I promise."

"Is that why you brought condoms? Because you weren't making assumptions?"

I'm smiling, so he knows I'm teasing, although I am intrigued, too.

"I thought it was best to be prepared," he says, pushing me down onto the mattress and leaning over me, his lips brushing against mine.

I love it when he does this. It's the intensity of it that I love most… almost as much as I love him. I think I've loved him for some time now, although I'm making a conscious effort not to say that out loud. It's too soon.

Even I know that.

He pulls back, both of us breathless, and he leans up on one arm and smiles down at me.

"I think I'd better go get my things… and then I can take you in the shower."

He kisses the tip of my nose, and goes to pull away, but I grab his arm, making him stop. "D—Do you mean you want to bring me with you into the shower, or…"

He shakes his head, his hand wandering down my body, resting on my breast for a moment and then moving lower, until his fingers find that sweet spot between my legs and I let out a gasp at the contact. "I mean, I wanna take you, Remi. Hard." I let my head rock back, loving his words, and what he's doing to me. "I wanna f—" He stops talking and I raise my head, looking up at him.

"You wanna what?"

"Make love with you."

I don't for one second believe that's what he was going to say, but I like the sound of it, and I smile up at him, biting my bottom lip. Gabe notices, his eyes dropping, and he straddles me, leaning in, nipping at my lip and sucking it into his mouth. His arousal is pressing in to me and I raise my hips as far as I can, letting him know what I think of his suggestion. He moves his legs between mine, pushing them apart and shifts down slightly, the tip of his erection finding my entrance with ease. I grind my hips and he nudges inside, stretching me in the most perfect way imaginable. He growls out something incoherent as he slides all the way in, then pulls out and slams back in again, making me scream, not with pain, but with pleasure. It's like he knows that, and he repeats his actions, again and again. It feels so good, our tongues dancing, our bodies in perfect harmony… until he stops, hesitates for a second, and then kneels up, pulling out of me.

"What's wrong?" I ask. He's staring down at me, sucking air into his lungs, pushing his fingers back through his hair.

"You've made me lose my mind… again."

"Excuse me?" I don't know what he's talking about, but before I can ask anything else, he leans over, his hands on either side of my head.

"The same thing happened last night, when I was inside you. It was like…" He pauses, frowning, as though he's trying to find the words. "It was like there was nothing else in the world, except us… nothing that mattered, anyway. You filled every part of me."

"I felt the same," I whisper, raising my hands and resting them on his chest. He closes his eyes, moaning quietly, although I don't pull my hands away. I love touching him.

He opens his eyes again, smiling down at me. "You have no idea how happy that makes me. But the problem is, losing my mind isn't always a good thing."

"It isn't?" It felt pretty good to me.

"No."

"Why not?"

He leans in, kissing my lips ever so gently. "It makes me do crazy things."

"Like what?"

"Like making love to you without a condom." I gasp and he drops to his elbows, barely giving me time to move my hands aside.

"You forgot?"

"Not exactly. I was aware of what I was doing. It's just that my need for you was more important than logic, or reason, or anything else."

I smile, even though I know I shouldn't, and he smiles back. "Was it more important than the thought that I might not be on birth control?"

"No. That's why I pulled out, and I promise I'll try not to lose my mind like that again." He gazes down at me and then chuckles.

"What's funny?"

"You are."

"I am?"

"Yes. You looked so sad then."

"Do you blame me? I liked you losing your mind. I like the way you feel."

"I like the way you feel, too, but I'll be more careful in the future, I promise."

"I wish you didn't have to." He frowns and I panic, realizing what I've just said. "Sorry. I wasn't suggesting we should... I mean, we've only been together for a few days. I'm not implying it would be a good idea for us to have a..."

He leans closer. "I get it, Remi. I know that's not what you meant," he says, and I nod my head as he brushes his lips against mine, tracing a line of kisses to my ear. "But let's not abandon the idea altogether." It's like something ignites inside me. I pull back, gazing up into his eyes. There's concern, insecurity, happiness... and something else. It's something I can't quite identify, but it makes me feel wanted, and needed, and... loved?

Can it be?

Is it possible?

"I—I won't," I mumble and his lips twist upward into a smile as he nods his head.

"In the meantime, I'll take better care of you."

"I like the sound of that, although I could..." I can't get the words out and he frowns at me.

"You could what?"

"I could maybe look into some kind of contraception, just for the time being. Something that's reliable, but that means we can make love and feel each other properly?"

"Like the pill, you mean?"

"Yes."

"I can't make that decision for you, baby," he says. "But we could look into it together, if you want?"

I nod my head, because that sounds perfect, and he kisses me again, harder than ever.

That has to go down as the best weekend of my life.

And what makes it even better is that it doesn't have to end, even though it's Monday morning, because neither Gabe nor I are going to work for the next couple of weeks. I hadn't fully appreciated that yesterday morning when I first woke up... but it seems spending the night with Gabe had more of an effect than I'd anticipated. How else could I have forgotten his presence? The thought of that makes me smile and I turn over in bed to find he's staring at me, his lips twitching upward.

"Hello, beautiful."

I don't think I can possibly look beautiful. My hair has a habit of getting in a spectacular mess during the night, but he doesn't seem to care, and pulls me into his arms, his arousal proving the point.

"What do you wanna do today?" I ask, teasing him, because I know perfectly well what he has in mind... and I feel the same.

"I'll need to go home." His answer surprises me and I pull back as far as he'll let me.

"Home?"

"Yeah." He smiles. "I don't have any more clean clothes, and we only have one condom left."

I don't know why that's a surprise. It shouldn't be. He's made love to me so many times... not just twice on Saturday night, but in the shower yesterday morning, in the living room by the fire later in the afternoon, and then again in bed last night. Each time seemed to be better than the last, and when I fell asleep in his arms, I realized what he'd meant about lasting longer. Our shower might have been hard and fast, and just what we both needed after our conversation in bed, but lying with him by the open fire, discovering each other's bodies and taking our time over it... that was just spectacular. I touched him for the first time, surprised by how hard he felt, and yet how soft he was to caress. He showed me what to do, and then let me experiment by myself, seeming to enjoy what I did, if the noises he was making were anything to go by. Then he made love to me, so, so slowly, the firelight glimmering off of our skin and sparkling in our eyes. It was romantic, and such a struggle not to scream, "I love you," when I came... which I did, several times before he finally let go, with such a howl of pleasure, it filled the room, and my heart.

As for last night... I can't help smiling about it, even now.

"What's funny?" he asks.

"Nothing's funny. I was just thinking about last night, that's all."

"And it made you smile?"

"Yes."

"Because you enjoyed it?"

"Of course I enjoyed it. Didn't you notice?"

He chuckles. "What did you enjoy the most?"

"You want me to choose?"

"Not necessarily. Just tell me what you liked, and if there was anything you didn't." He cups my face with his hand. "It's important we communicate about this."

He's probably right and I suck in a breath, wondering how to say the things that need saying. "I—I like it when you lick me," I whisper and he nods his head.

"I like licking you, baby. You taste like nothing else on earth."

I nod my head. "I like feeling you inside me, too."

"In what position?"

"Every position." There were so many last night, it's hard to choose. "Being on all fours was good."

"Because…?"

"Because it was so deep."

"Yeah, it was. It was a struggle not to come."

"But you managed it."

He chuckles. "Yeah. I seem to have worked that out at last."

I rest my hand on his chest. "I honestly wasn't complaining about anything you were doing before."

"I know, but now you know what it can be like…?" He leaves his words hanging in the form of a question and I tilt my head, gazing into his eyes.

"I love it when it goes on for hours, like it did last night… but I also love it when it's quick and unexpected, like it was in the shower yesterday morning."

He frowns, just slightly. "What was unexpected about it?"

"Everything. I've never done any of this before, Gabe. It's all unexpected to me."

He nods his head, his smile returning. "You liked being taken in the shower, did you?"

My body tingles at the memory of being held up in his arms while he penetrated me so hard. "Y—Yes, I did." His smile widens. "I just wish you didn't have to go home."

"So do I, but if we wanna keep fu… to keep doing this, I don't have much choice." I giggle and he leans in, kissing me and capturing the sound, turning it into a desperate moan as he rolls me onto my back. "What do you wanna do with our last condom?" he murmurs, his lips still brushing against mine. "Do you wanna stay here in bed, or go shower?"

"Shower," I say, without a second's hesitation, and he laughs against my lips, leaning up.

"I'll see what I can do to make it as unexpected as yesterday."

He succeeded. He didn't hold me up in his arms this time, but pushed me back against the tiled wall and raised my left leg, hooking it over his right arm, entering me in one swift movement. It was just as hard and fast as yesterday, though, and we came together, in a loud crescendo of kissing, splashing water, and unspoken love.

Now, I can't take my eyes off of him, even as I sip at my coffee and nibble at my toast.

"You won't be long, will you?"

"No, but while I'm gone, do you wanna try calling the doctor's office to see if we can get an appointment for sometime this week?" I put down my cup, resting my elbows on the table. "Unless you've changed your mind?" he says, clearly misinterpreting my hesitation.

"Not at all. I want you, Gabe… all of you. And I want to do this. I just don't want you to feel you have to come with me. We agreed to look into it together, but that doesn't mean you have to come see the doctor, if you don't want to."

His brow furrows, and he pushes his plate aside, his toast only half eaten. "Obviously, if you don't want me there, I won't come, but… but…"

"But what?"

"I told you I'll always be there for you, and I will. I want to understand the implications of what's being discussed."

"You do?"

"Of course. You're my responsibility, Remi."

I can't help smiling, because that sounds so good. "I like that."

"Good. Now, do you want me to come with you or not?"

"Yes… as long as you don't mind."

He reaches over, taking my hand in his. "I don't mind in the slightest." He kisses my hand, then stands, moving around the table and pulling me to my feet. "The sooner I go, the sooner I can get back."

"What are you gonna bring back with you?" I ask, leaning against him and looking up into his eyes.

"Aside from as many condoms as I can carry, I thought just some clothes, my razor, my toothbrush…" he says, his voice fading and a look of confusion crossing his eyes. "Is that a problem?"

"No. Of course not." I want to ask him to bring everything he owns, but it's too soon for that, just like it's too soon for 'I love you', and I shrug my shoulders. "You can bring as much as you like."

He smiles, like he's finally understood what I've been failing to say. "In that case, why don't I bring enough for a few days? Then maybe you can come stay at my place for a while."

"Don't you like being here?"

He pulls me closer. "I love it, but I've got a bigger fireplace… and a bigger bed."

"That sounds interesting."

"Believe me, it'll be better than interesting." He stops talking and tips his head to one side. "Why don't we stay here until maybe Thursday, and then you can pack a bag and come to my place for Christmas?"

"With your big fireplace and bigger bed?"

"Exactly."

I giggle and he smiles. "If I don't go now, we're gonna have a problem."

"We are?"

"Yeah. Because I want you again, only I don't have any more condoms."

I laugh and he joins in. "In that case, you'd better go… and hurry back."

"I will… and don't forget to call the doctor."

He kisses me again before I get the chance to tell him I won't, and then he leaves. I notice he's carrying the bag he brought in with him yesterday and realize he must have packed it while I was drying my hair. Not that it matters. What matters is, he'll be back soon, and I've got things to do.

First, I clear the table, stacking everything into the dishwasher, and then I sit back down again and look up the number for the doctor's office, placing a call.

It's answered on the third ring by a young and pleasant sounding woman, who listens while I explain that I want to see the doctor, although it's not urgent… even if it feels like it is.

"Doctor Dodds has a slot at two-thirty this afternoon," she says, surprising me.

I wish Gabe was here, so I could check if that's okay, but I can't see why it won't be, and I agree, giving her my name and number before I hang up.

I can't wait to tell him now, and to keep myself occupied, I go into the bedroom, smiling as I cross the threshold. We didn't make the bed this morning, and it's a mess… although the reason for my smile has nothing to do with that. It's because I'm thinking about Gabe's bed, and how much fun we can have in it.

I step forward, just as my phone rings, and I dart back to the kitchen, flipping it over and letting out a gasp when I see the word 'Dad' on the screen.

He hasn't called for ages, and I wish he hadn't now... not when everything is so perfect.

I could ignore him, but I know if I do and he doesn't leave a message, I'll only worry, so I answer, holding the phone to my ear.

"Hi, Dad."

"Remi, angel... how are you?"

He called me 'angel'. I don't even remember the last time he did that, and for a moment I'm lost, although I find my voice, eventually. "I'm good. How are you?"

"Not too bad. I can't talk for long, but I was wondering if you're gonna be coming home for the holidays?"

I hadn't expected that, either, and I'm thrown by the question. I haven't been home since my first year at college, and although Dad doesn't know why I've stayed away for so long, this is the first time he's actually invited me to visit since then. What should I say? How can I get out of it? Or is he just asking because he needs to check I won't be?

"Why? Have you got plans?" I ask, buying time.

"No. But it's been a while." It has. It's been four years, to be precise. Still... I can't think about that now. The problem is, I don't know what to say. "You're not working, are you?"

"No, I'm not working until after New Year," I say, then clench my fist and slam it against the outside of my leg. He just gave me the perfect 'get out of jail' card, and I blew it. All I needed to do was say 'yes' to that question, and I'd have bought myself the ideal excuse. Instead of which, I'm stuck... really stuck. I wish Gabe was here. Not that he'd understand. How could he? "I'm seeing someone," I say, my thoughts turning to him.

"You are?" I hate that my dad sounds so surprised, and I sit at the table.

"Yes."

"And I guess that means you'll be spending the holidays with his family?"

"No. They're in England, so…" What's wrong with me? That was another excellent opportunity to pass on my dad's invite, and it's just gone begging.

"I see. Well, in that case, I guess you'd better bring him along."

He doesn't sound as keen to meet Gabe as I'd have hoped, but what can I say?

"When do you want us to come?"

"If you're not working, why don't you drive down tomorrow?"

Tomorrow? But we had such plans.

"I—I'll ask him."

"Okay." The phone falls silent.

"He's not here at the moment," I say, when I realize Dad's waiting. "He'll be back soon, though."

"That's okay. Just send me a text message when you've spoken to him. What's his name, by the way?"

"Gabe. Gabe Sullivan."

I half expect more questions, but instead Dad just says, "Okay… well, text me if it's a problem, but otherwise we'll see you tomorrow."

We end the call, and I let my phone drop to the table, my head falling into my hands… my old life and my new one colliding uncontrollably around me.

I'm still sitting here when the doorbell rings and I jump out of my skin, getting up and rushing to open it.

Gabe takes one look at me and frowns. "What's wrong?" he asks, stepping into the house and putting his bag down by the wall as he pushes the door closed behind him.

I throw my arms around his neck and he lifts me, waiting a second for me to wrap my legs around his hips before he walks us into the living room and sits down on the couch, me on his lap, his arms tight around me.

"I—I had a call."

"Oh? Who from?"

"My dad."

He raises his eyebrows, as surprised as I was, even though he knows nothing about my family… or maybe because he knows nothing of them. "What did he want?"

"To invite me to go visit for the holidays."

His face falls. "Does this ruin our plans?"

"Yes, and no." His brow furrows and I rest against him, playing with the button on his coat, which he's still wearing. "We can still be together… but only if you agree to come with me."

He pulls back slightly, and I look up at him. "You mean, I'm invited too?"

"Yes. I told my dad about you and he said he wanted to meet you." Did he? I can't remember him using those exact words now, but what does it matter?

"Should I be scared?" he says, his smile returning.

"No. He'll wanna check you out, but nothing he says or does is gonna change how I feel about you." I've gone too far. I've given away too much, but before Gabe can say anything or question me, I lean back in his arms and let out a sigh. "It's not my dad you should be worried about."

"It's not?"

"No. It's my stepmom."

His frown returns. "You have a stepmom?"

"Yes."

He lets out a sigh, nodding his head. "I get the feeling there's a story behind this and that you've been avoiding it since we met."

"You're not wrong."

"About the story, or you not wanting to talk about it?"

"Both."

He pulls me closer to him. "If I'm gonna meet your family, baby, don't you think I should know at least some of what's gone before... even if you can't tell me all of it?"

"Thank you," I say, and he frowns yet again.

"What on earth for?"

"For giving me the option to not tell you everything... for trusting me."

"I trust you implicitly, Remi. If you don't wanna..." I raise my hand, silencing him with my forefinger across his lips. He kisses it and I smile

"I want to tell you all of it... because you trusted me not to." He smiles and nods his head, sitting back a little and bringing me with him, so I can nestle against his chest.

"Okay," he says, and I wonder where to start.

At the beginning, I guess...

"My mom died when I was twelve," I say. That's about as close to the beginning as it gets.

"I'm sorry," he whispers, and I can hear how much he means it.

"She had cancer, but didn't find out until quite late on, so we only had a few weeks between her diagnosis, and the end..." My voice cracks and he holds me tighter. "Dad was... Dad was devastated. To be honest, I thought he'd never get over it, and for years, he just went through the motions of living. It was horrible to witness him being brought so low, unable to pick himself up at all. I—I decided I wouldn't go to college, because I was worried how he was gonna fend for himself, and I couldn't leave him... not like that."

"That was a brave decision," Gabe says, and I lean away from him.

"Was it? It didn't feel brave at the time. It felt like the only option I had, and I honestly didn't mind or resent him for it. He needed me. Or I thought he did… until Celine came along."

"That's your stepmom?"

I nod my head. "I've only got myself to blame, really."

"What for?"

"The two of them meeting in the first place."

"Why?"

"Because I'd persuaded him to take up tennis, just to get out of the house… and that was how they met. Suddenly, he was like a new man. He wasn't even like my dad anymore, but someone completely different. I didn't realize what was going on until one evening, he didn't come home from the tennis club. He stayed out all night. I was worried sick, but he didn't call, or let me know where he was. He finally came home around ten the next day, and when I asked where he'd been, he told me straight out he'd spent the night with Celine."

"How did you feel about that?"

"Relieved, I think… at least to start with. He'd talked about her a lot over the previous weeks, and was clearly happy with her, so I was happy for him… until I met her."

"Why? What was wrong with her?"

"She was only seven years older than me."

"Excuse me?"

"I was eighteen, and she was twenty-five."

"How old was your dad?"

"Forty-eight." He raises his eyebrows. "It's okay, Gabe. You're allowed to say it."

"Say what?"

"That the age gap was enormous."

He shakes his head. "Is this where your thing about age gaps comes from?"

"If it does, I have good reason."

"Okay, but just so you know, I don't see age as a barrier to love."

I can't help smiling. He just said the 'L' word, even if he didn't wrap it up with 'I' and 'you'.

"Neither do I. Not now. But you haven't met Celine."

"Maybe not, but if they're happy…" He lets his voice fade and I shrug my shoulders.

"I'm not sure they are, but they have a little boy now, so…"

"They had a baby?"

"Yes. He's two. His name is Preston, and I'm pretty sure they're aiming for him to be a nuclear physicist… or, failing that, the President of the United States."

Gabe chuckles and I have to join in. "Nothing wrong with aiming high," he says, shaking his head and then resting his against mine. "So, you don't get along with your stepmom?"

"Not in the slightest. She moved into the house not long after I first met her, and they announced they were getting married about ten days later."

"Okay."

He doesn't seem fazed by the speed with which it all happened, but I guess we're not talking about his family… his father.

"I thought they were rushing things, and I spoke to Dad about it, only to be told it was nothing to do with me."

"That seems a little harsh. You were entitled to an opinion."

"I thought so, but I think he was blinded by her. He certainly didn't want to listen to anything I had to say. So, I enrolled at college in Boston, and left them to it. It seemed like the best idea at the time."

"To put some space between you?"

"Yes. I didn't feel welcome there anymore. My dad didn't need me, and my relationship with Celine was fraught with difficulties, so I figured I might as well get on with my own life."

"Good for you."

I take a breath, wondering how he's going to react to the next part of my story. "I—I haven't told you this before, but not long after I started at college, I met someone."

"A man?" he says, tilting his head, surprise showing in his eyes.

"Yes. His name was Leon."

Gabe pulls away slightly, looking deflated. "I didn't realize."

"I should have told you."

"Why? I haven't told you everything about my past."

"No. But that's because I asked you not to."

He nods his head. "Is there a reason you haven't told me about Leon before?"

"Only that it would have involved explaining about my stepmom, and I wanted to avoid that."

"I see. So you weren't in love with him? That wasn't your reason for keeping quiet?"

I'm surprised by his question, but shake my head. "No. Why do you ask?"

"Because I need to know," he says, surprising me even more. "You clearly didn't sleep with him."

I lean in to him, wanting to reassure him, if I can. "I didn't do anything with him, other than kissing. He was older than me, but…"

"How much older?" Gabe asks, interrupting me, like this matters.

"Eleven years."

"So he was twenty-nine?"

"Yes. He worked in the tech department at the college, and I went to him when I was having trouble gaining access to some of my online course materials on my laptop. He fixed the problem and then asked me to have coffee with him. We got along well, exchanged numbers, and met up again about a week or so later.

It started very slowly, but at Thanksgiving, I went home and had such a terrible time with Celine, I couldn't wait to get back to college. When I did, Leon said he'd missed me, and I realized I'd missed him, too." Gabe sucks in a breath, and I sit back, looking up into his eyes, seeing a sadness there that astonishes me. "It… It wasn't like us, Gabe. It wasn't anything like this."

"I know." He smiles and means it, his eyes sparkling into mine. "Go on with your story."

"You're sure?" He nods and I nestle against him once more, his arms coming around me tighter than ever. "We talked about going away somewhere for spring break, but in the meantime, we decided we didn't want to spend the holidays apart, so I invited him to come home with me. My dad said it was fine, and I drove us down there."

"What did your dad say when he met your boyfriend?"

"I think he was surprised by Leon's age, and that he wasn't a fellow student, but he didn't say anything."

"He couldn't, really, could he?"

"Not without being incredibly hypocritical."

"How did the visit go?"

"To start with, it was better than I'd expected. This was before Preston was born, so we didn't have to worry about him, and his bedtimes, and mealtimes, or any of the other things you have to prioritize when there are kids involved. We went for long walks and had dinner out every night. It was surprisingly good, and to be honest, I even quite liked Celine, which shocked me… until a couple of days before Christmas, when I found her in bed with Leon." Gabe chokes and I sit forward so he can get his breath back. "Dad had gone to play tennis with a friend of his," I explain. "I went to find Leon to suggest we go into town for a coffee, and there they were, in the guest room, in his bed. They were… they were…"

"It's okay," he says. "I get it."

"Good." I'm still haunted by the sight of Celine bouncing up and down on top of Leon, both of them groaning and moaning, and I'm not in the mood for describing it.

"Did they see you?" Gabe asks.

"They didn't need to. I yelled at them. Leon pushed Celine off of him, and jumped out of bed, trying to tell me she'd seduced him, while she sat on the edge of the mattress with a dumb smile on her face."

"Can I take it Leon wasn't wearing anything while he was bullshitting you?"

"You can." I look up at him. "How else do you think I know you're not exactly average?"

"Because he was?" he asks, trying not to smile.

"Very."

He chuckles, kissing my forehead. "Did Celine say anything?"

"Only that it couldn't have been very serious between us if we weren't… you know."

He smiles. "I do, but I don't think it was for her to say, was it? How did she know you weren't sleeping with him?"

"I assumed Leon had told her, and that had provided the incentive she needed to seduce him."

"You believed him about that?"

"I preferred it to the alternative," I say, and he nods his head.

"I can't blame you for that."

"Maybe not, but I'm not sure it really matters. Even if he didn't make the first move, he didn't fight her off, did he? And what he did still hurt. I might not have loved him, but I'd looked up to him. He was older, and I thought he respected me and cared about me. And before you ask, this… this is where my problem with age gaps comes from. They mess with people."

"No, they don't," he says, calmly. "People mess with people. Their age has nothing to do with it."

"You don't think people of different ages have conflicting expectations?"

"Probably, but that doesn't mean they can't make it work. They've just got to communicate, be completely honest, and show some understanding… and they've got to want it. And if you don't believe me, I've got first-hand evidence."

"You have?"

"Yes."

"In whom?"

"Us. Our relationship might be new, but I believe in it, and I believe in us… although if you need further proof of what I'm saying, I offer my parents as another example. There's a nine-year age-gap between Mom and Dad, and they've been happily married and completely inseparable for nearly forty years."

"Us?" I say and he laughs.

"Did you hear what I said about my parents?"

"Yes, but… us?"

He kisses me, his lips lingering over mine. "Yeah, baby… us."

"You believe in us?"

"Of course." He tilts his head, kissing me a little harder, until I'm breathless with need, although before things go too far, he pulls back. "What did you do?" he asks.

"When?"

He chuckles. "After you'd found your boyfriend in bed with your stepmom."

"Oh… sorry. I'd forgotten all about them."

He laughs even louder. "I'm glad about that, but I think I'd like to know the end of the story."

I sit up slightly, trying to focus, even though my lips are still tingling, my body on the verge of combusting, and my heart so swollen with love for him, I think it might burst.

"I left," I say simply.

"Didn't you wait for your dad to come home so you could tell him?"

"I couldn't see the point. That might sound odd to you, but I didn't think he'd believe me."

"Why not?"

"He'd changed since he'd married Celine."

"How?" he asks.

"This is going to sound like I was jealous – or paranoid – but it was something I noticed at Thanksgiving, which was that he never took my side anymore. Not in anything. Celine could be quite mean if she wasn't getting her own way, but if I said anything to Dad, he'd always take her side and tell me I wasn't making allowances for her, or that I should be kinder." I look up into Gabe's eyes. "It was like I didn't matter anymore."

He holds me closer, all thoughts of kissing and what might follow forgotten. "If that's the case, why do you want us to go there now? I'm assuming you haven't been back since?"

"No, I haven't. But he called me 'angel' just now on the phone. It was his pet name for me when I was little, but he hasn't used it since Celine came on the scene."

"So, he's stayed in touch?"

"Now and then. But like I say, he hasn't called me 'angel' for years. I guess I'm worried something might be wrong."

Gabe nods his head. "You know that's not your problem, don't you?"

"Yes, but he's still my dad."

He smiles. "Okay. So, when are we leaving?"

I throw my arms around his neck, kissing his cheek, which makes him chuckle. "Would you hate me if I said tomorrow?"

He clasps my chin in his hand. "I could never hate you, baby."

"Maybe not, but it kinda alters our plans for the holidays."

"That doesn't matter. As long as we're together, I don't care where we are." I hug him again, loving him even more, if that were possible. I'm so tempted to say the words, but I don't want him to think I'm saying them out of gratitude... even if he has been so understanding. "Speaking of being together..." he murmurs, his voice dipping to a low groan as he flexes his hips upwards into me, letting me feel his arousal.

I lean back, smiling at him. "Did you bring more condoms?"

He nods and I gasp when I feel his erection pressing hard against my core. He moans softly, letting his head rock back, his eyes closing as I grind into him, loving every second of contact between us.

"Oh, fu... you're too much," he growls, sitting forward and then standing with me in his arms. "I need to be inside you. Now."

I giggle as he carries me from the room, bending to grab his bag before he whisks us into my bedroom, dropping me onto the mattress and his bag at the end of it.

He shrugs off his coat, letting it fall to the floor, then leans over me. I'm wearing dark gray pants, which he quickly undoes, pulling them off, before he unfastens his jeans and pushes them down, releasing his enormous erection. I can't stop looking at it as he opens his bag, pulling out a box of condoms. My experience may be extremely limited, but he really is magnificent, and I gaze at him as he tears through the foil packet and rolls a condom over his impressive length.

"Oh, God. I forgot." I sit up, taking him by surprise, his eyes widening, his hand stilling on his shaft.

"Forgot what?"

"I called the doctor's office while you were out."

He hesitates for a second, then sits beside me. "And?"

"We've got an appointment at two-thirty this afternoon."

"Seriously?"

"Yes. Is that okay?"

"It's perfect." He leans in, smiling at me. "The sooner I can stop using these things, the better."

"Hmm… I couldn't agree more."

Without taking his eyes from mine, he completes his task, rolling the condom down as far as it will go, and then tugs his shirt off over his head and pushes me onto my back, settling between my legs.

I'm still wearing my panties and I'm feeling a little confused by that, but he nudges them aside and slides into me, letting out a slow sigh as he thrusts all the way home. I love how this feels, but I still don't understand.

"Aren't you gonna take my panties off?" I ask.

He smiles down at me. "I will. For now, I just need to be inside you, babe. I need to fuck you." He stops talking, bites on his lip and shakes his head. "I'm sorry. I didn't mean to say that."

"Why not? Don't you want me?"

"You know I do."

"Then say it. Say it however you want to, Gabe. I might be innocent, but I'm not a prude."

"I've kinda worked that out," he says with a broad grin. "The thing is, saying things like that feels wrong."

"Why? I want you to be yourself; not to feel you have to be someone else, just because I'm so much younger than you."

"It's not that," he says, moving slowly in and out of me. "It's not the age gap. Or it's not just the age gap."

"Then what is it?"

"It's you, babe. You're different."

I'm not sure I like the sound of that. "In a good way?" I ask, raising my hips to his.

"Oh, God… yes."

"In that case, tell me what you want… no holds barred."

He gazes down into my eyes. "I wanna fuck you, Remi… so damn hard."

"Then fuck me."

He groans, stopping and sucking in a sharp breath. "Are you trying to make me come?"

"Not especially."

He moves again, a little harder and faster than before. "Say that again," he mutters.

"Not especially."

He chuckles, shaking his head. "Not that. You know what I wanna hear."

I part my legs a little wider, raising them up slightly. "Fuck me, Gabe."

He pulls out of me, kneeling up, panting hard, his eyes closed, like he's concentrating. I stare at him until he opens his eyes again, and he lowers himself over me, his lips brushing mine.

"There's something about you asking me to fuck you… it's so hot."

"It is?"

"Yeah." He lets his eyes roam over me, even though I'm still wearing clothes, at least on my top half. "You're so elegant, and so innocent, which feels like a weird combination to start with, but when you say 'fuck me' like that, it does crazy things to my mind… and my body."

He kisses me much harder, then kneels up again, reaching out and putting his fingers in the top of my panties. With a swift tug, he tears through the seams, then he grabs my ankles, putting them up onto his shoulders and leans over, bending me back on myself as he enters me… hard.

I let out a yelp, but he knows it's pleasure racing through me and he pounds into me, harder and harder. I'm incapable of speech, but I don't think we need it. We're both close within minutes, and as I tip over the edge into a spiraling climax, he follows, throwing his head back and howling out my name. I'm lost then, oblivious to everything as wave after wave of trembling need rushes through me, claiming my body.

It seems to go on and on, but eventually subsides into a mist of satisfied joy, and I open my eyes as Gabe lowers my legs to the bed and slowly pulls out of me, lying on the mattress beside me and turning my body to his.

"I don't feel very elegant, or innocent at the moment."

He grins. "Innocence is overrated."

"And elegance?"

"Who cares? You're mine, baby. You're all mine."

I smile and nestle in to him, because there's nothing I want more than to be his. All his.

Chapter Sixteen

Gabe

The doctor's office is just like any other, really. The waiting room has seats along two walls, with a low table in one corner providing a home for a few well-thumbed magazines. A receptionist sits to one side, behind a wide desk, her head bent, her fingers flying across a computer keyboard, and Remi and I seat ourselves in the corner of the room, as far away from her as we can, while we wait…

She seems a little nervous, although I don't know why. We both want this, even if we got here by accident… the accident of me losing my mind. Remi has that effect on me, but at least I realized the gravity of the situation in time, and now we can do something about it… because, like I say, we both want this.

That thought brings a smile to my face, just as one of the two doors in the back wall opens, and a man comes out, giving the receptionist a nod of his head before he leaves the building. Remi sits forward, and the receptionist looks up at us and says, "You can go in now."

We stand together, and I keep a hold of Remi's hand as we enter the doctor's room.

It's a little sterile, but that's to be expected, and the doctor gets up as we step inside, closing the door behind us.

I remember Doctor Dodds from Ryan's wedding, although he looks different today, wearing a white coat over his button-down shirt and gray pants.

He stares down at Remi and then raises his dark brown eyes to me.

"I've brought my boyfriend," she says. "I hope that's okay."

"If it makes you more comfortable." He nods to the chairs at the end of his desk and we both sit, waiting until he's back in his seat and has turned to face us. "What can I do for you today?" he asks, ignoring me and focusing his attention on Remi instead. His hair is almost black, and neatly cut, and he tips his head to one side, waiting. I wonder if Remi's gonna say anything, and I give her hand a squeeze, hoping to encourage her.

She clears her throat, glancing at me, and I smile.

"Do you want me to say it?" I ask, but she shakes her head.

"No, it's okay." She looks back at the doctor. "I want to take birth control pills." She blurts out the words like she's been holding them back and they've found a way of escaping her lips, tumbling over themselves on the way out.

Doctor Dodds nods his head, like he hears this kind of thing every minute of the day. "That's fine." He turns slightly, clicking on his keyboard a few times. "We've already got your medical history, Miss Fox." He scrolls up and down with his mouse. "It looks like it's been a while since you had your blood pressure taken, though... so we'd better do that."

He pulls forward an electronic monitor, wrapping a gray cuff around Remi's arm, and pressing a blue button on the front of the machine. We all wait as the cuff expands, and then sit back once it's deflated.

"How is it?" I ask, and he smiles.

"It's absolutely fine. Nothing to worry about." He pushes the machine away again, looking back at Remi. "You've never taken an oral contraceptive before, have you?"

"No." She shakes her head, paying attention.

"Okay. The best place to start is probably with the combined pill." He sits forward. "The one I'm going to give you has twenty-one pills in each pack, and you take one each day, after which you take a break for seven days. During that time, you'll menstruate, although you'll probably notice it won't be the same as the periods you're used to."

"In what way?" she asks.

"Most women find their periods are lighter, or don't last for as long. It's impossible to say how or even if you'll be affected." Remi nods her head, and the doctor glances briefly at me. "Can I assume you want to use the pill as a method of contraception, rather than because your periods are causing you issues?"

"Yes," Remi says.

The doctor glances at me again, taking a little longer over it this time. "In that case, I just need to make sure you're aware that the pill provides excellent protection against unwanted pregnancy, but doesn't offer any protection at all from sexually transmitted diseases."

"I know that," she says. "But I've never been with anyone before."

"I have," I murmur, stating the obvious before the doctor can, and Remi turns to me.

"I know that, too."

"Well… I'll leave you to discuss that between yourselves," he says, clearly feeling his job is done. He's alerted her to the dangers, and now he can move on, and he does. "It's up to you when you start taking the pills," he says, leaning back in his seat. "You can wait and start them on the first day of your next period.

If you do so, you'll be protected straight away. Alternatively, you can start today, but that would mean you'd need to use condoms, or another barrier method of contraception for the next seven days."

Remi frowns, like she's thinking. "I only had my period ten days ago, so I think I'd rather start straight away." I squeeze her hand to let her know I agree, and she smiles up at me before looking back at the doctor. "If I do that, does it mean my next period won't arrive when it usually would, but in that seven-day gap you talked about?"

He nods his head. "It means exactly that."

"Okay. I'll do that then."

I try not to sigh out my relief that our appointment is over, although when we get outside, I'm grateful that we walked here, despite the snow. It'll give us a chance to talk on the way back to Remi's place.

"That went okay, don't you think?" she says, looking up at me. I'm holding her hand to make sure she can't fall.

"I think so."

"And you agree about starting straight away?"

"I think we'll survive seven days, don't you?"

She grins, tipping her head to one side and then the other. "It'll be a struggle, but we'll cope."

I can't help laughing and she leans against me. "I liked the little warning he gave you."

"What warning?" She looks up at me, her brow furrowing.

"About my past." Her frown deepens.

"When did he do that?" I love how naïve she can be sometimes.

"When he was telling you about sexually transmitted diseases. He'd obviously noticed the age gap between us, and realized there might be some discrepancy in our levels of experience." I can't think of another way to phrase that, but it seems I don't need to, as Remi nods her head.

"I'm not sure he was warning me. He was just stating the obvious."

"Yeah… that I've got a past, and you don't. But I want you to know, I've always been really careful… at least until I met you." She chuckles, leaning in to me. "And just to set your mind at rest even further, I was tested a couple of months ago."

"You were?" She seems surprised.

"Yeah. Ryan changed our insurance provider, and we all had to have medicals. The company sent someone to the office to do them."

"I see. I'm assuming everything was fine?"

"Of course."

"And you haven't been with anyone since?" she says, like it's a foregone conclusion, my heart sinking before she's even finished her sentence.

"I have… just once."

She stops walking, and I do too, looking down into her bemused face. "W—When?"

"About a month before we met."

"Who was she?"

"No-one from here. It happened when I went back to Boston on business."

"Was she someone you already knew? An ex-girlfriend or something?"

"No. I told you, I've never done the whole girlfriend thing before. She was just someone I met, that's all."

"So, she was a stranger?" I nod my head. "And you ended up in bed with her?"

"Yes. I hadn't been with anyone for a while. All I needed was the release of having sex, and I think she felt the same."

"Why?"

"I don't know. We didn't ask each other questions like that."

"You just had sex?"

"Yes. We didn't exchange numbers. I didn't even know her last name." Her eyes widen in surprise and she pulls her hand from mine, although I grab it right back. "Don't, Remi. I told you about this already."

"No, you didn't. You told me you went out with lots of women. You never said you slept with them all, or that you were so... so blasé about it."

She's right, I guess, and I step closer. "I know, but you said you didn't want details. Maybe I should have explained anyway, but I didn't want to shock you then, and I'm sorry if it's a shock now."

She lets out a breath, frowning up at me. "Is that how it always was? You'd just meet women and sleep with them?"

"Yes."

"So you didn't date them first? When you said you went out with them, that wasn't what you meant? You meant that you just slept with them?"

"That's exactly what I meant. Dating was never my thing."

"Never?"

"No."

"But you dated me. The first thing you did was invite me to have coffee with you. I might have declined, but you didn't give up, did you? We... we went to dinner, and for drinks. You came to my house. Those were dates, weren't they?"

"They were."

"Why did you do that if it wasn't your thing? What made you change?"

"You did." I study her face for a moment... her clear, delicate skin, her pink glistening lips, her brilliant blue eyes, so full of doubt. "I'm sorry if this wasn't what you wanted to hear, but it's the past and, like I said, there's nothing I can do to change it."

"I know," she says, her face softening as she leans in to me, thank God. "I'm being silly."

I release her hand, putting my arm around her and tip her head back, kissing her. She gasps, clearly not expecting such intimacy in the middle of Main Street, but I don't care. I need this. Like I need her.

"Can I tell you something?" I say, leaning back and gazing into her eyes again.

"If you want to." She sounds a little unsure, but given my most recent revelations, I can't blame her for that, and I hold her even tighter against my chest.

"The day I first met you, you cast a spell on me."

"I did what?"

"You cast a spell on me."

"Are you calling me a witch?"

"No. And I get that this sounds odd. But there's no other way to describe it, because that's exactly how it felt. I didn't even know your name, or anything about you, but the moment I saw you, I had this urge to put my arms around you and keep you safe. Even your voice did crazy things to me and I wanted to sit with you and just listen to you talk."

"You did?"

"Yes."

"You mean you didn't want to take me to bed?" She stops talking, a blush creeping up her cheeks as I lean in.

"Of course I did," I whisper, her blush deepening. "I wanted you more than I've ever wanted anyone. The thought of being inside you was driving me insane. But it was more than that. More than anything I'd ever felt in my life. It confused the hell out of me, but I think I knew even then…"

"Knew what?"

"That I'm yours."

"You're…"

"All yours."

I crush my lips to hers, wondering why I didn't just say 'I love you' instead of 'I'm yours'. Perhaps it's because of the conversation we've just had. It might seem too convenient to declare my love for her now, when she's still feeling doubtful about my past. Telling her I'm hers, and hers alone feels more real and more appropriate. My love isn't going anywhere and declaring it can wait... at least for now.

"You grew up here?"

I stop the car, turning to stare at Remi, who gazes at me with something like embarrassment in her eyes, and I have to smile. That look is certainly better than the confusion that was etched there yesterday morning on our walk back from the doctor's office, and it's different to the gratifying wonder she couldn't disguise when she sucked my cock for the first time last night. I don't know whether she felt she had a point to prove, but she didn't. We'd resolved our differences by then... if we ever had any differences in the first place. And as far as I'm concerned, Remi will never have a single point to prove to me. But she asked if she could try, and I wasn't about to say 'no'. For someone with no experience, what she did was incredible, and I think she enjoyed it almost as much as I did.

"It didn't look like this when I was growing up," she says. "Celine added the two wings onto either side, and the pool house."

I look back at the property before us, noting the original Colonial structure in the center. It's been added to, and not very sympathetically, although no expense has been spared, I'd have said.

"What does your dad do for a living?" I ask, edging the car down the driveway.

"He's a marketing manager. He earns well, but I think Celine must be working her way through my mom's life insurance payout."

"Why do you say that?"

"Because Dad doesn't make enough to pay for all this." She rolls her eyes and I reach over, resting my hand on her thigh.

"It'll be okay."

She sighs. "I wish I had your confidence."

"I'm here, and I won't let anyone hurt you."

She turns, smiling up at me, and I park the car just as the front door opens. A man steps out. He's a little under six feet tall, with salt and pepper hair, and a reasonable tan for this time of year. He's in good shape and is wearing casual pants and a sweater. Remi notices him as he walks toward us, springing from the car before I can get out myself.

"Dad!" she cries and runs into his arms. He hugs her and I climb from the car myself as he releases her, looking over her shoulder at me, a frown settling on his face.

"Mr. Fox." I hold out a hand, approaching them, and he reciprocates, giving me a very firm shake.

"Call me David." His voice is deep and commanding, and I'm not about to argue.

"Dad, this is Gabe," Remi says, completing the introductions.

The age gap must be obvious to her dad, and although he doesn't comment, his frown is doing the talking for him.

"You didn't wait for me, Davey." The sound of a female voice makes us all look up, and David turns, all of us watching the woman who's doing her best to get down the steps at the front of the house. She's made it hard on herself by wearing excruciatingly high heels and the tightest mini skirt I've ever seen. Her ludicrous outfit doesn't end there, either, because even though the snow is lying just as thick on the ground here as it was in Hart's Creek, she's only wearing a thin white blouse, which is undone sufficiently to reveal her very ample bosom. This has got to be Celine, and I find it hard to believe she's the kind of woman I used to go for. Except she is… although God knows why. Compared to Remi, she's nothing.

David walks back to her, offering his hand, which she takes, using it for support as she totters over to join us, and I put my arm around Remi, sensing the tension in her already.

Celine ignores her step-daughter, her eyes alighting on me as she flicks her strawberry blonde hair over her shoulder and pulls her hand from David's, holding it out to me, like she expects me to kiss it, not shake it. I disappoint her, giving her the firmest of shakes.

"You must be Remi's boyfriend," she says, or maybe purrs would be more accurate.

"I am… very much so."

"Where's Preston?" Remi asks.

"In his playroom." Celine dismisses Remi's question with a wave of her hand.

"Maybe we should go inside," David says. "Do you need any help with your bags?"

"No. I can manage." I reluctantly let go of Remi, knowing that Celine is too unstable on those heels to come after me, and I grab the bags from the trunk of my car, following them all into the house.

We've barely closed the door when I hear the sound of footsteps, and eventually a small child comes running through from the back of the house. He's holding a plastic dinosaur in one hand, and has a grin fixed on his face. His blond hair is a similar shade to his mother's, and he steps straight over to me, holding up the toy.

I put down the bags and crouch, taking it from him.

"You must be Preston."

He nods his head, looking up at Remi, reminding me they've never met before. I'm not sure what to say. I can hardly introduce her as his half-sister, and in any case, I feel like his mother or father should be the ones making the introductions. Or should that be explanations? I can't tell. Either way, neither makes a move, so I smile at him and say, "I'm Gabe, and this is Remi. She's…"

"We don't need to bother with any of that," David interrupts, and I raise my head, looking up at him. He's glaring at me, but I give as good as I get. It feels like he doesn't want his son to know he's related to his daughter… like he's trying to airbrush her out of Preston's life, in which case, I have to wonder what we're doing here.

"Why don't you take Preston back to his playroom, while I show Gabe and Remi upstairs?" Celine steps forward, breaking the frosty atmosphere, and for once, I welcome her intrusion.

Preston wanders to his father, holding up his hand, which David takes, the two of them heading for the back of the house, and I pick up our bags again, as Celine makes for the stairs.

"I know the way to my room," Remi says, following her as I bring up the rear. "Unless you've moved them around."

"No. Your room is still just as it was."

That's something, I guess. For a moment then, I half expected her to say they'd changed everything since Remi left and maybe eliminated her from her childhood home, too.

At the top of the stairs, we turn left and Celine opens the first door we come to. Remi steps forward, peering inside and nodding her head, making it clear to me that this is her bedroom. I can't see much, other than some floral drapes and pink walls, which show this room hasn't received any attention for years.

"Gabe's opposite," Celine says.

"You mean we're not sharing?" Remi blurts out her question and Celine turns to her with a smirk on her lips.

"No."

I'm not sure whether that was David's decision or Celine's, but it doesn't matter. Not really. The point is, we won't be sleeping together while we're here and Remi nods her head, looking up at me, her disappointment obvious as I drop her bag just inside the door before Celine turns away and then stops, clearly waiting for me to follow. Remi tags along, thank God, and Celine goes to the door opposite Remi's, throwing it open with a flourish.

"I take it this is me?" I say, looking down at her, and she flashes me a dazzling smile.

"It is. Hopefully, you'll find everything you need, but if not, just ask." She tilts her head, then licks her lips, letting her eyes rake down my body and back up again in a very deliberate move.

I'm not about to go inside the room alone, not with Celine standing there. But I can hardly drag Remi in there with me, either. Celine would be bound to object. Instead, I put down my bag where I am and make it clear I'm going nowhere for now.

Celine seems confused by that move, although she rallies quickly, stepping a little closer to me.

"I meant to say, Preston isn't great at sleeping through the night yet, so if either of you hear footsteps in the early hours, don't worry about it."

"Okay, thanks," I say with a nod of my head. "I'm sure we can take it from here."

That throws her, too… but what can she say? She can hardly invite herself into my room, even though I think she'd like to, and after just a second's hesitation, she steps back.

"We eat early because of Preston, so I'm afraid you've only got about thirty minutes to freshen up."

"We'll cope," Remi says, sounding as dismissive as I ever want to hear her.

Celine narrows her eyes at her step-daughter, and then turns, slowly making her way down the stairs.

We wait until she's gone, and then I look down at Remi. "I'm sorry," she whispers before I can get a word out.

"What for?"

"The separate bedrooms. I didn't realize Dad would do that." She's clearly holding her father responsible for the decision.

"He wasn't to know we're sleeping together."

"No."

I pull her close. "Shall I sneak into your room later?"

She smiles, letting out a sigh. "I'd love to say 'yes', but you heard Celine. If Preston's in the habit of waking up, and she or Dad have to go to him in the night, it probably wouldn't be wise."

"No." The last thing I need is to bump into either of them while trying to get into Remi's room.

"I'm gonna miss you," she whispers, putting her arms around me.

"Oh, baby… I'm gonna miss you, too."

I've already gotten used to falling asleep with her and waking up by her side, and while we have to respect her father's wishes, that doesn't mean we have to like it.

Dinner was an unmitigated disaster.

It started okay, with Remi and her father talking animatedly about her job and her house, making it clear he hadn't paid any attention to what Remi has been doing for a long time. The problem was that David kept trying to include Celine in their conversation, and she clearly wasn't interested. She couldn't take her eyes off of me. She'd spent the entire meal flirting, and whenever he said a word to her, she'd snap and snarl at him, glaring at Remi and ignoring them as much as possible. As the evening wore on, David obviously noticed his wife's behavior, and withdrew into himself.

Remi tried to keep their conversation going, but he'd already lost interest and, no matter what she said, he didn't seem to care.

I couldn't blame him for that. Celine was being really obvious, and anyone would have had to be blind not to notice what she was doing. I was powerless to shut her down without being rude. It was embarrassing, though, and horrible to watch how a husband and wife could behave toward each other, and how David took it out on Remi. None of it was her fault, and I longed to take her away from it all… somewhere she could feel safe, because she clearly didn't with him.

We've moved to the living room now we've finished eating, which at least means I can hold Remi's hand, and hopefully make her feel a little better… a little more wanted. But I haven't had the chance to speak with her about it, and am surprised by how late Preston goes to bed, considering we ate early for his benefit. It's gone nine by the time Celine even suggests bedtime to her son, and it takes another hour of cajoling and persuasion to get him up the stairs.

"I think we'll head for bed, too," Remi says, once Celine and Preston have left the room.

Her father looks up, nodding his head, like he's not even aware of her anymore. "Okay. See you in the morning." He appears very detached, and Remi frowns at him before turning to me. I shrug my shoulders. What can I say? I don't know the man, and it feels like she doesn't either… not anymore.

I stand, holding out my hand and pulling her to her feet.

"Goodnight, Dad," Remi says.

"Goodnight." He doesn't call her 'angel', and I know that will have hurt. It would have been easy enough. It's one word, and I can't help resenting him for not using it.

I lead her from the room and up the stairs, the sound of Celine's voice echoing from somewhere near the back of the house.

We don't have long and I daren't risk sneaking in to Remi's room or having to sneak back out again. Even so, there's no way I can let her go like this.

"Are you okay?" I ask, pulling her into my arms outside her bedroom door.

"I—I thought he wanted me here, Gabe, but he doesn't, does he?"

I can't answer, not without hurting her more, so I offer the only solution I have. "Do you want to leave?"

"No. We can't… not yet."

She's probably right. It would look odd, and probably rude to leave straight away. "I wish I could sleep with you tonight."

"So do I."

"I'll risk it if you want me to."

She hesitates for a second or two, then shakes her head. "I'll be fine."

"You're sure?"

"Yes."

I bend my head, kissing her, just as Celine's voice gets louder. "Mommy's going downstairs. You go to sleep now, Preston."

She's clearly coming this way, and I break the kiss. "I'd better go, baby."

Remi nods and I dart into my room, giving her a smile and a wink before I close the door.

"Fuck me," Remi whispers, looking at me over her shoulder. She's on all fours in the middle of the bed, and I'm kneeling behind her between her parted legs, slamming into her wet pussy. Fucking her without a condom is better than I'd imagined, and I can't get enough.

"You want my cock?"

"Yes! Yes!" She throws her head back and although she's not coming yet, I need her to. How does she do this to me? I thought I had control. I thought I was good at this, but she's gonna make me come, her walls tightening around me.

"Come for me, Remi... come now."

She rocks back in to me, making the struggle even more difficult. I need this... I need...

I startle awake, coming out of my dream as the bedroom door clicks closed and a smile forms on my lips. She's here. She couldn't keep away.

Thank God.

I lie still, waiting, barely daring to breathe, my dick aching for her to make my dream come true, even if we will still need to use a condom, and I listen to the sound of soft footsteps on the thick piled carpet.

The covers are tugged down and the bed dips behind me. I turn over, letting out a long sigh as she shifts across the mattress.

"I'm so fucking hard for you, baby."

She doesn't reply, but I feel the tips of her fingers slide gently up and down my cock, my brain flipping out. Remi hasn't touched me that often, but something's wrong here, and just as she puts her hand around me, I realize what it is.

"What the fuck..." I pull away and turn over, switching on the lamp beside the bed, and then look over my shoulder. Celine is lying on the mattress, smiling up at me, her full and unnaturally rounded breasts peeping above the covers. I leap out of bed, almost falling over in the process, and realize too late that I'm not wearing anything. My erection might be dwindling, but I still have no wish to be exposed to this woman and I grab the blanket from the end of the bed, wrapping it around my waist.

"You're..." She pauses, rolling over and kneeling up, then crawling toward me, like a cat eyeing its prey. "You're magnificent." She reaches for the blanket, but I step back.

"Get the fuck out of my room."

She smiles, kneeling back, her hands resting on her thighs now. "You know you don't mean that."

I turn slightly, focusing on the picture above the bed, rather than looking at her. "I mean every fucking word."

She clambers off of the mattress, standing before me, making it hard to look anywhere else, although I keep my eyes fixed on her face, not allowing them to roam. Even so, I jump as she places a hand on my chest, and I take a moment to bat it away. "Don't be like that." She pouts, looking up at me through her eyelashes.

"Don't touch me." My voice is a whispered growl, born of a desperation not to wake everyone in the house, while getting Celine to understand I don't want her.

"Why not? We both know a man who's built the way you are needs a real woman."

"I've got one already, thanks."

She smiles, shaking her head. "Remi isn't a real woman."

"Yeah, she is. She's all the woman I need. And before you say anything else, I know what you did with her boyfriend when she was at college."

"Which kinda proves my point, doesn't it? She didn't know how to please him, either."

"You never gave them a chance to find out."

She steps closer, and I move back, almost stumbling over the chair behind me. "She was aiming too high with him, just like she is with you... and I didn't notice Leo trying to stop me."

"His name was Leon, not Leo."

She waves a hand. "Whatever. We weren't paying too much attention to names at the time."

I'm reminded of my past, but I dismiss the thought. This isn't about me. "I'm sure you weren't... but how does your *husband* feel about you cheating on him?"

I emphasize the word 'husband' in the hope it'll bring her to her senses, that she might even see it as a threat that I'll expose her to him, although its clear from her complacent smile that there's no chance of her feeling threatened by anything.

"You don't have to worry about David. We have an arrangement."

"I'm not worried about David." I'm worried about Remi. "But are you telling me he knows?"

"Of course he does. He knows about all of them."

"All of them?" She nods her head. "Even Leon?" She nods again, and I take a moment to understand that, and its consequences. "What's wrong with you? Both of you? Don't you have any sense of remorse?"

"No. If Remi had been keeping her boyfriend happy, he wouldn't have been so ready to fuck me the moment I offered, would he? And as for David, what did he expect when there's such a big age gap between us?"

"That his wife might not behave like a slut, maybe?"

She raises her right arm to strike me, but I grab her wrist while still holding the blanket with my other hand. "You're an asshole," she hisses.

"Not anymore. That's who I used to be, before I met your step-daughter."

She narrows her eyes, pulling away from me. I let her, and move back, going around the chair, rather than falling into it. "I'll make you pay for this."

"Can I get this straight? Is David aware that you're here?" I ask, refusing to show fear to her, even though it's coursing through my veins now.

"What do you think?"

She struts across the room, bending to grab her robe from the floor. It's over by the door, where she must have dropped it when she came in.

I can't be entirely sure what her answer means, but if David knows about 'all of them', I have to assume that includes me. There's something sick about that, given that his daughter is my girlfriend, and she's sleeping just across the hall, but before I have the chance to say a word, Celine leaves.

"Jesus," I mutter under my breath, sitting on the chair now, and letting my head rock back.

What the hell just happened? And more to the point, what am I going to do about it?

Chapter Seventeen

Remi

I look up into his eyes, holding the tip of his erection against my lips as I kneel before him. The fire glimmers beside us, providing the only light in the room, but it's all we need. I can see the shimmer in his eyes and the smile on his lips as he flexes his hips, letting me know what he wants, and I smile, opening my mouth and taking him inside. I swirl my tongue over him, round and round, and he lets out a low groan.

"Fuck, that's good." His words spur me on and I suck him in a little deeper, feeling his hand come behind my head. "Take my cock, baby," he growls and I feel a tingle of anticipation rush through my body, my eyes never leaving his as I nod my head, acknowledging that he has control. He sucks in a breath, his hands either side of my face now, and he flexes his hips, although he doesn't go too far, careful not to make me gag, before he pulls out and stares down at me.

"You like that?"

"I do."

He smiles. "Enough to keep going?"

"Yes."

"Enough to let me fuck your perfect mouth?"

"Oh, God… yes." I breathe, and he smiles, tapping his erection against my lips.

"Remi?"

"*Yes?*"

"Remi?"

My body's on fire with need. Why is he waiting? Why is he saying my name over and over?

"Remi, baby… wake up."

I open my eyes, my dream fading as the outline of Gabe's face comes into focus. A smile forms on my lips and I sit up slightly.

"What are you doing here? I thought we agreed…"

He puts his finger over my lips and even in the dim moonlight, I can see he's dressed. Fully dressed in jeans and a sweater, and I pull his hand away.

"What's going on, Gabe?" I whisper, and he sits on the bed beside me, letting out a sigh.

"We're leaving."

I can't have heard that right, and I shift a little closer. "Did you say we're leaving?"

"Yes."

"Why? What's happened?"

He reaches over, switching on the lamp beside the bed, and I blink against its brightness for a moment, before I focus on him again. He looks worried, and my imagination goes into overdrive. Has something happened back in Hart's Creek? Are his friends okay? Is it his parents?

"I can't tell you now," he says, shaking his head. "But I will. I promise."

"When?"

"Later." He twists around, taking my hands in his and looking down into my eyes, his own filled with something that definitely looks more like fear than worry. "Do you trust me?"

"Of course I do." *I love you.*

"In that case, will you do as I ask?"

I think about that for a second. He may not be telling me anything, but something is clearly very wrong, and whatever it is, he needs us to leave. While that's not ideal, I have to do whatever it takes to help him… because that's what you do when you love someone. I nod my head. "What do you need?"

"Can you get dressed while I pack your things?"

"Okay."

He kisses my hands, then stands and I throw back the covers, smiling as he moans softly.

"I wish I had time to do something about that."

"About what?" I ask, getting to my feet and standing before him.

"You."

I smile and lean up, kissing him. "You can, if you want."

He shakes his head. "I'm sorry, babe, but we've gotta go. Now."

There's something about his voice that concerns me… something in the urgency of it. "Won't you tell me what's wrong?"

"Not yet."

"Why not yet?"

He sighs. "Because it's more important that we get out of here first."

"And you'll tell me once we have?"

He nods and I copy him, accepting his answer. He must have a good reason for this. Gabe isn't the kind of man who'd do something as drastic as this on a whim.

I step away, going to the chair by the window, and grab some clothes from my bag, choosing my dark gray pants and pale pink sweater, along with some underwear, which I bring back to the bed.

"There isn't much to pack," I say, looking up at him. "I had a shower last night, so my shampoo and body wash are in the bathroom, and my toothbrush and toothpaste are by the sink. Other than that, everything is still in my bag."

He nods, heading for the bathroom, and returns a few seconds later, carrying everything I've just mentioned, which he packs away.

"Do you need to do anything with your hair?" he asks.

"Just brush it."

"And your brush is…?"

"In the side pocket of my bag."

There are two, and he opens the wrong one first, but finds my brush on the second attempt, bringing it over and sitting beside me while I finish dressing. Once I've fastened my pants and pulled my sweater over my head, he hands me my brush and I quickly make myself look presentable.

"What's the time?" I ask, realizing I don't have a clue. It's still dark outside, but at this time of year, that could mean anything.

"Just after one."

That's a shock. I'd thought it was later, but I suppose my dream must have fooled me into thinking I'd been asleep for longer. Still… I can't think about my dream right now. My mind is too full of other things, none of which make sense.

I pull on my boots, zipping them up and turn to face Gabe.

"Can't you tell me anything?"

He stands, holding out his hand, which I take, letting him pull me into his arms as he shakes his head. "I'll explain it all later. I promise."

Before I can reply, he dips his head, his lips meeting mine in a breathtaking kiss, although he doesn't give me time to respond, and pulls back, glancing around the room.

"Have you got everything?"

I nod my head. "I think so."

"Okay. Let's go."

He keeps a hold of my hand, flicking off the light, and grabbing my bag with the other, he leads me across the room. As he pauses by the door, I notice he's left his bag on the floor and he bends, putting mine down and throwing his over his shoulder, before opening the door and grabbing mine again, never letting go of me… not even for a second.

It seems dark in the hall outside my room, but I know the way well enough, and rather than letting him lead, I head for the top of the stairs, guiding him instead.

Fortunately, these stairs have never creaked, but we tiptoe down them anyway, and at the bottom, I stop and look up at Gabe.

"I can't leave without telling my dad."

"No!" His voice is louder than it was upstairs, and even he startles at the sound of it, and then steps closer to me, shaking his head. "No, baby. You can't wake him. Just… just write him a note."

"Saying what? My boyfriend's decided we need to leave, but won't tell me why?"

He sighs. "Tell him… tell him something's come up at my office and we've had to go back to Hart's Creek."

"Can I take it that's not true?"

"It's not."

"So you want me to lie to my father?"

He opens his mouth, then closes it again. "I'm asking you to do this for me… for us."

I gaze up at him in the gloomy light. "This isn't fair, Gabe. Things may not have gone very well last night, but how can I hope to make it better if I'm not even here?"

He lowers his gaze, shaking his head, like he's thinking, and then he puts down the bags and pulls me into his arms. "I know I'm asking a lot, but I need you to trust that I wouldn't do this if I didn't believe it was in your best interests."

"*My* best interests?"

"Yes. I told you, you're my responsibility. I'm doing this because…" He pauses, pulling me even closer to him. "Because I honestly don't know what else to do to keep you safe."

"Are you saying I'm in some kind of danger?" I have to smile because that sounds so unbelievable and melodramatic, although I notice Gabe remains grim-faced.

"Not physical danger, no."

"What other kind of danger is there?"

"Emotional… mental…" His voice fades. "I'm trying to protect you, baby. All I'm asking is that you let me."

I stare up at him, wishing he'd tell me more, even though I know he won't.

"I'll write Dad a note," I whisper, pulling away from Gabe. He lets me and I feel him watching as I head for the kitchen. He follows, leaving our bags behind, and keeps his eyes on me as I tear off a piece of paper from the notepad on the island unit, and write…

Dad,

Really sorry about this. Gabe had a call in the early hours to say there's been a problem at his office in Hart's Creek, so we're going back there.

Didn't want to wake you, or risk waking Preston.

Will call soon.

Have a good Christmas.

Love, Remi xx'

"I don't feel comfortable lying to him," I whisper, folding the piece of paper in half and writing the word 'Dad' on the outside.

"I know," he says, coming over and standing beside me. "I'm sorry. If I could think of another way around this, I'd take it."

"If you told me what the problem was, I might be able to help."

He shakes his head, making it clear that confiding in me isn't an option and I push the piece of paper to the middle of the island unit, so it should be obvious for anyone to see, before I turn back to Gabe.

"Ready?" he says and I nod my head, even though I'm feeling less and less 'ready' with every passing minute.

He takes my hand again, leading me back to the front door, where he hands me my coat from the hook, helping me on with it before he shrugs on his own, and picks up our bags. He lets us out into the chill night air, closing the door as quietly as possible, and then holds my hand as he helps me across the icy footpath to his car, where he throws the bags onto the back seat and helps me into mine, neither of us saying a word.

I don't look at him, but wait while he closes the door and walks around the front of the car, getting in beside me.

He starts the engine and waits, turning to face me.

"Fasten your seat belt, Remi."

"Not until you tell me why we're leaving." I fold my arms across my chest, staring out through the windshield.

"I can't tell you yet."

"But you said you would."

"I know, but I can't."

"Why not?"

He sighs. "Because I can't. Okay?"

"No, it's not okay. Stop treating me like a child."

"Then stop acting like one."

I turn and glare at him, even though he's blurring before my eyes. "How could…? How…"

He reaches over, lifting me onto his lap, the steering wheel digging into me. "I'm sorry," he says, pulling me closer. "I'm sorry, baby. Forgive me. Please?"

"Tell me why we're leaving."

"I can't."

"Why not?"

"Because what I've got to tell you is gonna be really hard for you to hear, and I need for us to be a long way from here before I say anything."

I'm scared now, and that fear makes me lean in to him. It's an instinct... like I know he's my safe place. "How far is a long way?"

"England."

"Excuse me?" I pull back again, staring at him. "Did you say England?"

"Yes. We're going to stay with my parents. I've made all the arrangements already."

"They're okay, aren't they? There's nothing wrong with them?" That wouldn't make much sense of anything else he's said so far, but I can't understand why else he's taking me there.

He smiles. "They're fine. But thanks for thinking of them."

I don't know what else to do... what else to say.

"You're assuming I have a passport?"

His face pales, even in the dim light. "You do, don't you?"

"Yes. You remember me saying Leon and I talked about going somewhere for spring break?"

His face darkens, but he nods his head. "Yeah."

"Well... we hadn't decided where we wanted to go, but it seemed a good idea to get a passport."

"I see." He smiles now. "In that case, we'll go back to Hart's Creek, pack a few more things, collect our passports, and head for the airport."

"And then you'll tell me?"

"Once we're on the flight, yes."

I suck in a breath. "Okay."

He leans in, but hesitates before kissing me. "Am I forgiven? I didn't mean to accuse you of being a child."

"I didn't mean to act like one."

He smiles, closing the gap between us. His kiss feels just like it always does and I relish the familiarity of it, even though I'm struggling with just about everything else.

Chapter Eighteen

Gabe

I'm asking a lot of Remi. I know that.

But what else can I do?

I thought this through. I really did. And this was the only solution I could come up with.

We're sitting on the plane now, and it's the first chance I've had to catch my breath since I jumped out of that chair at roughly twelve-thirty this morning. Everything since then is a blur, although I don't think I'll ever forget the hurt expression on Remi's face when I accused her of behaving like a child. That was my fear talking, but I hated myself for saying it, and even though she said she's forgiven me, it's going to take me a while to forgive myself.

We're the last passengers to board, and within moments, the aircraft begins to taxi. Remi isn't showing any sign of nerves, considering this is her first flight, and she settles back in her seat, getting comfortable. It's easy when you're in first-class, and although Remi baulked at the cost, I couldn't have cared less. It was that, or wait for this evening's flight, and I didn't feel like waiting.

Take-off is smooth and I feel myself relax for the first time in hours, although when I turn to look at Remi, she's staring at me, with a frown etched firmly on her face, and I take her hand in mine.

"Will you tell me now?" she says and I suck in a breath.

"Would you hate me if I said 'no'?"

Her frown deepens, and she tries to pull her hand away, although I don't let her. "I—I wouldn't hate you, but I'd want to know why."

"Because I don't think thirty-thousand feet over the Atlantic, in a confined space, surrounded by strangers, is the best place for this conversation."

Her eyes widen. "Y—You're scaring me, Gabe."

"I don't mean to." That said, I'm terrified myself, mostly of how I'm going to protect her from what's coming.

"Are we gonna be okay?" she whispers, leaning in a little closer.

"We're gonna be just fine."

"Really?"

"Truly."

She nods her head, then rests it against my shoulder. That feels good, and I tilt my head against hers. Within just a few minutes, I hear her breathing change and realize she's fallen asleep… which isn't a bad thing. I woke her six and a half hours ago, in the early hours of the morning. Considering the day we've got ahead of us, she's going to need all the rest she can get.

Our landing was just as smooth as our take-off, and although I didn't sleep on the flight, I feel a lot better for knowing there are three thousand miles between us and our immediate problem. The distance feels necessary… and very welcome.

"Are your parents expecting us?" Remi asks once we've cleared the baggage hall and immigration. We're on our way to collect a rental car and I gaze down at her.

"Yeah. I texted my dad before I woke you."

"That was the middle of the night."

"Not in England. It was around six-thirty in the morning here, and my dad's always been an early riser. I knew he'd be awake."

"What did you say to him?"

I know she's trying to get me to tell her why we're here, but I'm not that easily fooled. "Just that we'd be catching the first flight here, that I'd rent a car, and drive to their place. I texted him again just now, when you were in the ladies' room, to let them know we'd landed."

"What time is it? Here, I mean… not at home."

I check my watch. "It's just after seven-thirty."

"In the evening?" I nod my head. "And how far away is your parents' place?"

"About a ninety-minute drive. Mom said she'd have something ready for us to eat."

Remi tilts her head, looking up at me. "You've thought everything through, haven't you?"

"Not at all. I'm making almost all of this up as I go along."

We have to wait for the woman at the desk to finish a phone call, and while she does, Remi leans in to me, studying my face. "Which parts aren't you making up?" she says, keeping her voice low enough that no-one else can hear.

"The need to protect you, baby. That's built into me. It starts in here…" I'm holding her hand and I raise it, placing it over my heart. Remi lets out a sigh, but before she can say anything, the woman behind the desk coughs, letting us know she's finished her call… which is a shame.

The car is a Range Rover, almost exactly the same as the one I drive at home, but with the steering wheel on the other side, and once I've signed all the necessary documentation, we set off for the Cotswolds. It's dark and cold, but at least there's no snow and the car eats the miles. Fortunately, I've made this journey several times before, and am familiar with all the turns I need to make, which is just as well, because exhaustion is getting the better of me now.

As we get into the village where my parents live, I hear Remi suck in a breath.

"This is pretty," she says, gazing out the window at the tiny shops and houses, all lit up with Christmas lights.

"It is… although it looks just as nice during the day. I'll bring you out tomorrow, so you can see the village properly."

She doesn't reply, and I feel a shudder of fear, wondering if she'll still be talking to me tomorrow.

No. Don't think like that.

I turn into the driveway, slowing down as we approach the house, and Remi gasps.

"Oh, my God."

I turn, smiling at her. "Don't be too impressed. I didn't grow up here."

"Maybe not, but it's beautiful."

The house is well lit, with two lamps by the door and fairy lights in the tall pine trees, which make it look magical, although I'm a little concerned about who put them there.

My dad's Mercedes is parked in front of the garage, and I pull up alongside it, switching off the engine.

Both of us seem to deflate at the same time. I think that's tiredness more than anything, but before I can say a word, the front door opens and Mom and Dad come out.

"I know you're desperate to talk, but we'd better say hello to my parents."

"Of course." Remi nods her head, smiling at me. "I wouldn't be so rude as to drag you off somewhere, when they've gone to so much trouble for us… even if I don't know why."

"You will. I promise. I'll tell you."

I take her hand, kissing her fingers and she manages a slight smile, before I let her go and climb from the car.

I give Mom and Dad a wave as I wander around and help Remi out. We carry the bags between us, going over to the front door, where Mom and Dad step aside letting us in, and wait while we dump our bags at the foot of the stairs, closing the door before they make their impatience for introductions too obvious for words.

"This is my girlfriend, Remi," I say, noticing the smile on my mom's face as she steps forward, giving Remi a hug.

"That's a lovely name. You must call me Gwen."

Remi smiles, taken aback by my mom's affectionate greeting, I think.

"And I'm Joseph… but I only usually answer to Joe," Dad says with a smile, taking Mom's place. The expression on Remi's face is priceless. It's a mixture of shock and wonder, and I have to chuckle.

"You'll have to forgive my parents. I've never brought a girl home before."

"No, you haven't," Mom says, narrowing her eyes at me, although she's grinning as she puts her arms around me. "It's good to see you, Gabe. You're looking well."

"I'm feeling well. But please tell me Dad didn't put those lights in the trees outside."

Mom rolls her eyes at me. "Of course he didn't. I'm not so crazy that I'd let a sixty-nine-year-old man climb a high ladder like that. Your father held on to it while Jude arranged the lights."

"Jude the gardener?"

"Yes," Dad says, giving me a wink. "Your mom only has to flutter her eyelashes at him, and he does anything she asks of him."

"Oh, behave." Mom blushes and ushers us through to the kitchen.

"Are you okay?" I whisper to Remi, and she looks up at me, nodding her head.

"Your parents are lovely."

"I think so."

Mom's set the table, with a bottle of red wine in the middle, along with a basket of bread rolls, and dishes all set out. "I've made a chicken casserole," she says. "I hope that's okay?"

"It's perfect," I reply, showing Remi to her seat, which is next to mine, before I help Mom with fetching the casserole from the Aga.

"I can manage," she says, independent as ever.

"I know, but it's heavy, and besides, you don't have to manage when I'm here."

She smiles up at me, and as I set the dish on the table, she sits opposite Remi, waiting for me to take my seat.

"I hope you're hungry," she says, pulling off the lid.

"I am," Remi replies, leaning forward. "We only picked at the food on the plane."

"I don't blame you," Dad says. "Airline food is atrocious."

That wasn't the reason for our lack of appetite, but we both nod our heads, watching Mom dish up large portions of casserole for all of us. Once she's done, she offers around the bread rolls, while Dad pours the wine.

"So… how did you two meet?" Mom asks, the moment we're all settled and eating the delicious, tender chicken.

"I drove into Remi's car."

Dad puts down his fork. "You did what?"

"It was an accident, but I drove into her car."

"Goodness me." Mom focuses on Remi. "Were you okay?"

"I was fine. And it was my fault, not Gabe's."

I turn to her, taking her hand beneath the table. "We've talked about this, and we both know it was entirely my fault. I wasn't concentrating."

"Was there a reason for that?" Dad asks, getting back to his food.

"Yes. I was distracted by the beautiful woman whose car I was about to hit."

Mom laughs. Dad joins in, and within seconds, Remi's giggling, too.

We finished dinner about thirty minutes ago, and although I know Mom would love for us to stay down here and talk, we've got a conversation of our own to have, and Remi has been more than patient.

"It's been a tiring day for us, so we're gonna go to bed," I say, getting to my feet. Remi follows my lead and Mom stands, too.

"I'll show you up."

"I think I know the way, Mom."

She shakes her head. "Except you're not in your usual room."

For a horrible moment, I wonder if she might have put us in separate bedrooms. Given the conversation I'm about to have with Remi, the very last thing we need is to be apart, and I'm about to object when Dad gets up, too.

"Your mother decided your room wasn't big enough for the two of you to be comfortable, and she thought it might be easier if you had your own bathroom, so she made up the bed in the guest room at the back of the house. Consider yourselves honored."

I almost sag with relief, giving my mom a smile. She smiles back, and leads us from the kitchen, while Dad gets on with clearing the dishes.

At the top of the stairs, instead of turning left, like she normally would to get to the room we've always called 'mine', even though

I've never lived here, she goes right, along the hall, all the way to the end, where she opens the door on the left.

"As Joe said, it's much bigger in here," Mom says, flicking on the lights. "I've left you some towels in the bathroom, although I didn't light the fire." She turns to Remi. "We never do. The central heating keeps the upstairs more than warm enough, and I don't see the point in lighting fires and then having to throw open the windows because you're too hot to sleep."

Remi chuckles, nodding her head as I put the bags at the end of the bed.

"Thanks, Mom," I say, leaning in and giving her a kiss on her cheek.

"You're welcome. I think you'll have everything you need, but if I've forgotten anything, just give me a shout."

"We'll be fine."

I feel like I'm pushing her out the door, but I need to be alone with Remi now, and with one last smile for both of us, Mom gets the message and backs out, closing the door behind her.

I let out a sigh, now we're by ourselves, and turn to Remi, who's standing in the middle of the room, looking around, before she lets her hands fall to her sides, her shoulders dropping.

"Talk to me, Gabe… please?"

Chapter Nineteen

Remi

As I said to Gabe when we got here, his parents are lovely.

I especially like his mom, who insists I call her Gwen. I worked out that, if Gabe's dad is sixty-nine, then his mom must be sixty, although she doesn't look it. She also doesn't look anything like Gabe, who clearly gets his coloring and build from his dad, while Gwen is much more slight, and has blonde hair, with not a trace of gray to be seen.

Now she's gone, I turn and look around the room we're standing in.

It's very homely, with wood paneling on the walls, and two chairs over by the window that's shrouded by heavy tartan drapes. There's a matching tartan blanket at the end of the enormous bed. As Gwen said, there's even a fireplace, and a door in the corner, which seems to lead to a bathroom… and while I'd love to explore, or just fall into bed with Gabe, I need to know why we're here in the heart of the English countryside, instead of at my dad's house in Connecticut.

"Talk to me Gabe… please," I whisper and he steps forward, taking my hands in his and sitting us both down on the end of the bed, the thick blanket beneath us.

He turns, looking right at me. "Your stepmom came into my room during the night."

I pull my hands from his and leap to my feet, backing toward the fireplace, my mind in turmoil.

"She… she…" I can't find the words and Gabe stands too, stepping closer and placing his hands on my shoulders, like he knows I need to be steadied.

"This is why I didn't wanna tell you on the flight, or in the car, for that matter."

"What did you do? I mean, what did she do?" I can't accuse him. It's not fair.

"I didn't do anything, baby. I promise. As for Celine, she snuck into my room and got into bed with me."

"Just like that?"

"Yeah. It was dark, and she didn't say a word, and to be honest, I assumed it was you. I thought you'd missed me and decided to sneak across the hall."

"W—What happened?"

"Nothing happened. The moment she touched me, I knew it wasn't you."

I pull back, my skin ice cold with fear. "She touched you?"

"Yes."

"Where?"

He lets out a long sigh. "She puts her hand on my cock."

No… I can't be hearing this. I look around the room, frantically searching for a way out… needing an escape, although there isn't one, and then I feel Gabe's hands on my waist as he pulls me close. "Were you…?" I ask, looking up at him.

"Are you asking if I was hard?"

"Yes."

He nods his head and I try to pull away again, although he won't let me. "I'd been dreaming about fucking you… about making love with you and not having to use a condom. Getting hard was a given, babe, but it had nothing to do with her."

"She touched you, though?"

"Yes, and the second I realized it wasn't your hand on me, I jumped out of bed, wrapped myself in a blanket, and told her to leave."

"Did she?" I ask.

"Not immediately. She tried to persuade me that not sleeping with her would be a mistake, but I told her I didn't agree, and eventually, she left."

"Eventually?"

"Yes. Nothing happened in between, though. I promise."

"W—What was she wearing?" I ask, trying to picture the scene in my head.

"She wasn't wearing anything."

"Nothing?"

"No."

"S—So you've seen her naked?"

"Yes."

"And you weren't tempted?"

"Not in the slightest. You're the only woman I want, Remi. I swear that to you on my parents' lives."

I can't doubt him, even if I hadn't just witnessed the bond he has with his mom and dad. There's too much truth in his voice for me to question his words, and I lean in to him as he holds me tight against him.

"This is awful, Gabe." I look up at him. "What's wrong with her?"

"All kinds of things."

"And what about my dad? He'd feel terrible if he knew what she'd been doing."

Gabe pulls away, looking down at me. "About that," he murmurs.

"About what?"

"Your dad."

"What about him?"

He shakes his head, rolling his eyes up to the ceiling before he lowers them to me again, a pained expression on his face. "This is the part that's gonna be hardest for you to hear."

"Harder than hearing that my stepmom tried to sleep with you?"

"Yeah." I can't see how that's possible, but Gabe walks us back to the bed, sitting down and pulling me onto his lap, holding me close. "I don't know how to put this into words, Remi, so I'm just gonna say it." I wish he would, because the suspense is killing me. "Your dad knows."

"Knows what?"

"About Celine."

I feel numb, and sick, and kind of dead on the inside, but I need to know exactly what Gabe means. "About her coming to your room, you mean?"

"Not just that. He knows about Leon, too... and all her other lovers."

"What other lovers? How many have there been?"

"I don't know. She wasn't precise about numbers. She just said your father knows about all of them."

Yeah... definitely dead on the inside.

"How? I mean, why?" I'm not making sense, and I know it, but Gabe nods his head, like he understands.

"They have an arrangement. That's what she said."

"An arrangement that she can sleep with my boyfriends?"

"Not specifically. The arrangement seems to be that she can sleep with whoever she likes."

"Including my boyfriends," I say and he nods his head.

"It seems that way. I asked if your dad knew she was in my room and her answer was, 'What do you think?'. Bearing in mind she'd already told me David knew about Leon and the others, I assumed he was aware of what she wanted to do with me."

"And he let her?"

"It would appear so."

"But why would he do that?"

"I don't know. I don't understand it, and to be honest, I was more interested in getting her out of my room than discussing the weird set-up of her marriage to your dad."

"How did you get her to leave? I know Celine. I know how determined she can be."

"So do I, but I think calling her a slut might have helped."

I smile despite the numbness. "You called her a slut?"

"Yeah. It felt appropriate."

I can't argue with that. "How did she react?"

"Not well. She tried to hit me, and called me an asshole, and then told me she'd make me pay."

"Pay? What for?"

"Rejecting her, presumably… or maybe calling her a slut. I don't know."

"How was she gonna do that?"

"Considering your father already knew what she was doing, I imagined she intended to tell you… presumably over a cozy family breakfast. Her words would have carried some weight, too, wouldn't they? It's not like I'd have been the first of your boyfriends she'd have seduced… or tried to. It occurred to me she might have embellished the outcome for your benefit, too."

"So you decided we had to leave?"

"Yes."

"You didn't want to stay?"

"And do what? Confront your dad with something he already knew?"

I can see his point, although I still can't take it in. Who could? "I can't believe this. I can't believe Dad knows what she's doing and puts up with it."

"I guess we can never fully understand what goes on in someone else's relationship. People get up to some weird things."

"As weird as this?"

"Weirder, I would imagine."

"Seriously?"

"Yeah, you'd be amazed by what some people consider as 'normal' in a relationship, although I don't think your dad's as happy with the arrangement as Celine is."

"I think that's understandable, considering he gets nothing out of it. But what makes you say that?"

"The way he was over dinner. Didn't you notice?"

"I noticed he got more and more bad tempered."

"But you didn't work out why?"

"Not really. I assumed he'd changed his mind about having me there; that our grand reunion wasn't what he'd hoped."

He pulls me closer still. "So you didn't notice Celine flirting with me?"

"No."

He smiles, shaking his head. "Okay. You're gonna have to take my word for it then."

"And you think my dad noticed? You think that's why he became so sulky?"

"I do. He'd have had to be blind not to see what she was doing. He kept trying to include Celine in your conversation and she kept knocking him back. I imagine he knew what was coming next. He'd probably seen the signs before, maybe even with Leon."

"How? I didn't see them."

"No, but you never know when people are flirting, do you?"

"I—I guess not. But if he's that miserable about it, why doesn't he stop her, or divorce her?"

"I don't know. I don't even know why he agreed to the arrangement in the first place."

Neither do I, and I think I might go mad trying to work it out. "I—I guess that explains…"

"Explains what?" Gabe says, tilting his head to one side.

"Why he was so keen to invite me home for Christmas, but then cooled off a little when I told him about you."

"Did he? You didn't tell me that."

"No. I didn't pay too much attention at the time, but he definitely seemed less keen once I told him I had a boyfriend."

"Maybe he realized what might happen, but didn't feel he could withdraw the invitation, having already made it."

"No, probably not." I wish he had, for all our sakes, and I snuggle against Gabe, needing to feel safe. "I thought he was happy with her… at least at the beginning."

"He might well have been. Although according to Celine, he should have seen it coming."

"How?"

"Because of the age gap between them. But maybe he thought she loved him as much as he loved her. Who knows?"

I remember my dad as he was when my mom died, the broken man who'd lost the woman he loved and couldn't seem to get over it, and try to think of him now, being manipulated by Celine… miserable in the life he's chosen, and willing to make me miserable too, just to appease her.

"Oh, God… Gabe." I throw my arms around his neck, tears falling down my cheeks. I've never cried in front of him before, but I don't care. There's too much turmoil inside me to hold back.

"Hey… it's okay." He strokes my hair, hugging me tight.

"How can it be? It's all such a mess."

He leans back, looking right into my eyes, shaking his head. "Your dad's mess is his responsibility. It's up to him to decide whether he wants to fix things with Celine, or divorce her, or carry on as they are now. You can't make that decision for him."

"I—I know." He's right. I can't interfere in my dad's marriage, no matter how unhappy he is. He's the only one who knows what's going on – and why – and what he can do about it.

"The only decision you need to make is whether you're willing to forgive him for what he's done to you."

I can hear every word he's saying, but I feel like I'm on shaky ground, like everything I've ever believed in is crumbling around me.

"I can't, Gabe. I can't decide anything. It's too much to take in. None of it makes sense." I swallow hard, trying not to cry again. "I don't even feel like I've had a home since my dad remarried," I whisper, giving voice to my fears, or at least trying to. "It was horrible after Mom died, but at least I still had my dad and the house I'd grown up in. It felt like there was some stability in my life. Then Celine came along and snatched that away... from both of us, I think. And now..." I lean back and glance around the beautiful room we're sitting in. "Now I'm three thousand miles from the place I've tried to make my home... and I don't even know where I belong anymore."

My voice cracks as I finish talking, more tears hitting my cheeks, but rather than holding me, Gabe leans back, clasping my face between his hands, steadying me, his eyes boring into mine.

"This isn't my home, either. I come over for a couple of weeks a year, at most. But that's part of the reason I brought you here. I thought it through, Remi... I really did, and I wanted you to know that when I said I'm yours, I meant it."

"So you brought me to England to prove that?"

"Yes. I wanted you to see me as I really am... the man who was lucky enough to grow up in a loving family. The man who cares whether his dad has been climbing ladders, and wants to help his mom with the dinner. I wanted you to understand, I'm not just about work and sex."

"I never thought you were."

"Maybe not. But if I were to let you see into my past, you'd probably take that back, because that's exactly how I used to be. Until I met you. You changed me, Remi. You made me better, and I don't ever wanna go back. Despite having the best parents in the world, and a place like this I can run to if I'm ever in trouble, you're all I need. You're my home."

"I am?"

"Of course you are. I love you."

He says the words so simply, but I can't believe I'm hearing them. "L—Love...?" It seems I can't speak either, and he smiles, resting his forehead against mine.

"I love you, Remi Fox, and I promise I will keep you safe. I won't let anyone hurt you, and I'll make us a home, wherever you want it to be."

He tips my head back, dipping his, and kisses me, his lips brushing against mine, over and over.

"I... love... you... too." I mumble between kisses, and he pulls back, gazing at me.

"You mean that? Don't say it because you think it's what I wanna hear."

"I mean it, Gabe. I might not know when someone's flirting, or very much about people and relationships, it seems, but I know my heart... and it's yours."

He kisses me again, so much harder, and while I respond to his hands roaming over me, I know my heart well enough to realize that I can't do more than this. Not tonight.

"I—I..." I lean back, breaking the kiss, and he gazes down at me. "I can't, Gabe. I'm sorry. It's just..."

"Hey... it's okay. You're tired, you're in a strange place, and you've had a shitty day. I get it. I'm just so damn happy right now." He smiles, leaning closer. "I don't expect you to feel happy, not after everything that's happened, but maybe tomorrow, or the next day, you might be able to give me a smile?"

I lean my head against his chest while he strokes my hair. "Thank you," I whisper. "Thank you for understanding."

"Any time, babe."

I wake with a start, knowing something's wrong… or at least different.

"It's okay." Gabe's voice filters into my brain, and I turn in his arms, looking up into his face. "You're safe, baby."

"I know I am. You're here."

He smiles, leaning in and kissing my forehead.

"We're at my parents' place in England," he says, clearly sensing my confusion, and the memories come back, washing over me like a wave of sorrow.

Celine and Gabe… and my dad. I still can't take it all in, and I snuggle against him.

"Hold me," I whisper, and he does, my body tight against his. I can feel his arousal, but there's nothing I can do about it, and he seems to get that.

"You opened the drapes," I say, picking up on the fact that it's light outside, and I can see the window now, which I couldn't last night.

"Yeah… you've been asleep for hours," he says, stroking my hair.

I look up at him. "I have?"

"It's gone eight-thirty."

I lean back. "What must your parents think of me?"

"Probably that you're jet-lagged, I imagine."

"Even so…"

He kisses the tip of my nose. "Don't worry about it. Mom and Dad are very laid back." He tilts his head slightly. "I was gonna make some coffee. Would you like one?"

"I'd love one."

He nods, briefly kissing my lips before he gets out of bed. He looks magnificent and I can't help admiring him as he pulls on his jeans and finds a t-shirt in his bag, before turning to face me.

"Is something wrong?" He tugs the t-shirt on over his head.

"No. I was just taking in the view."

He grins, leaning over, his hands on either side of me, although he doesn't kiss me. He just rests his forehead against mine. "I hope you liked what you saw?"

"I did, but…"

He leans back, breaking the connection. "It's okay, Remi. I get it."

"I know you do, but I hate feeling like this."

"It'll pass, baby. I promise. And in the meantime, let's just relax and enjoy spending some time together."

I nod my head, because that sounds perfect, and he smiles and stands up straight.

"Don't be long, will you?"

"No longer than I have to be."

He leaves the room, and I settle back against the pillows, trying to get comfortable, although I can't, because I need the bathroom. Throwing back the covers, I dash to the open bathroom door, switching on the light.

It's beautiful in here, just like the rest of the house, although the fittings are very modern. There's a walk-in shower in the far corner, and the walls and floor are tiled in white marble. It's very elegant, but that doesn't surprise me in the slightest.

When I'm finished, I go back out into the bedroom, stopping by the window. I approach it cautiously, because I'm not wearing anything, and I don't know who's out there, but once I see the coast is clear, I take a better look. The view is of a wide lawn, the grass covered with a crystal white frost, as are the bare branches of all the shrubs and trees. It's so thick, it almost looks like snow, and I shiver, running back to the bed and getting in, pulling the covers right up, just as Gabe opens the door.

He's carrying two cups, and stares across at me, shaking his head.

"What's wrong?"

"Nothing," he says, shutting the door, and coming over, putting the cups on the nightstand. "It's just so good to see you here."

"It's good to be here. Although I'm not sure we should be. Didn't you say you had to be on call over the holidays? In case of emergencies at work?"

"I did. But believe it or not, I can still answer the phone, even when I'm here."

"You're sure?"

"I'm positive."

I relax, and lean back into the pillows behind me. "Your parents have a lovely home."

"They do."

"I was just admiring the garden," I say as he hands me a cup of coffee. "It looks beautiful."

"It looks freezing, if you ask me." He smiles down at me. "Mom asked if we'd go with her into the village later this morning… or, to be more precise, if we'd drive her down there. Dad's gotta go to the wine merchant's or something, and she needs to collect a few things herself."

I nod my head. "When does she wanna go?"

"Whenever we're ready, so don't rush. We can shower, and then have some breakfast."

"You're sure?"

"I'm positive." He leans in, kissing me briefly. "Just relax, Remi. We're gonna have a good Christmas. I promise."

No matter how strange everything feels right now, I believe him.

I'll always believe him.

Because I love him.

Chapter Twenty

Gabe

Christmas is a real 'thing' for my mom.

It always was, even when she lived in America, and everyone there made so much more fuss about Thanksgiving. That was something she never really understood, although she went along with it, for Dad's sake, and mine.

But in our house, Christmas was the main event, and in their house, it still is.

Even though it's still a few days away, there's an atmosphere of expectation about the place, and I know that's all Mom's doing. For her, it's as much about the preparations as it is about the day itself.

When I came down to fix the coffee, I wasn't surprised to find her already dressed and sitting at the kitchen table, reading the newspaper, with a cup of tea in front of her. Neither was I surprised when she looked up and asked if we'd slept okay.

"Fine, thanks," I replied. "I've just come to get us both a coffee."

"I'll make it for you, if you like." She went to get up, but I shook my head and she sat down again.

"I can make coffee, Mom." I glanced around the kitchen. "At least I can, if you tell me what you've done with your French press."

"It's in the cupboard above the microwave, and I call it a cafetière, in case you've forgotten."

"As if I could ever forget."

I retrieved the glass jug and two cups, putting the kettle on the Aga to boil before I turned back to her. She was staring at me with a smile on her lips.

"Remi's lovely," she said, and I nodded my head, smiling myself.

"I know."

"Can I take it from the fact that you've brought her here, and from the gooey look in your eyes, that you've stopped fooling around and have finally fallen in love?"

My mom always knew how to hit home, and I strolled over, sitting opposite her. "Gooey?"

"Yes. It suits you."

"Oh, does it now?"

"Yes, it does, so you can stop trying to change the subject and answer my question."

"I'll deny 'gooey' to anyone who suggests it, but I'll happily admit to being in love with Remi."

Her smile widened, and she reached her hand across the table, waiting for me to take it, which I did. "There's an age-gap, isn't there?"

"Yes. She's only twenty-two."

She nodded, unfazed. "Take care of her, Gabe."

"I intend to."

"Good." She sat back. "Did you have any plans for today?"

"No. Everything about this trip is so last minute, we haven't had time to make plans."

"In that case, do you think you could give me a lift to the village later this morning? I've got some things to collect, and your father's taking the car to the wine merchant's."

"Of course we can take you into the village."

"Thank you. That'll save me waiting for Joe to get back." She folded the newspaper closed and then looked up at me. "Is there a reason you came over in such a hurry? We're thrilled to have you here, but…"

"There is a reason, Mom, but it's to do with Remi's family, and to be honest, I don't feel like I can share it. It's kinda her story, not mine."

She nodded her head. "Is she okay?"

"Not yet, but she will be."

She smiled. "We'll find things to keep her occupied, to take her mind off whatever it is."

I stood, leaning over, and kissed her cheek. "Thanks, Mom."

Mom was as good as her word, and once I'd driven her and Remi into the village, she insisted on linking arms with her, walking down the small high street together. We had to call at the butcher's to collect Mom's Christmas order, which they'd already boxed up for her. It was heavy, and I took it straight back to the car, finding Mom and Remi in the florist's two doors away. Mom had an idea about making a wreath for the front door.

"I've been meaning to do it for ages," she said. "But I keep forgetting."

I wasn't sure if that was true, or if this was one of her ideas for keeping Remi busy. Either way, they had fun choosing things together, and I picked up some mistletoe, which made Mom smile.

The village has a very well-stocked deli, and we went in there to buy some things for lunch before heading back to the house to find Dad had just returned from the wine merchant's.

Between us, we unloaded the two cars, then settled down to lunch, after which Mom and Remi cleared the kitchen table and set about making the wreath. I hung the mistletoe in one of the little alcoves by the stairs and then helped Dad re-organize his wine cellar. He's always enjoyed wine, and discovering the house had a cellar made moving here easier for him, I think... although I know he'd have gone anywhere with Mom, and I get that now.

"Your mom and I had given up hope of you ever settling down," he said to me as I handed him a bottle from one of the boxes he'd just brought back from the wine merchant's.

"I guess I was waiting for the right woman to come along."

"She didn't exactly come along. You drove into her."

"By accident."

He chuckled, putting the bottle on the rack that filled one wall before he turned back to me. "However it happened, I'm pleased for you, son."

He was nowhere near as pleased as I was, and once we'd finished with the wine, I couldn't wait to get back to Remi, who was just helping Mom put the finishing touches to the wreath.

"That looks fabulous," I said, walking into the kitchen and pulling Remi into my arms, her back to my front. She nestled against me, turning and looking up into my face.

"We've had great fun."

She looked back at their creation of green foliage, interspersed with cinnamon sticks, bows, and dried sliced oranges, and nodded her head at my mom, who smiled back, and then looked up at me. "I think I'll make some tea, and I've made some mince pies, too." She was trying not to smile, and I narrowed my eyes at her.

"Mince pies?" Remi sounded confused, which wasn't surprising, and I don't think the interchange between me and my Mom was was helping.

"They're an acquired taste," I said, and she looked up at me again.

"What are they?"

"They're the devil's work."

Mom laughed. "They're not. They're just something Gabe's always hated, ever since he was a small child." She shook her head at me. "I made some ginger cake for you, but to explain to Remi, mince pies are small pastry tarts, with a sweet filling made of dried fruit."

"They sound okay to me," she said.

"Try one, and then tell me they're okay," I replied, and she giggled, which was like music to my ears.

Remi surprised me by liking mince pies, but I've forgiven her. I'd forgive her anything.

After we'd finished our tea, she and I hung the wreath on the front door, and then I made a point of pulling her into the alcove in the hall… the one where I'd hung the mistletoe.

I glanced up at it, smiling down at her, and she tilted her head.

"You know what it is, don't you?" I said.

"Of course. I'm just surprised you need the excuse."

I laughed and kissed her… hard.

The next day, we went on a long walk together, leaving Mom and Dad at the house. Remi still wasn't in the mood for making love, but I was okay with that. I knew she'd get back to me eventually. She'd been through a lot, and I had to give her time to work it all out.

Being there for her while she did it was the least I could do.

The weather was freezing, but we were wrapped up against it, our gloved hands entwined as we trekked through the countryside.

"Can I ask you something?" I said, a thought suddenly occurring.

"Sure." She turned, tipping her head up to look at me.

I stopped walking then, feeling the need to focus.

"When we get home, will you move in with me?"

She leaned back, like she hadn't been expecting that, which I guess was understandable. I'd only just realized that we couldn't stay in England forever, but that I didn't relish the prospect of returning to even remotely separate lives in the States.

"M—Move in with you?"

"Yes. I can't bear the thought of being away from you."

She blinked, and then smiled, resting her glove-clad hands on my chest. "Neither can I."

"So, will you? I'd say I could move into your place, but mine's probably more practical. It's nearer to where you work, and…"

"And what? It's got a bigger fireplace?"

"There's that, yes, but that's not what I was gonna say."

"Oh?"

"No. I was gonna say I've got four bedrooms."

"I see. Whereas I've only got one. I guess that makes a difference when your parents come to stay, doesn't it?"

"It does, although I wasn't thinking about my parents."

She frowned. "You weren't?"

"No. I was thinking about us."

"Why would we need…?" She stopped talking as the penny finally dropped.

"We kinda talked about it already, and although there's no rush, we might as well be prepared."

"Even though I've only just started taking birth control pills?"

"Yes." I was suddenly scared she might have changed her mind… that the situation with her father might have made her think twice about having a family of her own. "I thought we agreed not to abandon the idea. We said…"

She stepped closer, and I stopped talking. "We did, and I'm not abandoning anything." She lowered her eyes, blushing, but then looked up at me again. "I'd love to move in with you, Gabe."

"And make use of all the bedrooms... sometime in the future?"

"All of them?"

"Okay. As many as you want."

She nodded her head, and I smiled, capturing her face between my hands as my lips met hers.

We made love that night.

It wasn't at my suggestion, but when we got up to our room after a lovely dinner with Mom and Dad, Remi turned to me, with a familiar sparkle in her eyes. And when I kissed her, she pressed her body against mine, moaning softly into my mouth.

"Please," she whispered. "Please, Gabe."

I didn't need to ask what she meant, or what she wanted, and I walked her backwards to the bed, lowering her to the mattress. Our hands were everywhere. Tongues, and lips, and fingers, too.

"I wanna fuck you, baby," I murmured, yanking off her sweater. She stilled, surprising me, and I stopped, my hand on her bra strap, looking down into her perfect, flushed face. "What's wrong?" Was that too much? Had I gone too far?

She took a breath, letting it out slowly. "I—I had a dream."

"When?"

"The night we kinda stayed at my dad's place. I was dreaming of you when you woke me up."

It was a relief she could talk about that night, and I smiled, pushing a few of her stray hairs aside and tucking them behind her ear. "Were you dreaming about me fucking you?"

She smiled back. "Not exactly."

"What does that mean?"

She blushed, frowning slightly. "I—I don't know how to put this."

"You can say anything to me, Remi. You know that. What were we doing in your dream… tell me."

"You said you wanted to fuck my mouth."

I grinned then, unable to help myself. "Did you like that idea?"

"I did in my dream. I didn't even realize it was a thing in reality."

"Well… it is. Would you like to try it?" She nodded her head, her breathing already ragged, but I pushed her over onto her back and flipped around, kneeling up before I undid my jeans, pushing them down as far as they needed to go to release my aching cock. Then I straddled her, shimmying backwards until I was above her head.

"That's a nice view," she whispered, making me chuckle as I leaned forward, sliding my dick into her open mouth. I gave her an inch or two, pausing before I started to move, giving her just a little more. She moaned, parting her legs and without breaking my rhythm, I leaned over and unzipped her pants, pushing them down, pulling her panties aside, and running my tongue along her swollen folds. She was drenched, and I lapped her up, her arms coming around my thighs, pulling me in a little deeper. I felt her kick off her pants and raise her legs, giving me better access, and I inserted my middle finger into her soaking hole as I flicked my tongue over and around her. She was bucking off of the bed, and I knew she was close. All it took was one more finger, and she came apart, flooding my mouth and hand. I swallowed her down, my cock gagging her cries as she writhed beneath me.

I held on, although God knows how, and once she was calm, I kneeled up, pulling my cock from her mouth.

Her eyes were glazed, her cheeks flushed, and I flipped around again, quickly pulling off her panties and bra, throwing them to the floor, to be joined by the rest of my clothes.

"Did you like that?" I asked.

"Yes, but you didn't…" She looked down at my cock.

"No. I didn't wanna come in your mouth. Not yet."

"But you will?"

"If that's what you want."

She nodded her head, and I gazed down at her, wondering how I got so lucky. Then I leaned over, retrieving my wallet from my jeans and pulling out a condom.

"How many more days until we don't need those?" Remi asked, watching me roll it over my cock.

"We'll be good to go on the twenty-seventh."

She nodded her head. "Will we be back home by then?"

I leaned back on my ankles. "You want to be?"

"Yes. I'm grateful to your parents and I want to spend Christmas here with them, but I want our first time to be at home… your home."

"Our home, baby." I raised myself up, my hands on either side of her head, and plunged into her. She gasped, parting her legs a little wider, and I rocked my hips back and forth, loving her like never before. There was something about the way we moved together. It wasn't urgent or frenzied, but it felt more intense than anything we'd ever done. I never took my eyes from hers… not for a second, and when we came, it was together, our cries hushed through a deep and passionate kiss.

I booked our flights home the next morning, although I didn't tell Mom and Dad. I saved that until Boxing Day, which was another 'thing' that Mom had to explain to Remi.

I broke the news of our imminent departure to them while we were all out after lunch, taking a walk, and although I could tell they were disappointed we weren't staying longer, they understood.

"We've both gotta get back for work," I said, which wasn't the real reason for our leaving, but it was accurate enough. The New

Year was beckoning, and with it, a return to the office, for both of us.

"Your father and I have been talking about coming to see you in the summer, if that's okay?" Mom's words didn't surprise me in the slightest.

"Of course it's okay. I'm guessing you're gonna make it sometime in July, so it coincides with Dad's birthday?"

"That's what we were thinking." She smiled up at me. "Our plan is to spend a few days in Boston, catching up with old friends and then drive up to Hart's Creek."

"Sounds great. We'd love to have you stay with us, wouldn't we?" I looked down at Remi and she nodded her head, smiling.

Mom seemed confused. "I—I didn't realize you were…"

"Living together?" I said, finishing her sentence. "We weren't, but we will be when we get home. We've decided Remi's gonna move in with me."

"Oh… but that's marvelous news."

I could tell how pleased she was, and so was Dad. They had no idea why we'd arrived out of the blue, or what the problem was that had driven us to seek sanctuary with them, but I think they knew they'd played a not insignificant part in helping us move our relationship forward to where it needed to be.

To where it is now…

It might have taken us two days to move all of Remi's things into my place, but it was worth every second. She hasn't put her house up for sale yet, but it's on the list of things to do in the New Year… along with buying more closets, because I don't have anything close to enough space in my dressing room. I went out yesterday, and when I came back, I found Remi moving her clothes around for the third time, trying to fit them in.

"Leave it, baby. We'll work something out." I turned her around. "No-one needs a mirrored wall like this." I pointed to it and she studied our reflections. "I've never thought it was very flattering anyway. We can take it out and put in some more closets, so you'll have as much hanging space as you need."

"Really?"

"Yes." I bent my head and kissed her then, before helping her to put back her clothes as best we could in the space available.

Aside from the lack of hanging space, Remi seems to like my house, her favorite places being my bedroom, and the living room... or more specifically, my open fireplace, which is a lot bigger than the one at her old place.

On our first night back here, we made love on the rug in front of it. I don't think either of us was capable of waiting until we got upstairs. Our seven days were up, and the idea of there not being any barriers between us was too much.

The reality of it was, too. I reverted to type – or the 'type' I am with Remi, it seems – coming in no time at all, although she got there with me, thank God. It was everything I'd ever dreamed of, and so much more, and after we'd recovered our breath, and kissed for a while, I made up for my shortcomings, making her come three more times before I had to fill her again.

We haven't talked about her father, or what happened, and she hasn't heard from him, either, which makes me wonder if he saw through Remi's note... or if Celine maybe told him a version of events in my bedroom that best suited her ends. I don't know what that might have been, but I doubt it would have been the truth. Either way, the silence between Remi and her father seems to have returned, at least for now. It may not last, but I'll be here for her, whatever happens, and whatever she decides, and she knows that.

In the meantime, we've had plenty to keep us occupied. Between moving Remi's things in, and making love at every opportunity, we've also been preparing for New Year's Eve.

I asked Remi yesterday if she wanted to go out somewhere, but she shook her head.

"I'd rather stay here and cook," she said. We were lying on the couch at the time and I held her a little closer.

"Together?"

"Of course." She smiled up at me, and I had to admit, I preferred her plan to mine. "It feels like it's been a momentous year."

"We only met a few weeks ago."

She chuckled. "I wasn't just talking about that. We've both moved house…"

"You've moved twice."

"That's true, and I've started a new job."

"I've moved offices. My best friend got married."

She nodded. "A lot's happened… not all of it good."

That was clearly a reference to that night at her dad's place, and I turned us onto our sides, so we were facing each other.

"It's ended well, though."

"It has. Which is why I'd like us to spend the evening together, so we can celebrate and look forward."

"That sounds perfect."

It's looking even more perfect now.

We've created a menu all by ourselves. Our appetizer was home-made cauliflower soup, which tasted amazing, and was followed by fennel-crusted pork, served with roasted vegetables, and once we'd eaten it and cleared away, we moved into the living room, bringing our dessert with us. It's a chocolate fondue, and I put it in front of the fire, along with a bowl of strawberries and marshmallows, which I've been feeding to Remi, occasionally taking one or two for myself.

"This is so lovely," she says, lying back on the rug.

I'm so turned on now, I'm tempted to feed her a lot more than the few remaining strawberries, but I hold back.

There's one more thing I need to do… and I'd like to do it before midnight.

Before I can even get started, though, I push the fondue aside, licking the chocolate from my fingers as I kneel beside her. Remi sits up slightly, tilting her head to one side.

"Is something wrong?"

"No." I take her hands in both of mine. "I wanted to thank you."

"What for?"

"For everything. All of it. I suppose most of all, for saying 'yes' to having that first dinner with me, even though you weren't convinced I was right for you."

"I was wrong about that."

"Maybe. But you took a chance."

She smiles up at me. "Things haven't been easy over the last week or so, but I'm glad I took that chance."

"So am I."

"While we're thanking each other, I wanted to say I'm grateful to you for taking me to meet your parents."

"You don't have to thank me for that."

"Oh, I think I do. It can't have been easy for you."

"Why not? I love my mom and dad. It wasn't a hardship to spend Christmas with them."

"I know, but you said you'd never taken a girl home before. It was a big step and you must have had to think twice about it."

I shake my head, shifting closer to her. "Not at all. When you find the woman you wanna spend the rest of your life with, you don't have to think twice about telling the entire world, let alone your parents."

Her eyes widen. "Th—The rest of your life?"

"Yeah. If you'll have me." Shifting onto one knee, I suck in a breath and Remi gasps, clearly guessing what I'm about to do.

"I love you. I want to spend forever building a home with you, and keeping you safe… as Mr. and Mrs. Sullivan." She blinks hard, like she's trying not to cry.

She nods her head, and I pull her up into my arms, holding her close. "Yes," she whispers, without me having to ask. "Yes, yes, yes."

I pull back, but only far enough that I can cup her cheek with my hand, and then I kiss her, our tongues clashing, our bodies fused in perfect harmony.

It takes a while before we pull apart, and when we do, we're both breathless, and I'm impatient for more, unfastening the buttons of her blouse. She grabs my hand, though, surprising me, and I frown, staring down at her.

"What's wrong?"

"Y—You don't think we're rushing things?"

I pull my hand away. "Why? What did you wanna do?"

"Nothing." She giggles. "I meant getting engaged… getting married. You don't think we're taking things too fast? I thought Alex was being hasty getting engaged to Jacques after meeting him at the beginning of November. You and I haven't even known each other that long."

"So? No two people are the same. No two couples are the same. Besides, at my age, I can't afford to wait." She laughs, throwing her head back, but then focuses on me again. "I don't care if we didn't know each other a month ago. It's irrelevant. What matters is that I love you, and you love me."

"I do. But can I just ask… does this have anything to do with Celine?" Her name hasn't crossed either of our lips since the night we got to England, and I let out a sigh.

"In what way?"

"Are you trying to prove a point?"

"About her? No. Although I guess I'm trying to prove that nothing can ever come between us, if that's what you're asking.

Not your dad, or your stepmom, or their weird relationship… or anything that anyone else does."

"And you really want to go from that man you were telling me about, who was all about work and sex, to being settled and married?"

"Don't forget the kids," I say, and she smiles.

"You really want all that?"

"With you? Yes. More than anything." I move a little closer. "I know it's all happened real fast, but we don't have to rush at this last part."

"Oh?"

"I'm not waiting forever, but I was thinking we might organize a summer wedding."

"For when your parents come over?"

"Yeah." She read my mind. "My dad's birthday is July fifteenth, but I imagine they'll come for a week or so either side. Once they've figured out their travel plans, we can fix a date… if that's okay with you."

"It sounds lovely." Her face falls. "Do you think my dad will want to come?"

"I don't know, but you've got time to think about that, and about whether you want him there. Because it's your choice, babe. No-one else's."

She nods her head and I hold her close to me for a moment before I remember something and I delve into my pocket, pulling out a tiny black box.

"You've… you've got a ring?"

"Yeah. Sorry. I got carried away just now. I was supposed to give it to you when you said 'yes', but kissing you seemed more important at the time." She giggles, and I open the box to reveal a diamond solitaire ring.

"Oh, Gabe… it's beautiful."

"I bought it yesterday when I went out." I place it on her finger and she gazes down at it. "Now the entire world knows you're mine."

"I am. I'm all yours." She throws her arms around my neck, and I kiss her, pulling her down onto the rug as the fire crackles and the clock chimes midnight, bringing in the most wonderful New Year.

The End

Thank you for reading *Grateful for Gabe*. I hope you enjoyed it, and if you did, I hope you'll take the time to leave a short review.

There will be more from Hart's Creek soon with the next installment – *Being with Brady* – a friends to lovers romance. Town sheriff, Brady Hanson has loved Laurel Bradshaw all her adult life. The problem is, she's taken, and he's doing his best to live with that.

When tragedy strikes, Brady has an opportunity... although it's one he can't take. Not just because Laurel is broken, but also because he's keeping secrets. Secrets that might cost him the only woman he's ever loved.

Printed in Great Britain
by Amazon

39182481R00165